PRAISE FOR

Lovely Girls

"What happens when mean girls are raised by tiger mothers."
—*Kirkus Reviews*

"Mean girls grow up to be mean moms with mean daughters in this entertaining domestic thriller from Hunt . . . Small-town gossip and teenage angst drive the brisk plot, which is elevated by fully fleshed-out characters and a palpable realism. Hunt remains a writer to watch."
—*Publishers Weekly*

"I couldn't turn the pages fast enough—mean girls, mean moms, the new girl in town, capped off by a superb mystery . . . Margot Hunt has such a deft hand with the clues that you'll never see it coming."
—J. T. Ellison, *New York Times* bestselling author

"When a body washes up on a Florida beach, anyone could be the killer—or the victim—in a town where the girls are raised to be ruthless and the mothers will stop at nothing to protect them. Pages turn themselves in this deliciously devious tale!"
—Wendy Walker, international bestselling author

"Every parent's nightmare . . . Hunt takes mean girls to a whole new level in her new novel, *Lovely Girls*. You won't want to miss this one!"
—Debra Webb, Amazon Charts bestselling author

Best Friends Forever

"[*Best Friends Forever*] constantly pushes forward, asking readers to question every conclusion and warning them to never completely trust anyone . . . The characters are well drawn, speaking easily for themselves and standing out as unique people who feel real."

—*Kirkus Reviews*

"Will please fans of psychological thrillers, especially those featuring unhinged, vengeance-seeking women."

—*Booklist*

"*Best Friends Forever* is a clever thriller that asks how far we'll go to protect our friends. Margot Hunt will keep you guessing until the final satisfying twist."

—Alafair Burke, *New York Times* bestselling author of *The Ex*

"Margot Hunt's richly drawn women wrap their hands around your throat and don't let go. A suspenseful page-turner that kept me puzzling over who did it until the last few pages. Fantastic!"

—Cate Holahan, author of *The Widower's Wife*

"*Best Friends Forever* is a page-turner of a read, delving into the often-fraught world of female friendships and the wreckage left behind when they implode. The women at the heart of this novel are full of secrets kept from loved ones, each other, and, most of all, themselves. You may think you know how this story is going to end. But trust me—you don't."

—Amy Engel, author of *The Roanoke Girls*

"Margot Hunt's cleverly constructed thriller kept me guessing till the very end."

—Peter Swanson, author of *The Kind Worth Killing* and *Her Every Fear*

"Friends or husbands? To whom do women tell more truth? Give more allegiance? Margot Hunt shocks and astounds as she explores these tugs of loyalty in *Best Friends Forever*, a psychological thriller that kept me off balance even after turning the last page."

—Randy Susan Meyers, bestselling author of *The Widow of Wall Street*

The Last Affair

"The action hurtles toward an astonishing conclusion. Fans of Paula Hawkins and Megan Abbott will be gratified."

—*Publishers Weekly*

"This gripping psychological thriller explores the reasons two marriages are unhappy and the ways vengeance-seeking women pursue their target."

—*Booklist*

THE
GUESTS

ALSO BY MARGOT HUNT

THE GUESTS

MARGOT HUNT

THOMAS & MERCER

Published by Thomas & Mercer, Seattle

www.apub.com

Amazon, the Amazon logo, and Thomas & Mercer are trademarks of Amazon.com, Inc., or its affiliates.

ISBN-13: 9781662514302 (paperback)
ISBN-13: 9781662513145 (digital)

Cover design by Amanda Kain
Cover image: © Sirichai Puangsuwan / Shutterstock, © Tony Arruza / plainpicture, © Roman Studio / Getty, © Carl & Ann Purcell / Getty

Printed in the United States of America

THE
GUESTS

PROLOGUE

The storm that raged around the boat felt alive. The air crackled with energy. It wasn't just the powerful wind, or the blinding rain, or the lightning that was striking so close. That would be scary enough. But it felt to her as if the hurricane had morphed into a living creature with sharp teeth and claws that could shred skin and a long powerful tail that could whip the legs out from under a much stronger person than her.

As if sensing she'd almost given up, the storm readied itself to kill her.

The forty-four-foot saltwater fishing boat felt as insubstantial as a kayak in the hurricane as it struggled to remain upright. Waves like rolling walls slammed into the vessel over and over with a terrifying ferocity. Every time the boat tipped, another huge swell of salt water rolled over the side, drenching her, stinging her eyes so that she couldn't see, washing away everything that wasn't tied down. Fishing gear, supplies, even the heavy Yeti cooler had been hurled out of the boat, fated to sink to the bottom of the ocean.

It was a miracle she hadn't been flung off as well. She figured it was just a matter of time.

He was still there.

At first, he had tried to steer the boat out onto the ocean. When it had quickly become clear that the boat was unnavigable, he'd sat huddled by the wheel. She could see his back occasionally when slashes of lightning lit up the darkness around him. Once he looked back at her, his eyes wide and panicked, his face hollowed out. Just like her, he knew the inevitable was going to happen.

They were both going to die that night.

PART ONE

10:22 update. The National Hurricane Center has issued a hurricane warning for southeastern Florida. Hurricane Celeste is expected to make landfall on Tuesday, September 5, at 15:42. This storm has wind speeds in excess of 150 miles per hour and has the potential to produce a storm swell of ten to twelve feet. This is a catastrophic event that may result in the loss of life. Preparations to protect life and property should be rushed to completion.

CHAPTER ONE

MARLOWE

Marlowe Davies stood in her spacious kitchen, her hands braced against the white marble countertop, and stared out the window at the wide sweeping view of the Intracoastal Waterway. Clouds were starting to gather, low and dark in the sky, but there were still occasional glimpses of the sun dappling against the low rolling waves. A pelican hunting for its lunch flew over the river, wings spread wide.

It didn't yet look like a Category 5 hurricane would be arriving in a matter of hours.

The only outward sign of the massive storm named Celeste that was circling slowly but purposefully toward the central east coast of Florida was the occasional gust of wind that fluttered the fronds on the foxtail palms in the backyard. It came in short strong bursts, whistling eerily as it blew past the window.

"Do you see Dorothy flying by in her house?" Lee asked.

Marlowe startled and turned around, and then she smiled ruefully at her husband.

"You scared me," she said, lifting one hand to her pale throat. "And that was a tornado in *The Wizard of Oz*, not a hurricane."

"Right." Lee stepped closer and kissed Marlowe on the forehead. "I didn't mean to startle you."

Her husband was a tall man with long limbs and an angular face. He'd aged into his looks, the way some men did. The streaks of silver in his hair and the creases at the corners of his pale eyes made him even more attractive than when they'd first met. He'd been handsome then, too, but also a bit awkward and gawky, traits that had been smoothed away over the years.

"I was lost in my thoughts," Marlowe said.

"I can't imagine why you're distracted." Lee raised one eyebrow comically, and Marlowe laughed weakly. He squeezed her shoulder in reassurance. "It's just a hurricane. We've ridden them out before."

"Not one like this." Marlowe shivered. "This one's going to be a Category 5 when it hits. We've never sat through a storm this strong."

They had gone to bed the night before thinking that Hurricane Celeste was heading well south of them. At that time, it had been projected to be a Category 3 storm when it made landfall. There had been no reason for them to evacuate. But then Celeste stalled overnight, feeding on the warm shallow waters of the Atlantic Ocean. It gained strength and speed as it shifted its course northward. Marlowe woke at six thirty that morning to her phone beeping out an alarm. She picked it up off the nightstand and stared down at an emergency alert. Hurricane Celeste had been upgraded to a Category 5. And the eye of the storm was headed straight toward their small coastal town of Shoreham.

Lee patted her arm. "How much different can it be? We'll get wind and rain. But we'll be safe enough. We're not in a flood zone." He nodded at their backyard, which angled gradually toward the Intracoastal Waterway. The height of the lot had been one of its selling points when they'd bought it fifteen years earlier. It allowed them to be on the river, without the threat of flooding during storms. "This house was built to withstand hurricanes."

Marlowe nodded. It was the third time that morning they'd had this exact conversation. Her anxiety would spiral upward, and Lee would soothe her back down. It was going to be a bad storm, sure. They would lose some trees or possibly even the fence that surrounded the perimeter of their property. But they would be safe inside their well-constructed home.

"Everything's almost ready. We put the storm shutters on the second-story windows yesterday," Lee said. He leaned back against the counter and crossed his arms. "The boys are almost finished hanging the ones on the first story at the front of the house. We'll leave these back ones until the very end. Once they're up, it's going to get dark in here."

Marlowe pressed her fingers against her temples. The drop in barometric pressure was giving her a headache. "I just heard on the weather forecast that the wind bursts might exceed one hundred and fifty miles per hour by the time the storm makes landfall. That's going to be devastating to a lot of people. Houses are going to be flattened."

"Then I guess it's a good thing we're having our storm shutters put up by two seventeen-year-old kids," Lee said.

Marlowe's eyes went round with horror. "I didn't think of that! I don't think Tom knows how to turn on the dishwasher, and we're trusting him with the storm shutters? And I seriously doubt Zack is up to the task." She glanced around to make sure neither her son, Tom, nor his best friend, Zack, had followed Lee into the house, but she still lowered her voice. "He's a sweet kid, but we both know that he's not destined to become a brain surgeon."

Lee laughed again. "God help us all if he did. And I was just teasing you. Mick is out there working with them."

Mick Byrne was a local handyman, although Marlowe had always thought of him more as a craftsman. He had designed their boathouse, had installed beautiful bookshelves in her home office and the living room, and ran a thriving business making custom mailboxes. He'd built their mailbox, a miniature version of their home. If Mick was in charge, she didn't have to worry. At least not about the storm shutters.

"I looked online. There are still hotel rooms available in Orlando," Marlowe said hopefully.

7

The Davies family had evacuated to Orlando once before during a hurricane, back when their twins were in elementary school. That storm had also been headed straight toward them but had taken a turn up the coast before it had come ashore. Since they were in Orlando and it ended up being a bright and clear day, Marlowe and Lee took the twins on an impromptu trip to Walt Disney World. It was lovely. The threat of the storm kept the crowds away from the park. They'd barely had to wait in line to ride Space Mountain and the Haunted Mansion.

"We have no way of getting to Orlando," Lee said. "Not today. The turnpike is a parking lot right now."

Marlowe knew he was right. She'd already checked the map app on her phone. It had informed her that the drive, which usually took about two hours to complete, would take ten hours in the current traffic, and she thought that might be optimistic. Everyone else in the area had also woken up to the news that the storm had strengthened and shifted. People were fleeing, and the roads were clogged. Celeste's imminent arrival was causing everyone to panic.

"It may be worth sitting in traffic if it gets us to safer ground," Marlowe said.

"It won't be safe if we're still sitting on the highway when the storm hits," Lee replied.

Marlowe wrapped her arms around herself. Why hadn't they left yesterday or even the day before? Right now, they'd be in a hotel, safe from the storm and planning where they were going out to dinner that night. But she knew why. Two days ago, they hadn't known the storm would be so deadly.

"Maybe she'll shift again," she said hopefully. "If Celeste hits north of us, we'll just have a bad tropical storm."

"I don't think we're going to get that lucky this time."

Lee looked unusually somber. And Marlowe knew he was right. This storm was going to hit them straight on. All they could do now was hang on and try to get through it.

"Hey." June padded barefoot into the room.

She's too thin, Marlowe thought with a familiar jolt of alarm. It was the same thing she always thought when she saw her daughter lately. She quickly smoothed her expression before June saw. Her daughter's temper flared up quickly.

June's weight was a subject they all danced around. She'd always been healthy and athletic. But the previous year, for no apparent reason, June had become convinced she was overweight. Marlowe had first chalked up June's strict diet and exercise obsession to general teen weirdness. But then the weight had fallen off her at an alarming rate. Now June's face was hollow, her clavicles painfully sharp, and the denim cutoffs that had once fit fell low on her hips. Marlowe worried June had an eating disorder, but her daughter refused to discuss it.

Marlowe knew June needed to see a therapist. Even if she didn't want to, she needed to. But Marlowe also knew that now was not the time to broach the subject while they were in the middle of preparing for the hurricane. Once the storm passed, Marlowe was going to make an appointment for June to talk to someone. She had to do it now, while June was still home. Next year, she'd be off to college, living a new life. This constant awareness that her children would one day grow up and leave had been a relentless timer counting down in Marlowe's head ever since the twins were born.

"What are you guys talking about?" June asked.

"We were discussing whether we made the right decision to stay here and ride out the storm," Marlowe said.

June looked up, alarmed. "But we're staying, right? I mean, we can't leave now."

"No, it's too late to go. We don't want to be sitting in traffic when the storm hits." Lee smiled fondly at their daughter.

June did not return his smile. Instead she looked at him coldly before turning to her mother. "Where's Tom? He's not in his room."

Marlowe glanced at Lee, who was rolling his eyes heavenward behind June's back. The ongoing strain between Lee and June was another issue they were going to have to address. But today was not that day.

"Tom's outside putting up hurricane shutters with Mick," Marlowe said. "Zack's helping them. You should be out there too. I'm sure they could use another set of hands."

June wrinkled her nose. "No thanks. I went for a swim when I woke up, and it was already scorching outside. Why does it get so hot right before a storm?"

"No idea," Lee said cheerfully. "There might be some sort of scientific explanation for it. Or it could just be that it's September in South Florida, and it's always hot this time of year."

Marlowe looked out at the long rectangular white-tiled pool. The aqua water was rippling in the wind. "Don't forget to put the pool cover on."

"It's on my to-do list," Lee said.

"June, if you're not going to hang shutters with your brother and Zack, then you can help Isabel and I pack up the artwork that's in my office," Marlowe said.

"Isabel's coming over?" June raised her eyebrows in surprise.

Marlowe nodded. "She didn't evacuate in time, either, so I invited her to ride the storm out here. It isn't safe for her to stay in her apartment on the beach. The hurricane that hit Tampa a few years ago completely washed away buildings on the shoreline. Don't you remember the footage?"

"I guess. But we barely know her."

"That's not true. She's been working for me for almost three months," Marlowe said.

"That's my point. You've only known her for three months. And now you're basically inviting her to join our family."

Marlowe laughed. "Stop being so dramatic. Having Isabel over for a night or two is hardly making her part of the family. And it's the kind thing to do. The storm is going to be dangerous and scary. I wouldn't want to be alone."

The doorbell rang, chiming in the front foyer.

"That must be Isabel now. Answer the door," Marlowe said to June. "And please be welcoming."

"I'll go let her in," Lee said. "And then I should get back outside. I have to put the rest of the patio furniture in the garage, and then we need to get the last of those shutters up. The storm's supposed to hit midafternoon." He glanced at the kitchen clock. "We're running out of time."

Marlowe shivered at his words. "Don't say that. It sounds so ominous."

Lee shrugged. "The storm's coming one way or another. We'd better be prepared for it."

CHAPTER TWO

JUNE

June's dad left to answer the front door. Her mother turned the volume up on the Weather Channel on the kitchen television.

"Aren't you tired of watching that?" June asked.

Marlowe shrugged but didn't take her eyes off the screen. There was an excited meteorologist wearing a slightly askew yellow tie and gesticulating at a graphic of the large swirling hurricane circling toward the east coast of Florida. The graphic of Celeste had been colored red to make it look extra scary, as though it were not just a storm but a giant fireball aimed straight at them. June's mother stared at the image, her face pale, her lips pinched tightly together.

"I can't believe how big it's gotten," Marlowe said softly.

June took the opportunity to rifle through the pantry. Her mom had obviously been stress grocery shopping, because it was fully stocked with junk food. June pulled down a container of peanut butter–stuffed pretzels and a red tube of Pringles, then grabbed a couple of tangerines off the fruit bowl on the counter. She was just about to make a break for it when her mom looked up and frowned.

"What are you doing?"

"Just getting a snack. I'm hungry."

"You're hungry? That's good!" Marlowe's face brightened, the storm forgotten for a moment. "Do you want me to make you breakfast?" She glanced at the clock on the stove, which displayed a bright-red 11:11. "Or brunch?"

June almost felt bad for her mom. She knew Marlowe was concerned about how much weight she'd lost and worried she was anorexic. June didn't have an eating disorder. Or, at least, she didn't think she did. She knew girls at school who bragged about how they lived on one boiled egg and half a banana a day. And while June didn't do that—intentionally starve herself or brag about it—she liked the way her baby fat had melted off her. She'd just meant to cut back a little, but then she couldn't quite seem to stop herself once she started. Most of her friends said she looked great, except for Emily, who rolled her eyes and said June was so thin she made her sick. June secretly liked both responses. But now seeing her mother's expression—a mixture of happiness and relief at seeing her daughter grabbing snacks—June felt a surge of guilt.

"That's why I bought so much," Marlowe said. "Storms always make everyone hungry. I'm going to bake brownies for the boys. They've been working so hard I thought they deserved a treat. Do you want to help me?"

"No, I'm good," June said. She turned and headed out of the kitchen before her mom could keep prattling on about food. When she reached the bottom of the staircase, she glanced at the front door, where her dad was wrestling Isabel's bags into the foyer. Multiple bags? How long was this chick planning on staying?

June didn't stop to chat. It wasn't that she didn't like Isabel. Not exactly. Isabel had always been perfectly pleasant to her, although she was her mom's employee, so she had to be nice to June. But there was something lacquered over about Isabel. She had a fake tan and fake eyelashes and applied blush and highlighter makeup to create fake contours on her face. At least today, for once, Isabel wasn't wearing her usual uniform of a skintight skirt and stiletto heels. In what was probably a concession to the storm that was about to hit, she was wearing a T-shirt and shorts, although both were formfitting and she'd paired them with towering espadrille wedges. Her perfume, a strong floral musk, filled the foyer.

June quickly headed up the stairs before Isabel could see her and draw her into one of those pointless conversations that adults loved having with teenagers. *Are you excited about your senior year? What colleges are you applying to? What are you planning on studying?*

June reached the top of the curved staircase, turned right, and padded down the hallway, which was carpeted with a striped runner. Her bedroom was at the end of the hall. She pushed open the door, closed it behind her, and said, "It's okay—it's just me. You can come out."

The accordion door that led to June's walk-in closet opened, and Felix stepped out. He grinned at her, which caused June's stomach to swoop.

Oh no, June thought. She kept hoping the stomach swooping would go away.

"What did you bring? I'm starving," Felix said.

June held up her arms, laden with snacks. She walked over to her bed, dropped the food on it, and gave a game show–hostess flourish. "All the junk food I could carry."

"Sweet," Felix said.

He sat down on the edge of her modern platform bed and reached for the Pringles. Felix was so tall, and the bed was so low to the ground, that his knees were bent awkwardly up in front of him. He popped a stack of chips into his mouth all at once. He munched happily, then swallowed.

"I'm starving," he said.

"You're literally always hungry."

"True enough. Pringle?" He held out the can toward her, and for a moment June considered taking one. She imagined the salty greasiness of it against her tongue and how good it would taste. But then she thought about how she'd been able to pull up her denim cutoff shorts without unbuttoning them first that morning and shook her head.

"No thanks," she said.

"Suit yourself," Felix said and grinned as he tossed another chip into his mouth.

He's so beautiful, June thought. Felix had high cheekbones and a broad, full mouth. His dark eyes and light-brown skin glowed as though he'd been dipped in light.

They'd been friends for years, ever since the sixth grade, when they had bonded over a shared love of comic books and vintage episodes of *Doctor Who.* They'd sat together in class, and at lunch, and at pep rallies. They'd kept one another company during the series of endless pool parties their classmates had thrown in the summers between eighth and ninth grade. They'd watched all the *Harry Potter* movies on repeat until they could recite the dialogue from heart.

But then, sometime during their junior year of high school, June had started to notice how broad Felix's shoulders had become. And how his face lit up whenever he smiled. And that he smelled amazing, a combination of soap and the spicy scent of his shaving cream. That was when the stomach swooping had started. Unfortunately, Felix's feelings toward her had not seemed to change at all. Not even a little.

"Tangerines? I definitely did not ask for fruit." Felix picked up one of the tangerines and tossed it suddenly at June. She tried to catch it but missed. The tangerine fell to the ground and rolled for a few feet, then came to a stop just inside the door.

Felix burst out laughing. "How did you not catch that?"

"It was a terrible toss—that's why," June retorted.

"I'm on the basketball team."

"So?"

"Compared to you, I'm practically a professional athlete." Felix leaned back on June's bed so that he was staring up at the ceiling, his expression suddenly serious. "Your mom doesn't suspect that I'm up here, does she?"

June shook her head. "She's too distracted by the storm."

"Yeah, I've been tracking it on my phone. This is going to be a big one. Thanks for letting me stay here."

"You know you're always welcome here," June said. Then she remembered and bit her lip in consternation.

Felix wasn't welcome at June's house. Her father had expressly forbidden June to have Felix over, ever since he'd been arrested and charged with stealing a car. Felix was innocent, of course. His cousin had stolen the car, and then he and his friends had used it to pick Felix up from his part-time job at a local golf course. A sheriff's officer had pulled them over a few miles down the road and arrested all the boys who were in the car. The case was still pending, although Felix's court-appointed lawyer was hopeful he could get the charges reduced.

June found it all outrageous: Felix's arrest, that his lawyer was pushing him to take a plea deal when he hadn't even done anything wrong, and especially that her father had decided that the boy they'd known for years—who had been over to their house hundreds of times, who'd accompanied them on family vacations—had suddenly transformed into a dangerous felon with whom June shouldn't associate. Her mom had tried to intervene on Felix's behalf, but she clearly hadn't tried hard enough. June would never forgive her father for trying to ban her from being friends with Felix—or her mother for not standing up to him.

I will never be that weak, June thought with a surge of resentment.

When Felix had told her that his mother had to be at the hospital where she worked as a nurse practitioner for the duration of the hurricane, June had immediately invited him over to her house. It wasn't safe for him to be home alone, she'd reasoned, and besides, her parents would never find out. Their house was huge. She could keep one seventeen-year-old boy hidden for a night.

Felix grinned at her. "Hey, stop worrying about it. I know I'm always welcome to hide in your closet."

"I know. It just pisses me off. My parents are so unreasonable."

"I'm the one who's going to end up with a criminal record," Felix pointed out. "Which means goodbye to my scholarship."

June wanted to argue with him, but Felix was right. He was a straight-A student and on track to win a coveted Bright Futures Scholarship, which would guarantee him free tuition to a Florida state college. But one of the requirements to get and keep the scholarship was to have a clean criminal record. Pleading guilty to stealing a car would mean forgoing the scholarship and everything he'd worked toward for years.

"It isn't right." June sat down on the bed next to Felix. She ran her hand over the pink floral coverlet. "You shouldn't be punished for something you didn't do. We have to fix this."

He nudged her with his shoulder. "Try not to worry. You never know. We might die in this monster hurricane, and then I won't have to worry about getting into college or how I'm going to pay for it."

"Oh, great." June shook her head. "That makes me feel so much better."

CHAPTER THREE

MARLOWE

"I really wish I'd transferred the collection to the Norton ahead of the storm. Then they'd be the ones worrying about keeping it all safe," Marlowe said ruefully. She sat back on her heels.

"We didn't know the storm was going to be this big until today," Isabel pointed out.

The two women were kneeling on the floor of Marlowe's home office, surrounded by dozens of paintings of various sizes, most of which were already wrapped in brown kraft paper.

Marlowe's office was small but, on normal days, had a gorgeous view of the river, although that was currently obscured by the storm shutters. Marlowe had hung paintings of the ocean—some traditional, some modern and abstract—all over the walls, gallery-style. There were built-in shelves along one wall full of glossy art books and a woven sisal rug on the floor. It was the only space in the house where she allowed herself to be messy. Papers were stacked on her desk and on the table where Isabel worked sometimes, and she had an inbox piled high with unopened mail.

Isabel took an oil painting, one of the last to be wrapped, and appraised it with a critical eye. It was an abstract of bright primary colors painted on a square canvas. The signature in the corner was illegible.

"I don't recognize this one. Who's the artist?" Isabel asked.

Marlowe glanced over. "Daniel Garwood. He was my art professor at Vanderbilt. Hugely talented, although he never gained the reputation he deserved. My mom and I went to one of his exhibitions when I was a sophomore. She fell in love with this piece." Marlowe smiled wistfully. "That was my mom. She was impulsive, but she had an excellent eye."

"Is it valuable?" Isabel asked.

Marlowe knew her assistant was wondering whether a painting by a relatively unknown artist was important enough to be included in the Bond collection, the lifelong obsession of Marlowe's parents, Thomas and Katherine Bond. It had been their plan to donate their collection to the Norton Museum of Art in West Palm Beach, as well as funding for the necessary construction to add an additional wing to the museum. When Marlowe's parents had died six months earlier in a car accident, the task to fulfill this dream had fallen to her.

Marlowe had been daunted by the scope of the project at first, especially taking it on while she was still grief stricken by her parents' deaths. Their spacious Jupiter Island home had been jammed full of artwork, much of which didn't have any documentation. Katherine had been just as likely to buy a piece that caught her eye hanging in a thrift store as she was to acquire a painting from a well-known art dealer in Europe. Marlowe had to sort out which pieces should be included in the Bond collection. It was a big task to curate the collection and the reason why she'd hired Isabel away from a Miami art gallery to be her assistant. And Isabel had impressed her. She had an excellent eye and was meticulous in her work.

"I think so," Marlowe said. "Once more collectors discover Daniel Garwood, the value of his paintings will only increase. And I know this is sentimental, but it was one of my mom's favorite pieces. It feels right to include it in the collection."

"I like it. His use of color and composition is extraordinary." Isabel laid the Garwood down on a square of Bubble Wrap and carefully began to package it.

Marlowe looked around the room and shook her head ruefully. The collection was insured, of course, but it was invaluable to her. It was the history of her parents, of their family. "This was not my best decision. I waited too long to get the paintings somewhere safe. What if we lose the roof in the middle of the storm? The whole collection will be ruined."

Isabel's eyes widened. She was, as usual, fully made up with layers of carefully applied eye shadow. Her long shiny hair had been expertly curled, falling around her shoulders in perfect glossy waves. Marlowe ran a hand through her own mess of curly hair and felt disheveled in comparison.

"Is that possible? Could the roof really blow off?" Isabel asked.

Marlowe smiled reassuringly at the younger woman. "No, we'll be fine. This house has been through several hurricanes, and we've never had any issues. I'm just letting my anxiety run a little wild."

Isabel nodded but still looked uneasy. "Are we going to leave the paintings in here?"

Marlowe glanced around. Her office was lined with large windows on two sides, which were covered by hurricane shutters, and a set of french doors made with hurricane-impact glass, which led out to a stone path that wound around the house toward the gravel driveway. But even with these fortifications, she worried about the damage that the potential wind and water intrusion could wreak on the art collection.

"No," she said. "We'll put them in my closet upstairs. I think they'll be safest there. They really should be in a vault, but this is the best we're going to do until the storm passes. I wonder where June went. She was supposed to help us wrap the paintings."

"We're done. This is the last one," Isabel said. She wrapped the Garwood in brown paper, which she secured with a length of packing tape.

"Not quite," Marlowe said. "There's still the Cézanne sketch."

"The Cézanne is here?"

Isabel looked so shocked Marlowe almost laughed. "Yes, it's here. I told you—I should have transferred the whole collection to the Norton. Mistakes were made."

"But . . . where is it?" Isabel glanced around, as if she'd somehow missed a Cézanne leaning up against a wall or tucked behind Marlowe's teak midcentury modern desk.

"It's in the living room," Marlowe said. "Come on—I'll show you."

The women stood, and Marlowe led Isabel out of the office, down the hall, and to the right through an arched, open doorway. The living room was a large tranquil space with two gray upholstered sofas that faced one another, a pair of low-slung brown leather chairs, and a huge round upholstered ottoman the kids liked to perch on. The room was usually flooded with light from the large windows that faced out toward their front yard and the street beyond. But with the hurricane shutters up, the living room was like a cave. It was so dark Marlowe had to turn on the large glass lamps on the end tables next to the sofas.

"But where . . . oh!" Isabel went silent as her eyes fell on the framed drawing that hung on the wall.

It was a modest pencil sketch of two apples and a pear sitting on a wooden table, the pear tipped to one side. But there was something about the curves of the fruit, the perspective of the picture, the sweeping lines of pencil that made the viewer stop and look closer . . . and then realize they were in the presence of something magical.

"Whenever I look at it, I wonder if it was something Cézanne spent time on or if it was just something he dashed off. You know he drew every day. His sketches are in collections at museums all over the world. But this one . . ." Marlowe stopped and shook her head in wonder. "I've always thought it was special."

"I can't believe you have it hanging in your living room," Isabel said.

Marlowe hid a smile at her assistant's censorious tone. Isabel was right, of course. The sketch should be hanging in a museum, not in a family home.

"That's where it hung when I was little. Well, not this living room, but at my childhood home. I used to curl up to read on this huge plaid armchair we had. I was always reading. And in a weird way, it felt like the sketch was looking down at me, keeping me company while I was lost in *Anne of Green Gables* or *A Wrinkle in Time*. It's like an old friend. I love it."

"But the light." Isabel looked at the now-covered windows with horror. "The sun's so strong. It could ruin the sketch."

"That's why I hung it on this wall. It doesn't get any direct light there. But I also don't think it should ride out the hurricane there."

"Definitely not," Isabel said. "Is it going in your closet too?"

"No." Marlowe shook her head as she carefully lifted the Cézanne sketch up from the wall. "Not this one. This one's going into the safe. There's room for it, and nothing will happen to it in there. Not even a hurricane can touch it."

———

While Isabel began carrying the wrapped paintings, one by one, upstairs to Marlowe's closet, Marlowe took the Cézanne into Lee's home office. They'd had a wall safe installed there when they built the house. At first, Marlowe had thought having a home safe was all a little overly dramatic. They had a safety-deposit box at the bank where they kept their passports and important papers, and it wasn't like they had a stash of gold bricks they needed to secure. But now, Marlowe was very glad they'd made the choice to install it. The Cézanne would be protected until the storm passed. And then it would be transferred to the Norton with the rest of the collection.

Although . . . Marlowe wasn't sure how she was going to part with the Cézanne sketch. She hadn't shared this with anyone—not Beatrize from the Norton, not Isabel, not even Lee. The sketch was a connection to her parents—her mother's love of art, her father's love for her mother. It was the most precious thing she had ever owned.

But Marlowe also knew Isabel was right. The sketch was too valuable to keep in their house, and it should be somewhere climate controlled and safe from the elements. And, she reminded herself, it would be selfish to keep it to herself. Art was something that should be enjoyed by everyone.

Marlowe set the sketch—now safely nestled in Bubble Wrap and brown paper—on the blotter that covered Lee's large desk. The safe was hidden behind a competent oil painting of a sailboat, which attached to the wall with hinges to make accessing the safe easier. She rotated the lock to the right, then left, then right again, and the safe clicked open.

There were the usual items inside—documents, a few pieces of jewelry in velvet boxes that had belonged to Marlowe's mother, a small amount of emergency cash, Lee's Rolex watch. Marlowe began to arrange everything to one side of the safe to make room for the sketch. But then her hand touched something plastic. Marlowe closed her hand around it and drew the item out.

It was a cell phone.

Marlowe stared down at it for a long moment. She didn't recognize the phone. She, Lee, and the twins all had iPhones. This one looked clunky and cheap and had **MOTOROLA** stamped on the back. Marlowe tapped the front, which lit up an unlocked screen.

Where had the phone come from? But Marlowe already knew the answer. She and Lee were the only two people who had access to the safe. The kids didn't even know the combination. The phone wasn't hers, so it must belong to Lee.

But that raised another, more disturbing question. Why did Lee have a phone that Marlowe didn't know about? And why was it stashed in their safe?

CHAPTER FOUR

MARLOWE

"Mom! Where are you?" Tom's voice rang out from somewhere near the front of the house.

Marlowe was still standing in front of the open safe, staring down at the strange phone, one hand lingering near her throat. At the sound of her son's voice, she started and looked back over her shoulder.

"I'll be right there," she called back. She slid the phone into the pocket of her khaki shorts and then closed the safe, twisting the lock for good measure.

Marlowe walked through the kitchen and out to the front foyer. Tom was standing at the open door, peering into the house. Her son was tall, like Lee, but had inherited her freckles and light-blue eyes. A gust of wind caused his dark shoulder-length hair to blow up into his face, and Tom pushed the strands back behind his ears.

"Why are you standing there with the door open?" she asked.

"I didn't want to track in dirt," Tom said, pointing down to his muddy sneakers.

"Good thinking. Do you know where your father is?" *I just found something weird,* she almost added but then, for some reason, didn't. She wanted to ask Lee about the phone first. It was probably nothing, she reasoned.

"He's in the back, putting the pool cover on. You need to come outside."

"Why? What's going on?"

"The police are here. They're talking to Mick."

"The police?" Marlowe frowned. "What are they doing here?"

Zack appeared behind Tom in the doorway. He was a gangly boy, with spaghetti limbs and sun-bleached hair that was so thick it stood up on end. "Hey, Mrs. Davies! Do you think the police are here to investigate a murder? That would be wicked cool."

"If there was a murder, they'd have sent more than just two police officers. There would be a whole crime scene unit here," Tom said.

"Maybe they're investigating a missing person, and they don't know where the crime scene is," Zack countered.

"I'm sure that whatever they want has something to do with the storm," Marlowe said. "Let's go see what they want."

Marlowe stepped outside into the thick humidity. The scent of the brackish river was always more pronounced just before a storm, a combination of salt air, vegetation, and something darker and moldy blew up from the water.

Two sheriff's deputies in uniform were standing on the front walkway, talking to the Davieses' handyman, Mick Byrne. Mick was in his late fifties and was tall with broad muscular shoulders and a pronounced paunch. He had been in the marines when he was younger and still held himself like a soldier, his posture straight. Marlowe joined the group, flashing the officers a friendly smile.

"I'm Marlowe Davies. Can I help you?"

The male deputy was in his midtwenties and had a cleft chin and shortly buzzed blond hair. He wore mirrored aviator sunglasses, and Marlowe could see her warped reflection in them.

"Hello, ma'am. I'm Deputy Jack Daley with the Cayuga County Sheriff's Department. This is my partner, Deputy Louise Perez."

Deputy Perez had a serious face and long hair pulled back into a neat ponytail. She nodded unsmilingly at Marlowe.

"It's nice to meet you both. How can I help you?" Marlowe asked.

"We stopped by to make sure everyone along the river is evacuating." Deputy Daley caught sight of Tom and Zack trailing behind Marlowe and frowned. "Your family is still here?"

"Why shouldn't they be? Did someone issue an evacuation order?" Mick asked. There was a slight edge to his voice, as though he found the officer's question intrusive.

"This neighborhood isn't in a flood zone, so there isn't an official evacuation order," Deputy Daley said. "But because of the size and strength of Celeste, the mayor and town council have strongly encouraged everyone who lives on or near the water to evacuate."

Mick crossed his arms over his broad chest and rocked back on his heels. "From what I hear, all of the evacuation routes out of town have turned into parking lots. They'll probably still be sitting there in gridlock when the hurricane makes landfall. I think those are the people you should be worrying about."

Marlowe glanced at Mick nervously, worried that he was offending the sheriff's officers. "My husband and I discussed leaving, but that's exactly what we were worried about. That we'd get stuck on the turnpike. At this point, staying put seems like the safest option."

Mick nodded approvingly. "Panicking is the worst thing you can do with a storm coming in. Everyone wants to feel like they're doing something, so they all run around, clearing the shelves at the grocery store, waiting in line for hours at the gas station. And in the end, the storm just passes, the way storms always do. There'll be some flooding, and some palm trees will get knocked over, but that's about it."

"Sir, this is a very serious storm. It's projected to make landfall as a Category 5 hurricane," Deputy Daley said. "We could see catastrophic damage, loss of property, even loss of life."

Marlowe felt a lurch of panic deep in her gut. What were they doing? Staying had been a bad choice, she thought. Even now, the wind was blowing so hard her curly hair was whipping around her face. She reached up to tuck it behind her ears. "But it's too late to leave now."

"Several of the local schools have been turned into emergency shelters," Deputy Perez said. "We're advising everyone still in the area to go to one of those designated shelters."

Marlowe looked at Mick, and he raised an eyebrow. She knew what he was thinking. The shelters were certainly helpful in protecting the members of the community who didn't have a secure place to ride out the storm. But the Davieses had a well-built house, storm shutters, a metal roof, and two generators that would kick in as soon as the power went out. Her family would be safe and far more comfortable in their home than they would be spending the night on foam mats laid out on the floor of the elementary school's gymnasium.

"I appreciate the offer, but we're going to ride out the storm here," Marlowe said.

Deputy Perez looked past the Davieses' home, out at the Intracoastal Waterway, which rippled with waves. "If there's a storm swell, you could get flooding."

"I think we'll be okay. We've been through three hurricanes here, and we've never had flooding or even any water intrusion." Marlowe smiled at the two sheriff's officers. "But I appreciate you checking in on us."

"Just so you know, if anything happens and someone's hurt or your home has structural damage that makes it not habitable for the duration of the storm, emergency services won't be able to dispatch any resources until the storm passes," Deputy Daley said.

Mick gave him a hard pat on the shoulder. "Don't worry, son. It's not our first hurricane."

Deputy Perez glanced at Mick and then at the two teen boys. "Are you all planning on staying here at this house?"

"I'm going to stay with my mother," Mick said. "She lives alone, and storms make her nervous."

"And the boys are staying with us, of course. They're mine." Marlowe patted her son's back affectionately. "Well, this one's mine. But Zack's over so often he's basically one of the family."

Zack blushed bright red and ducked his head.

Deputy Daley nodded and looked resigned. "If you change your mind, you still have time to get to the shelter. But don't wait too long. The storm's coming in quickly. There are worse things than sitting in the school gymnasium for a night."

"True enough," Mick said. "Stay safe out there."

The sheriff's deputies turned and headed back to their car.

Marlowe glanced at Tom. "Are the shutters up?"

"Almost. We just have a few more, and then we'll be finished."

"The boys have done a great job," Mick said approvingly. "They've been working hard all morning."

"Mick said we would make good marines. But they'd make us cut our hair," Zack said, running a hand through his straw-like blond hair so that it stood up on end.

"I think I'd prefer it if you'd both pick jobs where no one shoots at you," Marlowe said, smiling up at her son and his friend.

The boys headed toward the back of the house, and Mick and Marlowe turned to watch the sheriff's cruiser back out of the paved driveway, lined on either side by palm trees, and pull away down the street.

"The police have never gone house to house here ahead of a storm," Marlowe remarked.

"Like I said, everyone panics when a hurricane is coming onshore," Mick said.

"I know." Marlowe nodded. "We just have to get through it." She looked at Mick. "You're welcome to stay with us. We certainly have the space."

"I appreciate that, but I promised my mother I'd go over to her place. She's older, and . . . well. She shouldn't go through this on her own."

"She's more than welcome to come here too," Marlowe said quickly.

"No, she wouldn't be comfortable with that, but thank you for offering."

"Does she have a generator?"

"No," Mick admitted. "She's in a condo. It's a solid building, and it's inland. The maintenance guy there already reached out and said her shutters are up. She may lose power, but we'll be safe enough there."

"But she won't be comfortable if she loses power," Marlowe persisted. "We have generators here, so we'll have air-conditioning. And she can have her own room. We have a lovely guest room on the first floor."

"I'll pass your invitation along," Mick said. "But I don't expect she'll want to leave her home."

"Of course she won't." Marlowe sighed. "I get that. None of us want to leave our homes, especially during a storm." She turned toward the house but then stopped and looked at Mick. "But the offer still stands if you change your mind."

"I appreciate it," Mick said. He looked up suddenly, as if listening for something. Marlowe heard it, too, although it didn't make any sense, not with a hurricane so close to shore. It sounded like there was a boat out on the water.

"What's that?" Marlowe asked.

"I think it's a boat," Mick said. He walked to the side of the house, Marlowe trailing after him. As soon as they had a full view of the water, she could see the boat out in the distance, making its way down the dark, choppy river. Even from this distance, she could hear its engines straining with the effort, a long wake trailing behind it.

"It looks like they're heading toward our dock," Marlowe said in surprise.

Mick nodded grimly. "That's exactly what they're doing."

"Why would they come here?"

"You'd better tell Lee we may have guests. I'll go see what they want."

CHAPTER FIVE

—

Tom

"Where's June?" Zack asked casually as he slotted the last hurricane shutter in.

Tom, who was holding the aluminum shutter steady to keep it from sailing away in the wind, rolled his eyes. "Gross. Stop."

"Stop what?"

"Stop lusting after my sister. Seriously, dude. It's not okay."

Tom brushed his hands together and then shook back his shoulder-length dark hair. He glanced up at the sky, which had darkened, the clouds a foreboding gray. It had been stiflingly hot when they had started putting the shutters up earlier that day, but the thick cloud cover and bursts of wind were causing the temperature to drop quickly. Celeste was getting closer.

Tom's thoughts went, as they so often did, to the beach. The feel of the hot sand under his calloused feet. The smell of the salt water so pronounced on the air he could almost taste it. The sensation of holding his board as he charged out into the surf. It was where he always felt the most himself.

Zack looked wistfully out at the Intracoastal. "Dude, think about how big the waves are going to be when the storm hits."

"I know—it's going to be sick."

"We should go to the beach!" Zack looked excited, his brown eyes large and shining. "We could go later and bring our boards. Just think about it!"

Tom laughed. "Yeah, right."

"I'm serious! When will we get the chance to see waves like this again? If we ride them in, we'd be, like, heroes."

"No, we wouldn't. We'd be dead." Tom wanted Zack to drop the subject. It reminded him of a news story from when he was little. Two teenage boys had taken a boat out onto the ocean, trying to outrun a tropical storm. He remembered his mom had tried to hide the story from him and June, but she had kept anxiously checking online for updates to see if the Coast Guard had rescued the boys. The boat had never been found, and the boys' bodies had never been recovered. Tom loved the ocean, but he also respected its power. The sea would be lethal during a Category 5 hurricane.

"Lame, dude." Zack shook his head. "We're missing out on a major opportunity."

"To get washed out to sea?"

"No! To score chicks," Zack said, flinging his skinny arms out wide, his eyes popping open. He reminded Tom of a manic blond Kermit the Frog.

"Chill," Tom said. "I'm riding out the storm here. If I even thought about leaving the house, my mom would kill me. And I don't think this is the best time to get her mad."

"Oh, right." Zack's arms fell to his sides, and his expression turned somber. "You still haven't told them you're not going to college next year?"

"Shh." Tom hushed his friend furiously and then looked around, his heart banging in his chest. No, he had not told his parents about his college plans—or lack thereof. And he certainly didn't want them to find out by overhearing Zack talking about it. He'd managed to hide it from them when they had gone to tour college campuses the previous weekend, pretending to be impressed by the climbing walls and food courts their tour guide had pointed out.

"It must be tough to have expectations to live up to," Zack said sagely. He was the youngest of four brothers and had been basically raising himself since he was eight or nine years old. Tom didn't think that Zack's parents were neglectful. Not exactly. They just always seemed too exhausted to pay attention to their youngest child. They hadn't even minded that Zack was spending the hurricane at the Davieses' house.

It was the exact opposite of the situation Tom was in. He loved his parents, but his mother especially was overinvolved in his life. She wanted to know everything—his grades, his friends, where he was going, where he had been. And he knew both of his parents expected him to go to college. They would never understand why he was going to veer off the course they wanted him to take, and he wasn't sure how to explain it to them in a way that would avoid their inevitable freak-out.

The truth was Tom wasn't entirely sure why he had no interest in college. He was a decent enough student. He maintained a B average and usually pulled out As in history and Spanish. He would probably be able to get into a decent college. But every time he tried to envision his future—what he wanted to do, the shape of what his life would look like—college was never a part of that. He didn't want to live in a dorm, or juggle fifteen credits, or eat crappy food in a dining hall. When he walked around the college campuses with his parents, his sister, and the student tour guide, he couldn't picture himself there. And it wasn't like he had any professional aspirations that would require a college degree. He couldn't see himself becoming an engineer, or an architect, or a finance guy working on Wall Street.

His one true passion was surfing, and although he was a pretty good surfer, he wasn't talented enough to turn pro. But he could see himself running his own surf shop one day, selling everything from boards to swimsuits. And maybe, like the local surf shop in town, he could offer lessons and run a surfing camp for kids in the summer. It wasn't like he had a plan on how to get there. But it was the only future he could picture that felt like it might fit. And explaining any of that to his parents seemed impossible.

"Don't say anything. Let's just lay low tonight while the storm passes," Tom said. "Be warned—my mom got the board games out. She's going to make us play."

"Sweet." Zack smiled happily. "I love board games."

"That makes one of us."

"That's just because I always kick your ass at Catan."

"Right. Are you going to check in with your parents? You might not be able to get a call out once the storm hits. The cell towers usually stop working at some point."

"Nah. They know where I am. They're not worried about me."

"Must be nice," Tom said.

Zack's expression shifted, and he looked uncharacteristically somber. "It's a good thing that your parents care about you, dude. Don't wish for parents that literally don't care where you are in the middle of a monster-ass storm."

Tom shifted from one foot to the other, not sure what to say to that. Because in a way, he sort of did wish that was what he had. Not parents who didn't care. But maybe ones who didn't care quite so much. After high school, Zack could enroll in an electrician's course at the local community college, and everyone would be thrilled at his choice. Just the thought of knowing how his parents would react to his plan to not go to college made Tom feel queasy, just like he did after eating a fast-food burrito bowl, his stomach churning from the cheap grease and carbs.

"Where are your parents going to be for the storm?" he finally said. Zack's family lived in a modest house near downtown Shoreham. They weren't near the water and so wouldn't have to worry about a storm surge, but Celeste was coming for everyone. The winds alone would knock over trees and rip off roofs. The hurricane might even take whole houses down.

"My dad wants to stay home, but my mom was trying to talk him into going to one of the shelters. I don't know who will win that battle."

"Can't your mom go to the shelter on her own?"

"She could, but she won't. Whatever they end up doing, they'll do it together." Zack smiled so sweetly Tom felt his heart pinch. "That's one thing about my parents. They've always been joined at the hip. Even when they want to kill each other."

"I hope they go to the shelter," Tom said. "I think this storm is going to be bad."

Zack shrugged one shoulder and then squinted, looking out at the Intracoastal. "Dude, look. Is that a boat?"

Tom turned to see what his friend was looking at. He was used to boats passing by the house. But no one would be out on the water with a hurricane heading onshore. The water had turned dark and choppy, the usual placid waves of the river already cresting higher than Tom had ever seen them.

But Zack was right—there was a boat. It had a light-aqua-blue hull, and although Tom couldn't tell for sure from this distance, it looked to be around thirty feet long. There appeared to be several people onboard. And the boat was headed straight toward the Davieses' dock.

CHAPTER SIX

MARLOWE

"The police were just here," Marlowe said as she walked into the kitchen.

Lee was standing at the sink, washing his hands. He looked uncharacteristically grubby after spending the morning working outside in the heat. His gray T-shirt was soaked through with sweat, and he was wearing an old pair of paint-splattered shorts he reserved for yard work.

"The police?" Lee turned off the faucet and shook his hands dry. "What did they want?"

"They're going house to house to make sure everyone who lives on or near the water evacuated."

"It's a little late for that."

"They've opened the schools as emergency shelters. They want us to go there. They're concerned about the storm surge."

Lee shook his head. "We don't need to worry about that. We're too high up. I'm more concerned about the wind, and that will be an issue everywhere, including the emergency shelters."

Marlowe had a sudden vivid image of a crowd of people huddled on the gymnasium floor at the elementary school while the storm raged outside—and what would happen to them if the roof was ripped off the building. She shuddered.

Lee seemed to intuit her dark thoughts. "Stop worrying. It doesn't help. It's not like you can worry away the hurricane."

"I know." Marlowe sighed and slid her hands into her pockets. Her fingers wrapped around a foreign-feeling piece of plastic, and she suddenly remembered. The phone she'd found in the safe. She had forgotten all about it when the police had arrived. She pulled it out of her pocket and held it up for Lee to see. "I found a mysterious phone in the safe. Did you put it there?"

Lee nodded. "Yeah, I found it by the pool earlier when I was storing the patio furniture. I figured one of the kids' friends left it behind, so I brought it inside for safekeeping."

"Is that why you put it in the safe?"

"I'm not sure why I put it there. I don't remember doing that. I opened the safe to store the Batman before I went out to do the storm prep." The Batman was the nickname for Lee's Rolex, which had a black-and-blue bezel insert. Marlowe had given it to him as a birthday present a few years earlier. "I must have stuck the phone in there then by accident. Maybe I'm having hurricane-induced brain fog."

"The mystery is solved. My husband has become absent minded." Marlowe opened the phone and turned it on. She pressed a few buttons. "That's strange."

"What?"

"There's no information on here. There aren't any texts, or contacts, or even any outgoing calls. I wonder who it belongs to? I don't think many kids these days have these kinds of phones. They all have smartphones with apps."

"Who else would have left it by the pool?" Lee countered.

Marlowe shrugged and slid the phone back into her pocket. "No idea. Maybe one of the lawn-service guys? I guess we'll find out when its owner realizes it's missing and calls the number. Anyway, that's not why I came in to find you. Mick sent me to get you. There's a boat outside."

"A boat? What are you talking about? The storm's about to hit."

It was still early, only just past two in the afternoon, but Mick and the boys were just finishing hanging up the storm shutters. The house had been cast into a dark gloom. Marlowe could hear rain beginning to patter on the metal roof and against the aluminum shutters.

"I don't know why they're out on the water, but it looked like they were heading for our dock. Do you think they're planning on tying it up there?"

"I'm not sure. Do you know who it is?"

"I don't think so." Shoreham was a boating community, and friends passing by on their way home from a day out on the sandbar or on their way to one of the town's waterfront restaurants would occasionally stop by, tying up at the Davieses' dock and staying for a glass of wine. But they always called first, and besides, Marlowe hadn't recognized the boat or its passengers, at least not from so far away.

Lee wiped his hands on a towel and tossed it on the counter. "Let's go see what they want. But we'd better make it quick. I think that rain we're hearing is the outer band of the storm hitting. Conditions are going to deteriorate quickly." He shook his head and headed toward the door that led out to the garage. "What kind of an idiot would take a boat out in a hurricane? You'd have to have a death wish."

Marlowe grabbed her green raincoat off a hook in the laundry room and followed Lee out through the garage door. Their usually spacious garage was crowded. Lee had parked all the family's cars inside— Marlowe's SUV, his Mercedes sedan, the Honda Civic the twins shared. The patio furniture was crammed in Tetris-like next to the cars so that the wicker chairs and side tables wouldn't become projectile missiles in the storm.

As soon as they were outside, Marlowe knew that Lee was right— the storm was drawing closer to the shore. The sky was even darker and more foreboding than it had been just moments earlier when she had been outside talking to the sheriff's deputies, and the wind had picked up, whipping around and sending loose fronds on the palm trees flying. The rain was starting to come down harder, and she was glad she'd thought to put on her raincoat.

They walked around the house and out to the back, past the patio and pool, heading down toward the river. The boat with the aqua-blue hull had just reached their dock. One of the passengers onboard, a man who looked to be in his early thirties, jumped out and began tying up the boat.

"I don't recognize them. Do you?" she asked.

Lee folded his arms over his chest and shook his head.

"I wonder why they're here at our dock, instead of going to one of the public ones," Marlowe said.

Lee glanced down at her. "They're allowed to. It's an old maritime law. Boaters in distress can tie up at a dock out of necessity. The owner of the dock has to allow it."

"That's a thing?" Marlowe asked. It felt like such an intrusion, having strangers at their home just as a storm was about to hit. But just as Marlowe was wishing them away, she felt a simultaneous surge of guilt. It must have been terrifying to be out on the water with a storm closing in.

"I'd better go help them tie it up. If it isn't done properly, the boat could end up in our living room." Lee looked around. "Oh, good. There's Mick." He waved to get the handyman's attention, and Mick walked over to where they were standing.

"This looks like trouble," Mick said, nodding at the boat.

"I think they must be having some sort of an issue." Lee shook his head. "I don't love the idea of having strangers in the house, around the kids."

"They certainly can't stay out there on the boat in the middle of a hurricane," Marlowe said.

"I'll take them to the emergency shelter at the elementary school," Mick said. "I'll drop them off on the way to my mother's house."

Marlowe felt a familiar rush of gratitude for their handyman. He was a taciturn man who kept to himself, but he always seemed to know the right thing to do in any situation. Including, it seemed, handling boaters in distress who appeared just as a hurricane was about to hit.

"Maybe we should call the sheriff," Lee said.

"The sheriff's deputies were just here," Marlowe said. She brushed a damp curl back from her forehead. "They said they won't be responding to any calls until after the hurricane passes."

"We'll make sure the boat's tied up safely, and then I'll take them to the shelter." Mick glanced up at the sky. The clouds were moving rapidly across the sky, as if they, too, were fleeing the storm. "And the sooner, the better. The storm is going to hit soon."

The man on the dock was still working on tying up the boat. He was wearing a red long-sleeved T-shirt and dark-gray shorts. There were two additional passengers onboard—a second man, also in his thirties, who had a beard, and a young woman wearing a bikini. The three worked urgently as another huge gust of wind blew toward shore. The girl put her hands up, shielding her face from the gust.

Lee turned to Marlowe. "Go make sure the kids are inside. I don't think we have a lot of time."

His hand on her arm felt strong and reassuringly familiar. Marlowe felt a wave of gratitude that he was there, that she had him there to go through the storm with her.

Marlowe nodded and started to walk back up the sloping back-yard toward their house. She had always loved their home, had always thought of it as a warm and welcoming place. But right now it looked menacing with the storm shutters up, like a face without features. The thought made Marlowe shiver, and her skin broke out in goose bumps beneath the waxy lining of her raincoat.

The wind picked up again, whipping by her in short angry gusts. It roared up from the water with such ferocity Marlowe stumbled. Lee was right. This must be the first outer band of the storm hitting them. She turned to call back to him, to tell him that he needed to get back to the house, too, that everyone needed to take cover immediately.

That was when it happened.

A large navy-and-white-striped patio umbrella from their neighbor's backyard flew over the fence that divided the two properties. Marlowe watched in horror as it cartwheeled straight toward Lee and Mick, who had just reached the entrance to their dock.

"Look out!" Marlowe screamed.

But it was too late. The umbrella tumbled over again and rose up from the ground. Then, as another sharp gust of wind blew up off the river, the umbrella careened straight toward Mick, then struck him in the side of the head.

CHAPTER SEVEN

ISABEL

Isabel set the last of the brown-paper-wrapped paintings on its end in the master bedroom closet and then stepped back to survey her work. Although calling it a closet was laughable. It was bigger than Isabel's bedroom in her apartment, with clothing racks and shelves along three of the walls and an upholstered bench in the middle. Marlowe's clothes hung neatly on one side, while Lee's suits and dress shirts occupied the opposite. It smelled wonderfully of freesia and was wallpapered with a subtle sage-green stripe.

Isabel shook her head, marveling that an entire collection—one which would soon have its own permanent wing in the Norton Museum!—was stacked up in a closet, nestled next to the shelves that held Marlowe's Jack Rogers sandals and running shoes lined up in neat rows. But Marlowe was probably right. As an interior room, this was the safest spot in the house for the valuable art collection. They wouldn't be at risk from water or wind intrusion here. The only way the paintings would be damaged was if Celeste blew the roof off the house.

In which case, Isabel thought, *we're all fucked.*

She slowly turned, looking at the contents of Marlowe's closet. It was predictably boring. Despite having a slim figure that would look good in just about anything, Marlowe stuck to oversize button-down cotton shirts paired with khaki shorts, or Lilly Pulitzer shift dresses. Isabel spotted a few dressier garments off to one side of Marlowe's side of the closet. She pulled one out. It was a black silk sheath dress, simple but well cut and clearly expensive. Isabel stepped in front of the full-length cheval mirror and held the dress up to herself, posing with her head tilted in one direction and then another, her lips pouting seductively.

Pretty, but too conservative. Not at all her style, Isabel decided and returned the dress to its spot on the rack.

Isabel listened to hear if anyone was coming, but the only sound she could hear was the wind outside, which was starting to howl in a way that gave her the creeps. She poked her head out of the closet, but the master bedroom was empty.

Isabel returned to her snooping. She opened a few of the drawers, which held stacks of leggings and sports bras and workout shirts. One drawer contained a velvet jewelry tray, and for a moment, Isabel's pulse quickened. But she quickly realized that except for a thin gold bracelet and pair of possibly real pearl earrings that Marlowe often wore, the rest of it was costume jewelry. She supposed Marlowe wouldn't keep anything valuable in her closet when there was a safe downstairs. Isabel closed the drawer regretfully. She hadn't exactly planned to steal anything, of course, although had the right opportunity presented itself . . . but Isabel wasn't going to lose her job and ruin her professional reputation over some cheap costume jewelry.

She closed the drawer and quickly moved from the closet to the master bathroom, which was just as oversize as the closet. The bathroom had been finished with white marble and had a long vanity with two sinks, a huge walk-in shower with a rainfall showerhead, and a separate soaking tub big enough to comfortably fit three people. She closed the door behind her and turned on one of the square nickel sink faucets in case someone came looking for her. It would be odd to be found hanging out in her boss's personal bathroom, but she could always claim she needed an emergency pee.

There weren't any expensive lotions out on the sink, and anyway, pocketing face lotion was the quickest way for a thief to get caught. Isabel had learned that while she was in foster care, when her stays had been in far more modest homes. Women put on the same face cream every night and quickly noticed when it disappeared off their counter. It was easier to pocket nail polish or a lipstick, although these days, Isabel's taste had evolved. She wasn't interested in the sort of drugstore crap her foster mothers had bought. But a Chanel lipstick or a bottle of Tom Ford perfume might be worth her attention, if she could get away with it.

But a quick perusal of Marlowe's drawers left her confused and a little annoyed. Isabel had done her research before she'd accepted the job as Marlowe's assistant. She knew her boss's background. Marlowe came from big money. Her parents had owned Bond Marine, famous for their fleet of retail recreational fishing boats, and had been worth tens of millions, probably more. It was how they'd been able to procure their impressive art collection. Marlowe had grown up in a large house on Jupiter Island and had gone to the Benjamin School and then on to Vanderbilt, where she'd studied art history. Marlowe had never had to worry about finding a job to support herself or struggled to pay rent. And after all that wealth and privilege and the access to the sort of luxuries Isabel could only dream about, Marlowe's drawers were stocked with Olay moisturizer, MAC Cosmetics, and Nivea body lotion.

What the hell? Isabel wondered. If she had the money that Marlowe had, she would have only the best—Oscar de la Renta dresses, Hermès belts, La Mer moisturizer.

If Marlowe weren't so nice, Isabel would have hated her.

Isabel stilled. She thought she heard something other than the wind and the rain. She quickly turned off the tap so she could listen more closely. The hurricane shutters muffled some of the exterior noises, although she could still hear the rain sleeting against the roof and . . . something else? Yes, she could hear voices outside. Someone was shouting. Something was going on.

Isabel glanced around to make sure she hadn't left any of the drawers open and then quickly exited the bathroom. She needed to go downstairs and find out what was happening.

CHAPTER EIGHT

MARLOWE

Mick was lying on the ground. He wasn't moving.

Marlowe ran down the lawn, slipping on the wet grass and nearly tumbling over before she was able to right herself. The wind was now blowing up off the water so fiercely it felt like she was running straight into a wall. The rain blew horizontally, soaking every part of her that wasn't covered by the raincoat.

The striped umbrella that had struck Mick was lying on the lawn, twitching where it had fallen like an injured bird. But a fresh blast of wind suddenly caught the umbrella, and it rose up again, levitating for a split second. Then another wind gust off the water sent the umbrella careening wildly toward Marlowe.

"Marlowe!" Lee yelled. "Look out!"

She let out a cry and crouched down, barely avoiding being hit as the umbrella flew over her. She watched it take off again—it blew up the yard, past the house, and then out of sight.

What were the Coopers thinking, leaving out their patio umbrella in the middle of a hurricane? Marlowe wondered, feeling a surge of anger. How could they be so negligent? Everyone knew that unsecured items could become projectiles in a storm. She hoped the umbrella wouldn't do any more damage, that it wouldn't hit anyone else or break someone's window, which could be deadly in a hurricane.

Lee ran over to her and reached down to help her up. She clasped his hand and struggled to her feet.

"Are you okay?" he asked anxiously.

"I'm fine. How's Mick?"

They both turned toward where the handyman was lying prone on the grass, one arm flung out to the side, his legs splayed apart. Mick's eyes were shut, and from this distance, Marlowe couldn't tell if he was breathing. She hurried to his side and knelt in the damp grass, taking his hand in hers. It was ice cold. Marlowe was filled with a sickly dread.

"Is he dead?" she asked.

"No," Lee said, raising his voice to be heard over the wind. "He's breathing. I can see his chest rising. But he must have been knocked unconscious. We need to get him inside."

Marlowe was nodding, even as she was wondering, *How on earth are we going to do that?* Mick was tall and thickly built. He must have weighed at least two hundred and thirty pounds. She and Lee together wouldn't be able to move him, much less carry him all the way up the sloping lawn to the safety of their house.

"Mom!" Tom called out, heading down the lawn toward them, with Zack by his side. "Is he okay?"

Before Marlowe could answer, she saw that the passengers from the boat had disembarked and were now hurrying down the dock.

"Hold on! We can help! We'll be right there!" one of the men called out.

Marlowe watched as the three strangers ran toward them, the man in the red long-sleeved shirt in the lead.

How is this happening? Marlowe wondered. She looked down at Mick, who was frighteningly still as he lay on the soggy ground. His usually ruddy skin had turned gray. Should he have lost color so quickly? Marlowe wondered if she should call 911, then remembered the earlier visit from the sheriff's deputies. Emergency services wouldn't respond until the storm passed.

"We have to get him inside," she said to Lee.

"I know. But I'm not sure how we're going to move him."

"Hi there. I saw your friend get hit. Can we help?" the man in the red shirt asked, his voice ragged from the exertion of tying up the boat and running down the dock.

He looked to be in his thirties and seemed very fit. He had thick dark hair and a day's growth of stubble on his face, and had a battered-looking dark-green backpack slung over one shoulder. His male companion, standing behind him, was thin with a full beard. The second man leaned forward to brace his arms against his legs while he tried to regain his breath. The younger woman in the bikini hovered behind them, as if she wasn't sure what to do with herself.

Lee and Marlowe exchanged a glance, in which they held a silent conversation. Accepting their help meant they would be inviting strangers into their home and around their children. But bad people wouldn't come running to their aid, Marlowe reasoned. And if they didn't find a way to move Mick inside, he would die. It really wasn't even a choice.

"Thank you. I don't think we can move him on our own," Lee said. "We were on our way to help you tie up your boat when Mick got hit."

The man in the red shirt glanced back at the boat they'd arrived on. "I made sure it's tied securely. Or as securely as it can be with this storm coming in."

"We can help carry Mick too," Tom offered.

"Why don't you boys go open the doors on the patio?" Marlowe told her son.

Tom and Zack sprinted up the lawn, toward the house. Marlowe stood back while Lee and the man in the red shirt each positioned themselves by Mick's shoulders. The bearded man took his legs.

"On three," the man in the red shirt said. "One, two, *three*."

The men lifted Mick, grunting with the effort. Lee struggled, and Marlowe's heart lurched when, for a moment, she thought they might drop Mick. But the men braced themselves and, grunting with the effort, hoisted Mick back up.

"Let's go!" Lee shouted over the roar of the wind. The men started to walk crab-like up the sloping lawn, struggling to hold up Mick's prone body while the wind gusted behind them. They skirted around the pool and up onto the patio, toward the french doors that led into the house.

Marlowe turned to the girl, who was very tan and so thin her ribs were prominent. She had straight brown hair that the wind was whipping around her face. The girl's eyes were wide with fright, and she was shivering in her bathing suit, her arms wrapped around herself. Marlowe smiled at her, realizing that she didn't look much older than Tom and June.

"Come on," she said. "We need to get inside. It's not safe out here."

The girl nodded, and the two followed the men's path up to the house and onto the back patio. The wind blew behind them in such strong gusts Marlowe felt like it was pushing her all the way up the lawn.

Thunder rumbled close. Marlowe glanced back at the river. The water was churning, and the waves were roiling higher than she'd ever seen before. The palm trees around the house were bent under the onslaught of the wind, the heavy rain nearly horizontal as it sheeted down. The sky was eerily dark, despite the fact that it was only midafternoon. A bolt of lightning struck so close to the shore Marlowe was temporarily blinded. When she closed her eyes, she could still see the outline of the lightning bolt on the inside of her eyelids.

She's here, Marlowe thought.

Celeste has arrived.

CHAPTER NINE

MARLOWE

Tom and Zack were waiting at the french doors on the back patio. When the men carrying Mick reached them, they each quickly pulled one open, struggling against the gusting wind.

"Is Mick going to be okay?" Tom asked anxiously when Marlowe and the young woman from the boat reached him.

"I don't know. He's unconscious," Marlowe said. The wind roared through the open doors into the sunroom, knocking over an occasional table next to one of the wicker chairs, sending it crashing to the ground. "Come on—we need to close these doors!"

Tom nodded, and he and Zack shut and locked the french doors. The storm outside was still audible but now muffled, as though someone had dialed the volume down on a radio. Marlowe went to the wall and pressed a switch. A large storm shutter slid into place over the patio doors, closing with a metallic click, muting the sound of the storm further.

Marlowe saw the teen boys studying the young woman with interest. She was shivering violently.

"You're freezing," Marlowe said. She grabbed a gray cashmere throw blanket off the back of a chair and wrapped it around the girl's shoulders. Marlowe turned to Tom. "Please go find June and ask her to bring down some clothes for this young lady." Marlowe looked at the girl. "What's your name?"

The girl stared blankly back at her, and Marlowe wondered if she was in shock. But finally, the girl said, "D-Darcy."

She was so young and vulnerable looking. Marlowe didn't know why the three strangers had been out on the water, but she imagined it must have been terrifying out there. The lift and pitch of the swells would have tossed the boat around like it was a toy.

Marlowe smiled kindly at her. "Hi, Darcy. I'm Marlowe Davies, and this is my son, Tom, and his friend Zack. It's nice to meet you."

"Hey," Zack said, waving awkwardly.

"I didn't think we were going to make it to shore." Darcy looked dazed. "I thought we were going to die out there."

"Why were you out boating with the storm coming in?" Marlowe asked.

"I didn't know it was going to be that bad," the girl said, which wasn't really an answer. But Marlowe decided this was not the time to press her. The girl needed dry clothes and a chance to warm up. And Marlowe had to check on Mick. She glanced at Tom, who hadn't moved. He was frozen in place, staring at the girl, who was, Marlowe realized, quite pretty.

"Tom," Marlowe said gently. "Please go get June and have her bring down something for Darcy to wear. And get some towels too. Everyone's going to need to dry off."

Color flooded Tom's cheeks, but he nodded and hurried toward the front hall, Zack following close behind him. Marlowe could hear their heavy footsteps as they bounded up the stairs.

"Let's go see where the others went," Marlowe said to Darcy.

She led the girl from the sunroom, through the kitchen, and out into the front foyer. Marlowe could hear voices in the living room, so she headed there. Lee and the two men from the boat were helping get Mick situated on one of the charcoal-gray sofas, his head propped up on a cream throw pillow. Isabel had joined them, although she stood off to one side, watching silently. Mick's eyes were slitted open, and even in the dim lamplight, Marlowe could see he looked pale and unwell.

"Mick!" Marlowe went to his side, kneeling by the sofa. "I'm glad you're awake. You scared us. How are you feeling?"

"I've been better," Mick grunted. He raised a hand to the side of his head, where the umbrella had struck him. Marlowe noticed it was bleeding.

"We need to get that cleaned up," Marlowe said, touching his temple, just under the nasty cut on his forehead.

"He came to just as we were bringing him inside," Lee said.

Marlowe looked up. The man in the red long-sleeved shirt was gazing down at Mick, his face creased with concern. He was incredibly good looking, Marlowe realized. He had perfectly symmetrical chiseled features accentuated by unusual bright-green eyes and a lean, muscular build. He looked like he could be a model or a film star. Maybe an actor playing the part of a weathered and scruffy pirate, she amended. His dark hair was mussed, and he looked like he hadn't shaved in days.

The man beside him, who had a beard and wore a short-sleeved T-shirt with the slogan SHUCK 'EM ALL screen printed on it, was thinner and not as handsome but had the same green eyes. Marlowe wondered if they were related.

The man in the red shirt felt her gaze on them. He looked up and smiled, extending his hand to her. "I'm Bo Connor. This is my brother, Jason. You already met my girlfriend, Darcy. We're sorry to intrude like this."

"Thank you for helping bring Mick in," Marlowe said. "I don't think Lee and I could have managed to carry him on our own."

"Probably not," Bo agreed. "I guess it's a good thing we were there, although believe me—I wish it were under different circumstances. We got caught in that storm. I wasn't sure we were going to make it to shore."

"I told you we were going to make it," Jason said, tripping over the words. "I told you we would."

Marlowe wondered if Jason had a speech impediment or if he was just nervous. Or maybe, like Darcy, he was dazed from the storm. When Marlowe looked at him, Jason's gaze slid away, and his fingers drummed against his leg.

"Why were you out on the water with a hurricane coming in?" Lee asked.

"The owner of the boat lives down in Fort Lauderdale. He's an oral surgeon from up north, new to the area. Not at all experienced on the water. He panicked when he saw the size and strength of the storm and arranged indoor storage for the boat in Shoreham. He hired Jason and I to bring it up at the last minute. I thought we could beat the storm, but . . ." Bo stopped and shook his head, exhaling deeply. "It came in faster than I expected. A lot faster."

"You were trying to move a boat as the storm was coming in?" Lee asked. Marlowe could tell by the incredulity in his tone exactly what he thought about that decision. Lee had always maintained that the number one role to boat safety was not setting out in bad weather.

"The hurricane was still well offshore when we set out, but we got delayed down near Jupiter, running against the tide."

"I'm surprised the owner would want to take that kind of a risk with his boat."

"Like I said, the boat is new, and he was desperate. He was willing to pay us top dollar to run the boat up to the storage today. Enough that we decided to risk it."

Bo sounded resigned but not necessarily regretful. Probably because it wasn't his boat that was now tied up outside for the duration of the storm, Marlowe thought. And they had made it to safety, even if that was an unexpected stop at the home of strangers.

"The kids are bringing down something for Darcy to wear and towels for all of you," Marlowe said. "Would either of you like a change of clothes?"

"I can go get them," Isabel offered, stepping forward.

"No, thank you. A towel will do just fine," Bo said. "Much appreciated."

"We're used to being out on the water," Jason said. "Bo and I grew up on boats. We know boats inside and out."

"Isabel, would you mind getting a dish towel from the kitchen and dampening it with warm water? I want to clean off Mick's face," Marlowe said.

"I'm fine," Mick said, even though it was obvious he wasn't.

Isabel nodded, looking relieved to have been given something to do. She hurried out of the living room.

"I can't believe you set out on the water with a hurricane blowing in," Lee said, clearly not ready to give up this line of inquiry. "You could have all been killed."

"Like I said, the job paid well," Bo said easily.

And even though his tone was genial, Marlowe got the sense that the conversation could easily turn combative if Lee continued to question their guest's judgment. It was too late to call for help or drive them to a shelter. They were all going to have to be together for the duration of the storm, which would last for at least the rest of the day and probably into the early hours of the morning. Conflict should be avoided, if possible.

"You must be hungry after your ordeal. I'll go rustle up some food. Lee, will you get our guests set up with drinks?" Marlowe asked.

Lee met her gaze, and she could see the strain behind his eyes. Marlowe knew what her husband was thinking—these were strangers standing in their home. People they knew nothing about. But then Lee apparently made the same calculation Marlowe already had. It was going to be a long night, and they were going to be spending it together. There was no reason to make the evening more unpleasant than it had to be.

"What can I get you?" Lee asked, his tone more cordial. "A beer? A soda? Let's go see what's in the fridge."

"A beer sounds great," Bo said, and he and Jason followed Lee out of the living room.

Marlowe looked down at Mick, who was still lying on the sofa. He shifted and pushed himself up on one arm. Marlowe reached out a hand to stop him.

"You don't have to get up. What can I get you?"

"I'm sorry I didn't get a chance to take them to the shelter," Mick mumbled.

"Don't worry about that now," Marlowe said. "Do you want me to call your mother? I'm not sure how long we'll have phone service before it gets knocked out. I wish I'd kept the landline. I forgot how useful they are to have during hurricanes."

"I'd appreciate that. Thank you," Mick said. "Just don't tell her I was hurt. She worries too much as it is."

"I'm sorry we can't get you to the hospital. We'll take you to the ER as soon as it's safe to drive."

"I'll be fine," Mick said again. Marlowe thought he'd probably claim he was fine even if he'd just lost a limb. *I'm fine. It's just a leg. I can live without it.* "It's probably just a concussion. There's nothing anyone can do for that."

"You still need it looked at. I'm going to go get you a glass of water." Marlowe turned to follow Lee and the brothers toward the kitchen, but Mick's voice stopped her.

"Marlowe. Wait," he said, his voice low and urgent. "Listen to me."

She looked back. "What is it?"

"I don't trust them." Mick's expression was grim. "No one would go out on the water with a storm like that coming in. Not for all the money in the world. Something's not right here."

CHAPTER TEN

JUNE

June and Felix were lying on her bed, with June's laptop propped up between them. They were watching *The Breakfast Club* for what had to be the tenth time, but June had happily agreed when Felix had suggested it. She loved the movie, too, and it was soothing, watching something and knowing how it would end. They gazed at the screen in a companionable silence, with Felix occasionally saying the dialogue out loud with the actors and June trying to ignore how much she wanted him to move closer and take hold of her hand.

But just as June was reminding herself that she did not, could not, have a crush on Felix, there was a knock on the door. June froze, turning to stare at Felix. He stared back, his eyes wide. Then he leaped up and hurried into the closet, sliding the accordion door closed behind him. June was amazed that someone so tall could move so quietly.

"Hold on," June called out, but whoever was on the other side of the door rattled the knob. June frowned and went to the door, pulling it open to find Tom and Zack standing there. "I said hold on. That doesn't mean come on in."

"Why's your door locked?" Tom frowned. "You never lock it."

"Maybe to keep you two from barging in uninvited?"

Zack held a hand over his heart. "I want you to know I would never do that. In fact, if Tom ever tries to walk in your room without permission again, I'll tackle him before he gets through the door. Like, *boom*, I'll knock him right to the ground. You have my word."

"Um, thanks?" June said while Tom rolled his eyes. She waved the boys into the room. "Come in, but close the door behind you."

Tom and Zack complied, and June reached over to lock the door again.

"It smells really good in here," Zack said. "Like perfume and . . . something else. What are those white flowers that smell like honey?"

"Honey blossom?" Tom suggested.

"It does?" June sniffed. "I don't smell honey blossom."

"I love the smell of honey blossoms. I think it smells better than anything in the world," Zack said.

"Oh-kay," June said, drawing out the word. Zack had always been a goof, but lately it seemed like he'd ratcheted it up. And weirdly, at the same time, Tom seemed to have grown more serious and withdrawn. She had no idea what was going on with either of them. *Everyone thinks teen girls are weird,* she thought. *Teen boys are so much worse.*

"What are you doing up here?" Tom's eyes wandered across the room, taking in the now-empty can of Pringles and the half-eaten plastic tub of peanut-butter-filled pretzels. "Are you alone?"

"Not exactly," June said. "Felix, you can come out. It's just Tom and Zack."

The closet door slid open, and Felix stepped out, ducking to keep his head from bumping on the doorframe.

"Hey, man," Tom said.

Felix slapped hands with Tom and then bumped his fist against Zack's.

"Dude. How long have you been in the closet?" Zack asked, pointing at him.

"Funny guy," Felix said, sitting on the edge of June's bed. "I am persona non grata in the Davies household."

"You do know Dad will freak if he finds out he's here?" Tom asked June.

"I don't even care. Let him freak. But don't say anything, okay?"

"I won't say a word," Tom said. "My policy is that the less Dad knows, the better."

"Your secret is safe with me," Zack said. "I would never do anything to hurt you."

"That's good to know." June looked at Tom, confused by Zack's earnest declaration. Tom shook his head, silently telling her to ignore him. June sat down next to Felix. "What did you guys want?"

"You're not going to believe what's going on downstairs," Tom said.

"Mom has the board games out?" June guessed. "Or a two-thousand-piece jigsaw puzzle of Van Gogh's *Starry Night*? You know how Mom loves a jigsaw puzzle."

"Mick got hit in the head by an umbrella and had to be carried inside," Zack said excitedly.

"Wait. What?"

"The Coopers must have left their patio umbrella outside. It blew over the fence and hit Mick," Tom explained.

"It knocked him out," Zack said. "Like, *boom*. He went down hard."

June's eyes widened with horror. "Oh my God! Is Mick okay?"

"I don't know. He was unconscious when they carried him inside," Tom said.

"How did you guys manage that?" June frowned. "Mick's a big guy."

"That's what we're trying to tell you. There are *people* downstairs," Tom said.

"You mean your parents?" Felix asked.

"Well, yeah, they're here, obviously," Tom said. "But get this—there are three strangers down there. Two men and a woman. They were out on a boat as the storm was coming in. They had to tie up at our dock."

Felix let out a whistle. "They were out on a boat? That's crazy. There's been a marine advisory out since yesterday."

"Since when do you check the marine advisory?" June asked. Felix was terrified of the water. He never went boating. He didn't even like swimming in a pool. Whenever they'd both been invited to a pool party, she'd pretended she didn't like swimming, either, so he wouldn't feel lonely sitting off to the side by himself while everyone else splashed around in the pool.

"I don't. There was an alert on my weather app." Felix grinned at her.

Tom leaned against the wall. "I don't know who they are or why they were out on a boat, but now they're here. Downstairs. In our house."

"They're not planning on staying here, are they?" June asked.

"Where are they supposed to go?" Tom nodded toward her shuttered window. "In case you missed it, the hurricane's arrived. Don't you hear the wind?"

The four teenagers fell silent for a moment, listening to the wind howling and the rain pelting against the shutter. It sounded like a monster was outside, trying to claw its way into the house. For the first time, it occurred to June that when they'd locked out the storm, they'd also locked themselves in. Tom was right. No one would be able to leave until the hurricane had passed.

"It's weird to have strangers in the house. Especially overnight. This all sounds super sketch," June said.

"They seem okay," Tom said. "They did help carry Mick inside."

"Tom thinks the girl is hot," Zack chimed in.

"I didn't say that!"

"I know, but you thought it." Zack nodded knowingly at June and Felix. "He totally did."

Tom bumped his shoulder against Zack's. "Shut up."

"I think they might be on the run," Zack suggested. "Like, what if they're drug smugglers or something like that? And the police were after them, so they took off in their boat into the storm so that the cops wouldn't chase after them." Zack threw his arms out, and his eyes were wide. "Maybe that's why the police were really here earlier! Maybe they were looking for them and didn't want to scare us by saying anything."

"The police were here?" Felix asked.

"Yeah, they were going house to house, warning people to evacuate," Tom said. "They also said they're not going to be responding to 911 calls until after the hurricane is over."

"Or that's what they claimed. They might have been looking for the guys downstairs," Zack said.

"They're not criminals on the run," Tom said wearily.

"You don't know that. They could be. You could be harboring criminals and not even realize it." Zack's eyes slid to Felix. "Oh, sorry, man. I didn't mean to bring up a sore subject."

"Felix isn't a criminal!" June said hotly.

Zack turned so red he looked like he'd suffered a sudden acute sunburn. "Sorry, dude. I didn't mean anything by it," he muttered.

Felix laughed. "No worries. It's a sore subject for June. I'm fine."

"Mom sent us up here to find you. She wants you to bring down clothes for the girl," Tom said to his twin.

"Why does she need my clothes?"

"She doesn't have any. She's just wearing a bathing suit," Tom said.

"They were out on a boat," Zack said. "So that part's not so weird."

"All of this is weird." June raised her hands. "All of it."

"Tom! Where did you go? June?" their mother's voice called from downstairs, muffled through the door. "Please don't forget to bring down towels!"

"Towels?" June looked at Tom.

"They're all soaking wet from getting caught out in the rain."

June nodded. "We'd better go down before she comes up here. And I guess I need to bring this strange chick my clothes." June went to her closet and pulled out a charcoal-gray sweatshirt and a matching pair of joggers. She folded the clothes into her arms and then looked at Felix. "Are you going to be okay up here on your own for a bit?"

"Don't worry about me." Felix stretched out, plumping up one of the pillows behind his head. "I've got my movie; I've got snacks. I'll be right here chilling."

"I'll come back up as soon as I can get away."

Felix stretched out on her bed again, and June wanted to curl up next to him and finish their movie. But if she didn't go downstairs, her mom might come looking for her. So she smiled at Felix and then followed her brother and Zack out of her room, shutting the door softly behind her.

CHAPTER ELEVEN

MARLOWE

"No, Janet, he's fine," Marlowe said. She'd been relieved that her iPhone still worked, and she was able to get ahold of Mick's elderly mother, Janet Byrne. She hated to lie to Janet but knew Mick was right—there was no reason to cause the woman unnecessary worry. Marlowe pressed her phone to her ear, trying to hear the woman's faint voice over the roar of the wind outside.

"Please tell him I'm safe and snug here. I don't want him trying to drive anywhere right now," Janet said, her voice thin and reedy.

"I'll make sure he stays here for the duration of the storm," Marlowe promised. "Please don't worry."

Janet chuckled. "I never worry about Mick. He's always been able to take care of himself. Even when he was a boy. He once built a stone wall at the Audubon Society all by himself. He earned his Eagle Scout badge for it."

Marlowe laughed weakly. "Yes, I can just picture that. I'm sorry, but I have to get going, Janet. Please be safe, and let us know if you need anything."

"I will. And you—"

But whatever Janet was going to say was lost as the call disconnected. Marlowe looked at her phone and saw that the cell signal was gone. *The cell phone towers must be down,* she thought, resignedly placing her phone on the counter next to a flickering three-wick candle that filled the air with the scent of orange spice. It was inevitable that they'd lose contact with the outside world.

The sound of the shrieking wind and the rain splattering against the house was so loud Marlowe could barely hear the voices of her husband, Isabel, and their unexpected guests in the living room. But from the easy tenor of Lee's voice and Bo's laughter, it sounded like everyone was getting along. Marlowe released some of the tension she'd been holding in her stomach. It almost felt like they were hosting a party, Marlowe thought as she unwrapped a dish of spinach-artichoke dip and set it in the microwave to heat up.

She'd already arranged a cheese platter, with wedges of creamy goat and blue cheeses, a thick rectangle of sharp cheddar, sliced prosciutto, coins of salami, and an assortment of crackers. Lee loved her queso with chorizo, so she'd already prepared a bowl of that, paired with tortilla chips. She'd made brownies earlier as a treat for the boys, who had worked so hard getting the house ready, and they were cut into neat rectangles and stacked high on a glass cake stand.

"Mom?" June walked into the kitchen, with Zack and Tom trailing behind her. "I brought down clothes and the towels you wanted for . . . ?" June's voice trailed off, and she looked around.

"Darcy," Marlowe said. "Thank you, honey. Will you bring them to her? She's in the living room with the others. I'm sure Tom told you we have guests."

"Yeah," June said. "Is Mick going to be okay?"

"I think so. He's awake and alert, although I suspect his head hurts like hell. Not that he'd ever admit it. We're going to take him to the hospital as soon as the storm passes." Marlowe set the spinach-artichoke dip on a platter and unsheathed a sleeve of crackers around it. "I can't believe Dan and Julie didn't clear off their patio before they evacuated. Mick could have been killed."

"Mom," June said, her voice low. "Are you really going to let a bunch of strangers stay here all night?"

"What am I supposed to do? Send them away in the middle of a hurricane?" Marlowe gestured toward the windows. They could all hear the wailing wind and the rain beating relentlessly against the shutters. As if in response to her words, the house shuddered under the force of the wind. "It's not like this is a normal day. They need our help, and we need to help them. It's the right thing to do."

June nodded but looked unconvinced. "What are they like?"

"I don't know, actually," Marlowe said. "I've been in here getting the food ready. I haven't really had a chance to talk to them. They mostly seemed to be in shock, which is understandable. It must have been terrifying being out on the water in the middle of that."

"Brownies! Sweet!" Zack said. He started to reach for one but hesitated, looking at Marlowe for permission.

"Go ahead—help yourself." Marlowe smiled at Zack, whom she was very fond of. She was glad he had opted to stay with them during the storm. His family's house was older, built long before Hurricane Andrew had slammed into Dade County, killing dozens of people. After Andrew, most of the new construction in Florida was made from cement blocks, built to withstand hurricanes. Marlowe didn't know how Zack's home would weather the storm. She hoped his parents had opted to go to a shelter.

"Mom," June said, wrenching Marlowe's attention back. Her daughter's voice was a low hiss. "How do we know that they're safe?"

"Safe how?" Marlowe asked.

"We think they might be criminals on the run from the police!" Zack said.

"Shh," June shushed him. "They might hear you!"

"And we don't think that. You thought it," Tom added.

"We were all thinking it," Zack said mutinously as he popped an entire brownie into his mouth.

"Do you need any help?" a voice said from the doorway.

They all looked up, staring at Bo, who had materialized without anyone noticing. Marlowe wondered how much of their conversation he'd overheard and felt heat rise to her cheeks.

"Bo! Hi!" Marlowe said, her voice too bright. "You briefly met my son, Tom, and his friend Zack." Marlowe gestured to the teenage boys. "And this is my daughter, June."

"It's nice to meet you all," Bo said easily, casually holding a bottle of beer in one hand.

"Here's a towel," June said, handing a neatly folded striped beach towel to him.

"Thank you. I am a bit waterlogged," Bo said, taking it from her and draping it around his shoulders. "Do you mind if I leave my backpack here? I don't want it to be in the way."

"Sure, go ahead," Marlowe said.

Bo lifted the backpack off his shoulder and set it in a corner of the kitchen. "That looks like quite the spread, Marlowe."

"Yes, I might have gone a little overboard," Marlowe said, looking at the platters of food spread out on the counter. The kitchen timer dinged. Marlowe used an oven mitt to pull out a cookie tray lined with pigs in a blanket out of the oven.

"Pigs in a blanket! My favorite," Bo said, looking delighted.

Marlowe laughed. "Everyone loves them. They're always the first thing that gets eaten at parties."

"I guess we're having an impromptu hurricane party." Bo smiled ruefully. "Although I think that would mean Jason, Darcy, and I are officially party crashers."

"What's a hurricane party?" Zack asked.

"Just what it sounds like. Everyone gathers together, drinks a few beers, and celebrates the force that is Mother Nature," Bo said, raising his bottle toward a shuttered window.

"That sounds fun! I'll have a beer," Zack said brightly.

"No, you will not," Marlowe said.

"One beer won't hurt. It's not like we're going to be driving anywhere," Tom pointed out.

"And yet not happening," Marlowe said, patting his shoulder.

Tom smiled and looked away. Zack took another brownie from the platter and stuffed it into his mouth.

"Boys, will you take all of this food into the living room? And June, please bring those dry clothes to Darcy. She must be freezing."

"She's in the living room. You can't miss her." Bo tipped his head in the direction of the living room. "She's the one not wearing any clothes."

June looked startled, but she nodded and headed off with the clothes and towels bundled in her arms. Tom and Zack picked up platters of food and followed her.

"I'll help," Bo said, nodding toward the platter of pigs in a blanket Marlowe had just arranged, next to a dipping sauce of Dijon mustard mixed with mayonnaise.

"Thank you," Marlowe said. The words felt stiff and formal in her mouth. Unlike her guests, she hadn't yet had a drink, but she was desperately craving one. Alcohol was exactly what she needed. It would smooth the awkward situation she found herself in, playing hostess to strangers.

Bo picked up one of the hors d'oeuvres off the platter and popped it into his mouth. "Mmm," he said, once he'd chewed and swallowed. "That's an exceptional pig in a blanket. And I should know. I'm something of an expert on the subject."

"It's a mini hot dog wrapped up in puff pastry. They're kind of hard to screw up."

Bo laughed at her joke, but then his expression grew serious. "It really was kind of you to take us in."

"We couldn't leave you out in the storm."

"A lot of people would have," Bo said. "You seem like a nice person, Marlowe. And you have a lovely family."

Marlowe smiled to accept the compliment.

"And speaking of family . . ." Bo stopped and ran a hand through his hair. For the first time, Bo looked distinctly uncomfortable. He lowered his voice. "Please don't worry about Jason. I know he comes off as a little, well, awkward, I guess you could say. But he's harmless."

"I hadn't noticed," Marlowe lied.

"Well, he does. We didn't have the easiest time of it growing up." Bo paused again. "We lost our parents when we were young."

"I'm so sorry. That must have been tough."

Bo nodded philosophically. "It was. But especially for Jason. They kept us together, and I did my best to look out for him, but still . . . he was just a kid. It took its toll on him. I think that's why he gets nervous around people he doesn't know."

"I understand. And hurricanes make everyone nervous. I've been a wreck all day."

"At least you had the good sense not to get on a boat." Bo grinned and then glanced around the kitchen. "Do you need any help in here? I'm not much of a cook, but I'm happy to pitch in wherever you need me."

"No, I'm just about done. In fact, I was just thinking I'd like to sit down with a glass of wine. I've been bracing for the storm for days. Well, we all have."

"You wouldn't believe what it was like out on the water. The waves were pitching us around so much the boat was practically sideways a few times. Darcy got seasick, and I don't blame her. I was feeling it too."

"It must have been terrifying."

"It was what it was. We agreed to the job, so it's not like anyone forced us out there. Jason and I have been on boats all our life and have been out in plenty of storms, so I thought we could handle it. But that . . ." Bo stopped and shook his head, his eyes wide at the memory. "That was intense." He took a long drink from his beer and then held up the empty bottle. "Do you have a recycling bin?"

Marlowe took the bottle from him and placed it next to the sink. She always rinsed out bottles before they went into the recycling bin, to keep it from getting sticky.

"Would you like another one?" Marlowe asked.

Bo hesitated, but then he also glanced at the shuttered window, listening to the storm howling outside. "Why not?" he said. "It doesn't look like we're going anywhere anytime soon."

Marlowe retrieved a bottle of Blue Moon ale out of the Sub-Zero refrigerator and handed it to Bo. "Do you need a bottle opener?"

"No, I've got it," Bo said, twisting the lid off with his hand. He took a sip and looked around the kitchen, taking in the charcoal-gray cupboards, the marble countertops, and the sculptural overhead lamps that lit the room. "This is a really nice house you have here."

"Thank you," Marlowe said. If this were a real party and she knew her guest, this would be the point where she'd offer to give him a tour. She was proud of the home she and Lee had created. It was pretty, thoughtfully planned, and comfortable. But she didn't know Bo, and some part of her brain—the part that had been trained from an early age not to be alone with strangers—stopped her. "We like it here."

"You and Lee have clearly led very fortunate lives." Bo sounded wistful.

Marlowe tried to imagine seeing her home and her family from his point of view. Bo was right. They had been fortunate. Although they'd had hard times too. Maybe not financial hardship, but something far worse . . . Marlowe stopped her thoughts from veering down that path. She needed to keep it together right now.

"Would you mind bringing these into the living room?" Marlowe asked, handing Bo the platter of pigs in a blanket.

"Sure thing." Bo turned and started to walk out of the kitchen. But before he passed through the door, he turned back and smiled at her. "Thank you again for opening your home to us. We'll make sure that we don't inconvenience you more than necessary."

"You're very welcome," Marlowe said and watched while Bo disappeared through the doorway. Then she went to the refrigerator, took out a bottle of chilled Sancerre, and poured herself a very large glass.

CHAPTER TWELVE

ISABEL

When Isabel had accepted Marlowe's invitation to ride out the storm at the Davieses' house, it hadn't occurred to her just how dreary being stuck there with a bunch of teenagers would be. The two boys were joking about a meme they'd seen online and cracking themselves up. Isabel hadn't been able to figure out what they were talking about, much less why it was funny. The skinny blond kid had such an obnoxious, braying laugh she'd had to walk away. She'd tried talking to June about her college plans, but the girl's responses had been monosyllabic. The spoiled princess would no doubt be headed off to a prestigious private school paid for by her parents.

Rich kids were all the same. They had won the genetic lottery by being born into money and then were stupid enough to believe they deserved the privileges that came with it.

It was the downside to working in the art world, Isabel thought as she stood by herself off to one side of the room, sipping a glass of wine. Everyone who bought art was wealthy, which meant Isabel was forced to spend all her professional time with entitled assholes. She hadn't really thought that through when she'd chosen her career path.

Isabel had studied art history and conservation at Florida State University. She'd attended on a full scholarship, part of which had been merit based and part funded from a program the State of Florida had that waived tuition at state schools for foster kids.

As it turned out, the best thing her alcohol-and-pill-addicted mother had ever done for her was die and spare Isabel from having student loan debt.

"Would you like a pig in a blanket?" a male voice said from behind her.

Isabel turned and met Bo's very attractive green-eyed gaze. He was holding a large plate stacked with hors d'oeuvres, and when he smiled at her, dimples appeared in his cheeks.

"Come on—try one. They're delicious. I've already had three." Bo held up the plate temptingly.

Isabel found herself smiling back at him, despite her efforts to remain cool with the unexpected guests. She took a pig in a blanket and nibbled at it.

"There you go," Bo said. "You look like a pig-in-a-blanket kind of girl."

Isabel laughed, almost choking on her bite of food. She took a large sip from her glass of wine, even though she had planned to stay sober that night. "What does a pig-in-a-blanket kind of girl even look like?"

"Just like you. So." Bo looked around to see who was nearby. "You're the assistant, huh?"

"Yes. I work for Marlowe," Isabel confirmed. She wasn't about to go into any details about the Bond collection. It wasn't that she was above bragging, but she wouldn't want Marlowe—or her family, or Mick, who was glowering at everyone from his position on the sofa—to overhear her.

"Your employer must think highly of you. Inviting you to stay here in her very nice house for the hurricane."

"Or maybe she's just a nice person."

"She does seem nice." Bo leaned closer to Isabel. He smelled like the beach, a mixture of salt and coconut-scented sunscreen. "That's a rare thing these days. I haven't met many people who are genuinely nice."

"Neither have I," Isabel said. She curled a lock of her hair around one finger. It was a nervous habit that she kept trying—and failing—to break. "And how did you end up here? You just happened to be out boating in the middle of a hurricane?"

"No, I was out on a boat trying to beat a hurricane to shore," Bo corrected her. He smiled, flashing his dimples again. "I've been told I have bad timing."

"That sounds like a serious problem."

"It can be a burden."

Darcy appeared at Bo's side, wrapping her arm possessively through his. Isabel was instantly irritated by how pretty the girl was, with her doe-shaped brown eyes, high cheekbones, and long shiny brown hair. At least she was finally dressed in the clothes June had brought down for her.

"Hey," Darcy said shyly.

Isabel nodded at her. "You look warmer than you did before."

"I am. I have clothes on the boat, but they were already soaked from the rain by the time we reached shore. It was nice of June to lend me these." Darcy ran her hand over the sleeve of her borrowed sweatshirt.

"A nice girl who takes after her nice mom," Bo said.

Darcy took a pig in a blanket and popped it into her mouth. "I'm starving."

"There's a ton of food. Would you like a glass of wine?" Isabel paused and arched her eyebrows. "Wait. Are you old enough to drink?"

Darcy laughed, her face lighting up with delight. "Of course I am! I'm twenty-five. You're so sweet."

Bo gave Isabel a look that made it clear he, at least, knew she wasn't being sweet.

"Where did you two meet?" Isabel asked.

"Bo came into Schooner's for drinks. That's where I work as a wait-ress." Darcy snuggled into Bo's side. "He stood by the bar for three hours, waiting for a chance to talk to me."

"Actually, I was sitting on a barstool," Bo interjected.

"But you were hoping to catch my eye," Darcy continued. "Which you did. I noticed you as soon as you came in."

Isabel had a feeling that this wasn't the first time Darcy had recounted this story. "That does sound like a fairy tale," Isabel said dryly. "What girl hasn't gone to a bar looking for the love of her life?"

But her sarcasm was lost on Darcy, who beamed again. "I know, right? Only I was there for work."

"And I was just looking for a cold beer and a plate of nachos," Bo said.

"And instead you found me," Darcy said, curling against Bo's side and smiling up at him.

"If you'll excuse me, I'm going to see if Marlowe needs any help," Isabel said, detaching herself from what was becoming an increasingly nauseating conversation. She turned and walked away, hoping Bo was watching her as she did. Isabel had always had a nice ass. She wondered what Bo saw in his insipid younger girlfriend, other than the obvious physical attributes.

She was suddenly reminded of her mother, Sondra, who had been fond of drawling in her deep throaty voice, "That girl's about as sharp as a sack of wet mice." Isabel had never been exactly sure where the saying came from, but it did seem an apt description of Darcy.

Isabel walked out of the living room, turned left, and headed toward the kitchen, where she found Marlowe standing alone, glass of wine in hand.

"Do you need any help in here?" Isabel asked.

"No, everything's done." Marlowe took a large sip from her wineglass and then smiled weakly. "This is all just a little . . . overwhelming, I guess. The storm, our guests. I was taking a moment."

"Do you want me to leave you in peace?" Isabel asked, gesturing toward the arched door that led out of the kitchen.

"Not at all. Do you like Sancerre?"

"It's my favorite."

Marlowe opened the refrigerator and took out a chilled bottle of wine. She filled Isabel's glass. The wine was dry and cold, and Isabel hoped the numbing power of the alcohol would work quickly.

"How's Mick doing?" Marlowe asked. "I haven't had a chance to check on him."

"He's cranky."

Marlowe laughed. Her cheeks were flushed from the wine, and her curly hair looked as unruly as ever.

"He's always a little cranky," she said. "It's part of his charm. He's not happy about our guests being here."

"I can tell." Isabel leaned against the counter, wineglass in hand. "What do you think?"

Marlowe shrugged. "They seem rattled by the storm, which is understandable. I'm sure this isn't where they'd planned on riding out the hurricane."

"I bet not."

The two women fell silent for a moment, drinking their wine and listening to the wind howl outside.

"How long do you think the storm is going to last?" Isabel asked.

Marlowe shrugged helplessly. "I'm not sure. But I think we could be in for a long night."

CHAPTER THIRTEEN

TOM

Tom and Zack stood by the built-in bookshelves, watching Tom's parents and their unexpected guests standing around the living room, trying to make conversation.

"This is weird, right?" Zack asked, speaking louder than Tom would have liked.

Zack had never mastered the gift of speaking in a volume that couldn't be overheard by adults. Tom wondered if this was because Zack's parents had never paid attention to him. When they were in middle school, Zack had built an elaborate—and dangerous—set of increasingly high and steep ramps in his driveway, with the plan that he and Tom could jump their bikes over them. It had taken him three weeks to complete the course, but Zack's parents hadn't even noticed what their son was up to. They had been surprised when the sheriff's deputies had shown up at their front door, called by a neighbor who was worried that Zack would break his neck. That was about the same time Tom's mother had started insisting that Zack hang out at their house, instead of the other way around.

"Shh," Tom hushed him.

Zack turned so that he was facing Tom and away from the others. His friend was juggling a paper plate full of food in his hands and was talking through a mouthful of chips and queso. "No, but really. This is *weird*. You know what it reminds me of?" Zack's eyes widened with excitement. "That movie with those lizard aliens who were pretending to be humans by wearing skin suits."

"What movie is that?"

"I don't remember, and maybe it was a TV show. But it's that level of weird."

"I guess," Tom said, but Zack was sort of right. Not about an alien wearing a human suit, but there was definitely an odd vibe in the room. It was like a strange facsimile of a party, where everyone was standing around, drinking, and making chitchat, but in an artificial way. And it was all against the background of the storm roaring outside, so loud and powerful the house occasionally shuddered under its force.

Mick was lying on the couch, looking grumpy. Tom didn't blame him. The umbrella had clocked him hard. Mick's head, which now had a square bandage taped over the wound, had to hurt. Mick was sipping out of the glass of water Marlowe had brought him. Even from his prone, vulnerable state, he stared suspiciously at their guests, as though suspecting they might suddenly grab valuables and run out into the storm with them.

His mom was chatting animatedly with—or, more accurately, *at*—Darcy, who was still incredibly hot, even wearing June's least favorite sweatshirt and pants, the curves of her body clearly defined under the cotton fabric. His mom's face was flushed, and she kept gesturing with her wineglass as she pointed out how they'd built the house to face the water rather than the street.

"When our architect first gave us the plans for the house, everything was pointed in the wrong direction," Marlowe said, her voice sounding higher pitched than normal. "We had to tell him, 'No, the view of the water is the entire point of building here.'"

Darcy was nodding and smiling but not saying much. Isabel was standing with them, but she was checked out of the conversation and kept glancing at her phone, even though Tom knew the Wi-Fi wasn't working. Marlowe kept looking meaningfully at her assistant, clearly hoping to drag her into the conversation, but Isabel seemed impervious.

His dad stood on the opposite side of the room, talking to Bo, who still had a striped beach towel wrapped around his shoulders. Lee had changed out of his grubby work clothes into a cobalt-blue Lacoste polo shirt and neatly pressed khaki shorts. He shook the ice cubes in the glass of whiskey he was nursing. Bo—much like Zack—was a loud talker, and his voice boomed good naturedly.

"And I said to the guy, I said—get this, Lee." Bo was laughing so hard at his own anecdote he could barely get the words out. "I said to him, 'This isn't a bathroom; it's a bar. You should probably zip back up!'"

June was trying to talk to Jason, but it looked like she was having a hard time. Jason shifted his weight from foot to foot and stared down at his beer, as if he wasn't sure what to do with himself, and constantly drummed his fingers against his leg. It looked like her efforts at talking had stalled, and June was glancing over her shoulder at the staircase, clearly hoping she could escape. Tom knew she wanted to join Felix upstairs and resume watching whatever movie they'd been in the middle of when he and Zack had interrupted them.

"I think June might need rescuing," Zack muttered.

"What do you mean?"

"Look at her. She seems uncomfortable."

Tom studied his sister. She was standing with one arm wrapped around herself and had a pained expression on her face. But June always looked uncomfortable. She was even awkward when she was around Felix. Tom had read articles about twins who had a telepathy so pronounced they always knew what the other was thinking or feeling. He'd never experienced that with June. It wasn't that they didn't get along—they'd always had a low-conflict relationship, especially for two siblings sharing a home. But they'd never had a secret twin language or been able to read each other's thoughts.

"What do you mean? She looks like she always does."

"That guy keeps looking at her boobs." Zack tilted his head in their direction, in what he probably—wrongly—thought was a subtle way.

"Dude," Tom said. "Stop. She's fine."

But when he glanced at his sister and Jason again, he saw that Zack was right. Jason was mostly looking down at the bottle of beer in his hand. But every few beats, his eyes would slide over toward June's chest.

Oh no, Tom thought. He shifted uneasily, torn between feeling like he should rescue his sister from the situation and not wanting to have to talk to some weird guy he didn't know.

"She's fine," Tom said again, trying to convince himself that June was, in fact, fine. Unfortunately, she chose that moment to look at him with an expression of such exquisite misery he knew that he was lying to both Zack and himself.

"She's not," Zack said. "We have to go help her."

It bothered Tom that Zack had always been so much braver than him. Zack just acted, never stopping to think through the consequences of what he was doing. Tom was just the opposite. He couldn't keep his brain from churning out every possible worst-case scenario. It could be paralyzing.

"I'll see if she's okay," Tom said reluctantly.

"I'll go with you," Zack said, straightening up and thrusting out his chest, as though they were heading into battle.

But just then, Mick, thankfully, interrupted them.

"Boys," Mick barked. "Come here."

Tom set down the can of soda he'd been sipping from on one of the glass-topped side tables that dotted the room and headed toward the couch, where the handyman was stretched out, taking care to keep his feet off the upholstery.

"Hey, Mick. Do you need something?" Tom asked, glad for the interruption.

Mick gestured him closer, twitching two fingers toward himself. Tom knelt down next to Mick, hoping he'd ask for an aspirin or send Tom on some other errand. But instead, Mick pushed himself up on one elbow.

"Something's not right," Mick said, his voice low and urgent.

"That's what I was just saying!" Zack exclaimed. "They could be aliens about to tear their human suits off!"

Mick stared at Zack, who—Tom had to admit—looked even more like a very tanned, very blond Kermit the Frog in manic mode than usual. He'd thrown his arms out to the side, and his eyes were bugged out.

"What's he talking about?" Mick asked Tom.

Tom sighed. "Nothing. Just ignore him."

"Oh, that's nice," Zack said sarcastically.

"What do you mean something's not right?" Tom asked, making sure to keep his voice low enough so that only Mick and Zack would hear him.

"I'm not sure." Mick tried to sit up but instantly winced, his hand going to his bandaged forehead. "I want to find out what those people are doing here."

Tom wondered if it was possible that Mick's injury was affecting his ability to think clearly. They knew why their guests were there. They'd gotten caught out in the storm. Was it possible Mick didn't remember? He exchanged a concerned look with Zack, who seemed to be thinking the same thing.

"Skin suits," Zack said meaningfully.

Nope, they weren't thinking the same thing at all.

"They're just riding out the hurricane here," Tom said.

"No one would take a boat out with a storm like this bearing down," Mick said grimly. "And you need to keep an eye on your sister. I don't like the way that man is looking at her."

The boys turned to look at June. She had turned away from Jason and was walking over to join her mother, Isabel, and Darcy. Jason watched her go, his eyes roaming over her body. Tom was again struck by how he wanted to stop Jason from staring at his sister like that but also really didn't want to get into a conflict with the stranger. Jason noticed that Mick and the two teen boys were staring at him, and he started, his gaze sliding away. He took a nervous sip from his bottle of beer.

"I don't know what your parents were thinking letting those people into the house," Mick said.

Tom was about to tell Mick that there was no way they could have carried him inside without Bo's and Jason's help but decided not to. Mick seemed almost distressed, which was completely unlike him. Tom didn't want to make him feel responsible for them being here. It wasn't Mick's fault he had been hit in the head by a flying umbrella.

"They seem okay," Tom said instead.

Mick stared at him, his eyes narrowed. "I'm telling you something here isn't right. I can't quite put my finger on it, but from what I saw, there's—"

"How's the head feeling?"

Tom, Zack, and Mick all looked up at the interruption. Bo was standing just behind the teenagers, his arms crossed over his chest, his expression concerned as he gazed down at Mick.

"I'm fine," Mick said gruffly.

"It must hurt. That umbrella came flying at you." Bo shook his head. "I can't believe the neighbors here would leave out patio furniture with a hurricane coming in. That loose umbrella could have killed someone." He turned and looked at Lee. "Would that be considered a crime? Like, reckless homicide?"

"I'm not sure. My field is trusts and estates, not criminal law," Lee said. "But I would imagine they could be civilly liable if someone got hurt."

"Yeah," Bo agreed. "You can't just go around hurting people and not pay a price for it."

"I'm fine," Mick said again. He shifted irritably on the sofa.

"Is anyone still hungry?" Marlowe asked brightly. "I can make sheet pan fajitas. I have everything prepped in the fridge, ready to go."

"Marlowe, relax. You don't have to constantly feed everyone," Lee said.

"Actually, I do." Marlowe gestured toward the boys. "They're always hungry."

But before Lee could respond, there was a deafening crash from above. It sounded like a missile had hit the house, even though Tom's mind told him that simply wasn't possible. The house shook with the impact, and Darcy let out a high-pitched scream. And just as they were all looking around, wide eyed at the shock of the impact, the power went out, and they were left in a complete, unrelenting darkness.

CHAPTER FOURTEEN

MARLOWE

"What's happening?" Isabel's voice was spiked with fear.

"Something hit the roof," Lee said. "But I don't know what would have caused that kind of an impact."

"It was probably a tree. Maybe one of those palms out in back," Mick said.

Marlowe pictured the stately royal palms that lined the edges of their property and felt a pang at the loss. But if a downed palm tree was the worst damage Celeste would inflict that night, they'd be lucky. And, as if the storm were reading Marlowe's thoughts, the wind began shrieking, sounding even louder now that the power was out and the air-conditioning was no longer humming in the background. The darkness made the situation even scarier, and Marlowe felt her pulse skitter.

"Didn't you say you have generators?" Isabel asked. "Do they turn on automatically?"

"They're supposed to," Lee said.

Almost as soon as he spoke, the generators kicked in, and the lights turned back on. Everyone stared around, blinking at one another, their faces pale and drawn. Except for Bo, who oddly seemed amused.

"That was dramatic," Bo said, his mouth quirking up into a smile. "Imagine if when the lights came on, there was a dead body on the ground, with a knife sticking out of its back. And then we spent the rest of the night trying to figure out which one of us was the murderer."

"That would be so cool!" Zack said. "It would be like living in the middle of a murder mystery."

"I think it means one of us would be dead," Tom told him.

"That's true. I didn't think about that part."

There was a loud scraping sound that sounded like it was coming from the roof. Marlowe thought she felt the house shake under the movement and wondered if she was imagining it. Then she met Lee's worried gaze. He'd felt it too.

"What's going on?" June asked, moving to Marlowe's side. Marlowe put a reassuring hand on her daughter's back.

"The hurricane knocked something over onto the house," Marlowe said. "Mick's right; it was probably a palm tree. They can get uprooted in storms."

"Is it going to crash through the roof?" June asked.

"No, honey," Lee said. "The roof is solid."

"What if the storm picked up a car and threw it up onto the roof?" Zack asked excitedly. He pantomimed the motion of reaching down and tossing an invisible object up into the air. "And then it was just parked up there? How would you even get it down?"

"That would be funny." Jason laughed nervously. "I'd leave it up there and tell everyone, 'Hey, look! There's a car on my house! I just decided to park it there one day.'"

Bo chuckled and took a long drink from his bottle of beer.

"It's not a car," Mick said sternly.

"How do you know?" Zack asked. "Wasn't there a movie where a storm picked up a cow and carried her off?"

"That was a tornado in the movie, not a hurricane," Tom said.

"But there can be tornadoes inside of hurricanes," Zack said. "My grandma has one of those cages over her pool—you know to keep the leaves and stuff out of the water? Once, during a hurricane, a tornado touched down right where her pool was and crumpled the cage up like it was a tin can. After the storm was over, she went outside, and the cage was in her neighbor's yard. My grandma had to replace the whole thing."

Marlowe could feel her unease rise again. Zack was right. Not about a car landing on the roof—that was ridiculous—but about the possibility of tornadoes within the hurricane system. She remembered seeing news footage a few years earlier of an apartment building that had been struck by one. Most of the building still stood, but one section had been completely decimated. It looked like a train had run straight through it.

There was another loud shuddering, scraping sound as the tree, or whatever it was up there on the roof, slid again.

"I'd better go outside and check on it," Lee said.

"No!" Marlowe exclaimed. "Are you crazy? It's too dangerous! And anyway, it's not like we can do anything about it until after the storm passes."

Lee stepped closer to her and lowered his voice. "I need to make sure the roof is secure."

"And if it isn't?" Marlowe asked, remembering the sheriff's deputies telling her that they wouldn't be responding to any calls for help until after the storm had passed. And it wasn't like she could call the emergency services anyway, not with the cell towers down.

We should have gone to Orlando, Marlowe thought. She felt a sudden rush of fury at Lee for dismissing the idea when she had first brought it up a few days earlier—and equal anger at herself for not insisting on it. What if something happened to June and Tom and Zack, whom she was responsible for . . . Marlowe shook her head, not wanting her thoughts to go down that dark road. She needed to focus on keeping them all safe.

"I'll go check it out," Bo volunteered, setting down his beer on a side table.

"No!" Marlowe said again. "We need to all stay inside, where it's safe."

"I'll go with him," Lee said.

"It's okay, Marlowe," Bo said, smiling easily at her. "We'll just stick our heads out there and see what's going on."

She wondered how Bo was able to stay so calm, here in a strange place, in the middle of a hurricane, facing the real possibility of danger. He looked comfortable and loose, his posture relaxed, as though he had just volunteered to check on how much beer was left in the refrigerator. In stark contrast, she was stiff with anxiety, her jaw clenched, her shoulders so tight they hurt.

Mick struggled to sit up. "I'll go."

"Absolutely not!" Marlowe exclaimed.

Mick gave her a stern look as he finally pushed himself into a seated position. "This can't wait until after the storm passes. If there's been damage to the roof, we need to know about it now so we can make a plan."

"You have a head injury. You need to rest," Marlowe protested.

"As far as I know, I'm the only person here who's done construction." Mick glanced over at Bo and Jason, but Bo shook his head and shrugged.

"No, boss. Neither one of us has ever worked construction," Bo said.

"Then I need to go check to see if there's any damage," Mick said. He stood, and Marlowe thought he looked a little unsteady on his feet.

"I'm going with you," Lee said quickly.

"No, stay here and look after your family," Mick said.

"I'll go," Bo said. "I may not know construction, but I can grab onto your leg if the storm tries to carry you off."

"I'll go too!" Zack said, his eyes shining with excitement. "I want to see what it's like outside. I bet it's insane!"

"Absolutely not," Marlowe said. "You kids are all staying inside." Zack started to protest, and Marlowe raised a single finger. "That's not up for debate. And I want everyone to stay downstairs."

"I was going to go up to my room," June said.

"Wait until we find out what's going on with the roof first," Marlowe said. If there was structural damage, the second floor would be the least-safe place to be in the house, she thought.

Mick limped toward the front door, with Bo behind him. He opened the door, letting a gust of salt-tinged wind into the house so strong it sent an antique convex mirror crashing to the ground, the glass shattering into pieces. At the noise, Darcy cried out, and June covered her ears.

"Let's move!" Mick yelled. He and Bo rushed out the front door, Bo wrenching the door closed behind them.

Marlowe started toward the front hall, but Lee put up a hand to stop her.

"Stay back. There's glass everywhere."

"I'll sweep it up," Marlowe said, looking past Lee, hoping to see how badly damaged the mirror was. She'd bought it at an antique store in West Palm, not long after they'd moved into the house. It had been an impulse purchase, and she knew she'd paid too much for the piece, but it had looked perfect hanging in the front hall. She hoped it wasn't a total loss. Maybe they'd be able to salvage the frame. Marlowe was very glad she and Isabel had moved the Bond collection to her closet. The paintings, at least, were safe. For now.

"I'll go get the broom," Tom said, turning toward the kitchen. He returned a moment later with a broom and dustpan.

"I'll help," Darcy said. "I'll hold the dustpan."

Marlowe smiled her thanks. She took the broom from Tom and swept the glass into a pile in the middle of the glossy pale-blond wood floor while Darcy knelt down with the dustpan and Lee pointed out shards that she'd missed. The mindless task of sweeping soothed her, but even so, Marlowe kept glancing at the front door. How long had Mick and Bo been outside? Five minutes? Ten? How long would it take them to assess the damage?

"How do you know Bo and Jason?" Marlowe asked, trying to distract herself from her spiraling anxiety.

"Bo's my boyfriend," Darcy said proudly.

"How long have you been dating?"

"Two months. Well. One month and three weeks."

"Do you have experience piloting boats too?"

"No, I don't know anything about boats. But Bo called me yesterday and asked if I wanted to come along when he and Jason brought the boat up here."

Marlowe stilled midsweep. "I thought Bo said they were hired today to move the boat."

"Oh." Darcy tipped her head to one side, considering this. She shrugged. "Maybe I mixed it up."

Before Marlowe could press her further, the door flew open, and the wind rushed into the hallway, swirling as it entered. The force of it caused Marlowe to stumble. She put out a hand to steady herself against the wall as Bo struggled to close the door. He finally threw his body weight against it. The door slammed shut, closing out the force of the storm once again.

Marlowe stared at Bo. He was out of breath, his chest heaving with the effort of fighting through the storm. His hair was wild from the wind, and his clothes were soaked. He looked up at them, and for the first time since she'd met him, Marlowe realized that Bo was rattled.

He was also alone.

CHAPTER FIFTEEN

TOM

"This queso is on point," Zack said, dipping a tortilla chip straight into a stainless steel saucepan on the counter.

"Hey, leave some for me," Tom said, trying to reach in with his own chip before Zack finished all the dip.

After Mick and Bo had gone outside and the mirror had crashed to the floor, sending glass flying everywhere, Marlowe had shooed Tom and Zack away. They'd taken the opportunity to retreat to the kitchen in search of more food. They munched in companionable silence, occasionally fighting over whose turn it was to dip their chip.

"How can you two eat right now?" June asked as she walked into the kitchen. She opened the refrigerator, took out a pitcher of filtered water, and refilled her glass.

Tom looked up, his mouth full of chips. "Why shouldn't we eat?"

"Because Mick and Bo are outside in the middle of a very dangerous hurricane trying to make sure the roof isn't going to fall in," June said. She leaned back against the counter and stared at them over the rim of her glass.

"That's why we're eating. We're men. We need to keep our strength up in case we're needed to lift heavy things or go into battle," Zack explained.

June rolled her eyes. "Right."

"Was that Jason guy bothering you?" Zack asked.

June's eyes slid toward the hallway, checking to see if anyone was there listening. "Not really, but he seems a little . . . off," she said. She made a face that reminded Tom of the grimacing emoji.

"He was checking you out," Zack said.

"Zack," Tom warned him.

"What? He was totally checking her out."

"I didn't notice that." June wrapped one arm around herself and took another sip of water.

Zack nodded. "He was looking at you whenever you looked away from him."

"That's kind of creepy." June picked up one of the brownies still left in the pan. She considered it and then set it back down.

"Are you going to eat that?" Zack asked.

"No, I'm not hungry. It's all yours." June slid the pan of brownies down the counter, toward the boys.

"Don't mind if I do." Zack reached for the brownie and popped it in his mouth.

"Mick thinks they're lying about why they're here," Tom told June. "He said no one with any sense would be out on a boat in a storm like that."

June's eyebrows arched up. "He doesn't buy their claim that they were moving the boat to a storage space?"

Tom shook his head. "No, he said that no one would ever go out on the water with a hurricane coming on to shore. He thinks there's something fishy going on."

Zack looked indignant. "I said the same thing earlier! Before Mick said it!"

"You said that they're lizard aliens wearing human suits," Tom said.

"No, I didn't say they *are* lizard aliens. I said they're *like* lizard aliens. There's a difference."

"What are you two talking about?" June set her glass of water down on the counter and frowned at her brother and his friend.

"I think we need to make a plan," Zack said, spreading his hands out.

"To do what?" Tom asked.

"To find out what they're really doing here," Zack said. "What their true motive is."

"How are we supposed to do that?" June asked.

"We'll investigate. Like detectives. We'll talk to them and ask sneaky questions to trip them up. Try and break their cover."

"What's the point? It doesn't really matter why they were out on that boat. They can't go anywhere until the storm's over," Tom pointed out. "We're stuck with them until then."

"Well, they could be criminals. Drug smugglers on the run from the Coast Guard. I bet if they are, and we turned them in, we'd get a reward."

"I seriously doubt they're criminals," Tom said dismissively.

"And if they were, they'd never admit it to us," June added.

"We may need to get additional evidence," Zack conceded. He looked up, his eyes wide again. "I know! We need to take a look at their boat. See if there's any contraband onboard."

"Dude," Tom said. "You may not have noticed, but we're in the middle of a hurricane."

"Why am I the only one generating ideas here? This is supposed to be a brainstorming session."

"I need to go upstairs and check on Felix." June looked up at the ceiling. "I should bring him some food."

The front door opened and slammed shut again, letting in another violent burst of wind. It blew down the hallway and into the kitchen, startling all three teenagers. Tom could hear raised voices out in the hallway and knew that whatever was happening out there, it wasn't good.

"We'd better go find out what's going on," he said grimly.

CHAPTER SIXTEEN

JUNE

"Where's Mick?" June's mother's voice was high pitched and frightened.

June hurried out to the front hallway to find her parents there, standing side by side, Marlowe still clutching the broom she'd been using to sweep up the broken glass. They were staring at Bo, who was leaning back against the front door. He was pale and looked disoriented, his chest heaving with the effort of being out in the storm. Darcy rushed to his side and grabbed his arm.

"Babe!" she exclaimed. "Are you okay?"

Bo straightened and ran a hand through his damp, wind-tangled hair. His shirt and shorts were soaked through again.

"I'm fine," Bo finally said. He looked at June's parents. "Mick's fine too."

"Where is he?" Marlowe asked, her voice still shrill. June felt her stomach knot up in response. "Is he still outside?"

"The wind died down for a few minutes, so he decided to take advantage of the break and head home."

"Home," Marlowe repeated. "You don't mean he's driving in this? Why would he do that?"

Bo shrugged. "He didn't go into details. He just got out his keys and headed for his truck."

"But that doesn't make any sense," Marlowe said. "And the wind has been blowing nonstop."

"He was worried about his mother being alone during the storm," June said. "Maybe he wanted to check on her."

"Mick knows that it's incredibly dangerous to drive somewhere in the middle of a hurricane!" Marlowe exclaimed. "The roads could already be flooded!"

"It doesn't sound like something he would do," Lee agreed. June looked at her father—something she rarely did these days—and saw that his face looked drawn and worried. She knew how fond he was of Mick. They all were.

"He must be disoriented from his head injury," Marlowe said. "Which makes his driving even more dangerous. And we can't even call him to make sure he gets home—or to his mother's place. The Wi-Fi and cell towers are both down."

Marlowe threw her hands up and let them fall by her side. Lee put a hand on her back, and Marlowe turned toward him and rested her head on his shoulder for a moment.

June glanced toward the stairs. She wanted to go check on Felix, but she also didn't want to disappear when Mick was possibly in danger and her parents were upset. Although, her mom was right—what could they possibly do at this point? No one could get ahold of Mick anyway.

Would he really have tried to drive in this? June wondered. And as if by response, the wind let out a particularly violent assault and caused the house to shudder again under its force. Mick was tough, yes. But he was also smart and careful. His leaving like this didn't make sense.

June turned away from her parents, about to head for the stairs. But Marlowe snaked out a hand and gently placed it on June's arm.

"Honey, stay down here. We don't know how badly the roof was damaged," Marlowe said. "It might be dangerous to be upstairs."

If we lose the roof, will we be safe downstairs? June wondered. But for once, she decided not to argue. She'd never seen her mother look so pale, her freckles standing out in stark contrast against the milk white of her skin. It made June feel uneasy and off center. Marlowe had always been the sort of mother to smile and say, "You're fine!" This constant reassurance had been the background noise of June's childhood. But now, everything wasn't fine. And her mother couldn't fix what was happening with a freezer gel pack and an oatmeal cookie, like she had when June hit a curb on her bike when she was nine and flew over the handlebar, banging her knee and elbow when she hit the pavement outside their house.

"I just wanted to get a sweatshirt," June muttered, moving out of her mother's reach. "It's freezing in here."

"Not until we're sure it's safe," Marlowe repeated.

"The roof is fine." Bo ran a hand through his hair again. "A palm tree is up there, uprooted and laying against it, but Mick didn't think there's any serious structural damage, or at least nothing we could see from the ground. It looks like it's wedged against a dormer, so it will probably stay put for the rest of the storm. Once the storm passes, you're going to need a crane to come move it. But I don't think it's going to cause any additional damage."

Marlowe exhaled a sigh of relief, and Lee squeezed her shoulder.

"That's good news," Lee said.

"You should see it out there." Bo shook his head. "I've seen some crazy things in my life, but I think that might be the craziest yet. The wind is so strong the trees are practically bent horizontal."

"What other kinds of crazy things have you seen?" Zack asked loudly. "Anything involving a high-speed police chase?"

June had to make an effort not to roll her eyes. Was this Zack's idea of sneakily questioning the guests to figure out if they were really criminals on the run? Because it wasn't very subtle.

Luckily, Bo seemed oblivious to the purpose behind Zack's question. "Now that you mention it, I did once see the Miami PD chase a guy in a stolen Honda CRV going the wrong way down I-95." He smiled, dimples appearing. "That was pretty crazy. They had to clear the highway and then put one of those spike strips across the tarmac to puncture his tires."

"Cool!" Zack said, clearly forgetting for the moment his purpose in asking the question. "What happened next?"

"The Honda spun around and hit the concrete barrier. The airbags went off, and the police dragged him out of the car and handcuffed him."

"Tom, please go grab a towel for Bo. He's soaking wet again," Marlowe said.

Bo laughed weakly. "It does seem to keep happening. I'm sorry, Marlowe. I'm dripping all over your wood floors."

"It's fine," Marlowe said. She turned to June, her eyes softening. "June, will you go see if any of our guests need a refill on their drinks?"

June looked regretfully at the stairs, worried that she'd missed her opportunity to check on Felix. But no, that was silly, she told herself. The storm would go on for hours. She'd have plenty of time to slip upstairs. And then they could curl up together and watch one of the movies she'd downloaded on her laptop. Right now, there was nothing she wanted to do more. She was tired of making conversation with strangers.

"There's an open bottle of wine in the fridge," Marlowe said, interrupting June's thoughts. "Will you get that and see if anyone would like a top off? And check with the men to see if they want another beer."

"I definitely could use another beer after going out into that," Bo said. "It might not have been the smartest move I've made. The wind was crazy."

"I thought you said it died down while you were out there?" Lee asked.

Bo paused, as if only just realizing his mistake. "Well, it did die down a little. But it's still gusting. It was hard to stand up in it. I think maybe Marlowe was right and Mick might have been a little disoriented."

"This is bad," Marlowe said, wrapping her arms around herself.

"I'll go get the drinks." June padded in her bare feet to the kitchen. She opened the refrigerator and stood for a long moment, staring at the contents. Her mom had prepped the fajitas she was planning to make later—the chicken and vegetables were sliced up and mixed with spices and resting in a glass bowl.

Her stomach suddenly grumbled, and June realized she was starving. She'd successfully managed to avoid all the appetizers and brownies that everyone had been munching on all evening. But now she couldn't remember the last thing she had actually eaten. Just the Greek yogurt she'd had that morning. That was usually enough to get her through to dinner, but with the storm and the guests, dinner would probably be late. She wondered if she should eat something now, like maybe a slice of cheese on a cracker. A wave of shame washed over her at the thought, and she pressed her hand against her flat abdomen.

I'll have a fajita when they're ready, she decided. *I can make it until then.* June reached past the bowl of chicken and vegetables and grabbed the open bottle of wine, a cork sticking out of the neck. She closed the door, turned, and then started violently.

Jason was standing there, silently watching her from the doorway.

"Oh my God!" June pressed a hand over her breastbone. She could feel her heart hammering. "You scared me."

"Woah!" Jason held up his hands. "Sorry! I didn't mean to."

"It's okay—I just didn't hear you come into the kitchen," June said, clutching the bottle of wine to her chest while she waited for her heart rate to settle.

Something about Jason set her on edge, probably because of what Zack had said earlier about Jason watching her. She hadn't noticed Jason paying any particular attention to her. If anything, he'd been hard to chat with. But still. She didn't want to be alone with him. There was something unsettling about the way his eyes slid away whenever she looked directly at him.

"Your mom said I could grab a beer from the fridge," Jason said.

"Oh . . . right," June said. She stepped back, bumping into the counter behind her. "Help yourself."

Jason stepped closer and peered into the refrigerator. It took him a few beats to locate the beers, even though they were lined up neatly on the second shelf. He plucked one out, twisted off the cap, and then turned to face June. The refrigerator door swung shut behind him.

Suddenly, he was standing too close to her. So close she could smell the scent of salt water on his body and beer on his breath, along with the sour smell of his body odor. June wanted to step away from him, to escape back to the living room, but she worried that it would be rude to just abruptly walk away.

"Are you in here drinking by yourself?" Jason asked.

"What?" She was still clutching the bottle of wine. It was cold in her hands. "Oh. No. My mom asked me to get the wine for her. I don't drink. I'm only seventeen."

It seemed like Jason was suddenly even closer, although June hadn't seen him take a step forward. His unusual green eyes were no longer unfocused or sliding away. He stared so intently at her June felt pinned in place.

"Only seventeen, huh?" he murmured. He reached out and touched her hair, gently stretching out one of her curls. "You have really pretty hair. It's all curly."

"Please don't touch me," June said, hoping she sounded tougher than she felt.

"Don't be like that. I don't mean anything by it. We're just talking."

Jason was still holding a lock of her hair. It didn't hurt, but it felt like a violation. She wanted to get away, to put space between them. She wondered if she should scream to attract her parents' attention or if that would be overly dramatic. It suddenly annoyed June that he was the one making her uncomfortable, and yet she was worried about hurting his feelings.

"Seriously. Let go of my hair," she said more forcefully. "I don't want you to touch me."

"What's going on in here?" Zack asked loudly as he strode into the kitchen. Tom was behind him, his eyes wide with alarm.

Jason let go of June's hair and turned, but he didn't step away from her. He was so close she could see a bead of sweat trickle down the back of his neck. Zack stood with his chest puffed out and his hands fisted at his sides. He looked like a blond rooster, June thought.

"We're just talking," Jason said. "Right, June?"

June stepped stiffly around Jason, taking care not to let any part of her body brush his. She hurried across the kitchen to where Zack and her brother stood.

"Let's go back to the living room," Tom suggested. "Come on, Zack."

"You were touching her," Zack said accusingly. "I heard her ask you to stop."

Jason drew himself up, his shoulders squared, his body language reflecting Zack's. But where Zack was a skinny teenage boy, Jason was a grown man, wiry but muscular, and June was suddenly very aware of the size differential between the two. June put her hand on Zack's arm.

"It's okay," she said softly. "Tom's right—we should go back to the living room. My mom asked me to bring in a bottle of wine. She's waiting for me."

Zack ignored both June's and Tom's pleas to disengage. "You can't just come into someone's house and start touching people who don't want to be touched," he said.

"Maybe you should shut your mouth," Jason said. He kept his voice low, but his tone was now ugly and sneering.

June realized then that she had been very wrong about Jason. She'd assumed that his simple nature and lack of focus meant that he was harmless, like a sweet but not very bright Labrador retriever. That had been a terrible mistake. The man standing in front of them, his eyes hostile and his posture coiled up, suddenly seemed dangerous. She could feel the fine hairs on her arms stand on end.

"Come on, Zack," she said. "Let's go to the other room."

"Listen to her, boy," Jason said. "You should run away with the other kids. You don't want to mess with me."

Zack took an aggressive step forward. "What did you call me?"

Jason slowly looked him up and down, then chuckled. June felt a chill run through her. She had definitely been wrong to underestimate this man.

"I called you a boy." Jason's voice had a taunting note to it. *"Boy."*

Zack stepped forward, raising his fists in front of him.

"Zack, no," Tom said, reaching for his arm, but Zack shook him off.

"Please, Zack. Stop!" June pleaded.

Zack ignored them both and took another step toward Jason. June's mouth went dry, and she could feel her pulse accelerate. She wondered if she should call for her parents to come and help, to intervene. To stop whatever was about to happen from happening.

"I dare you to say it again," Zack said through clenched teeth. "Call me *boy* one more time, and I'll make you sorry."

June opened her mouth, ready to yell for her mother, her father, anyone. But before she could get the words out, Jason lifted a hand and slapped Zack across the face. The impact of his palm against Zack's cheek made a loud crack, and Zack staggered back a step, lifting his hand to the spot where he'd been hit. When he turned to glance back at them, June could see the angry red outline of Jason's hand on his cheek.

"Stop it!" June started to move forward, wanting to get between Jason and Zack before the fight turned even uglier, but Tom grabbed her arm, holding her back.

"June, no!" Tom said.

June looked back at her brother, wondering why he had stopped her, when someone obviously needed to put an end to this pointless confrontation. In the split second she turned away, she heard Zack let out a furious roar. By the time June looked back, Zack had launched himself at Jason, pinning him back against the counter.

"Mom!" June yelled. "Dad!"

Zack and Jason grappled together, their arms wrapped around one another. Zack got one arm free and punched Jason's chest, causing the older man to grunt with pain. They turned as they wrestled, so June could first see Jason looking incandescent with rage and then Zack's face red with exertion.

"What's going on in here?" Marlowe asked as she appeared in the doorway, Lee beside her.

"Stop this immediately!" Lee said, his voice loud and carrying. "What the hell do you think you're doing?"

Zack hesitated for a moment, turning to look at June's parents. And at that moment, Jason leaned back, uncoiled his body forward, and threw himself against Zack.

"No!" Marlowe cried out. "Stop!"

Zack staggered back, flinging his arms out to try and regain his balance. But then, almost as if in slow motion, he started to fall backward, his feet going out from under him. As he fell, his head hit the edge of the kitchen counter with a sickening thwack. The sound reminded June of when her family was on vacation in Key West, walking down the main street in town, and a man sliced open a coconut with a dangerously sharp knife to sell the pierced fruit to tourists passing by.

And then Zack's body fell onto the pale-blond hardwood floor with a loud thud.

PART TWO

18:05 update. The National Hurricane Center has issued an emergency warning for southeastern Florida. Hurricane Celeste has made landfall as a Category 5 storm. Conditions continue to deteriorate. This storm is producing a life-threatening storm surge, catastrophic winds, and devastating flooding. The Palm Beach International Airport reported a wind gust of 176 mph. Seek shelter for the duration of the storm.

CHAPTER SEVENTEEN

FELIX

Felix was lying on his back, his tall rangy frame spread across June's bed, watching the final scene in *The Breakfast Club* on her laptop. Judd Nelson walked across the football field, holding one fist triumphantly up over his head while "Don't You (Forget About Me)," by Simple Minds, played in the background. Felix sighed happily and laced his hands together behind his head. It was such a great movie. He just wished June had been there to watch it with him.

Where is she, anyway? he wondered. He thought she would have come up with an excuse to escape the gathering downstairs. Being forced to hang out with a random bunch of adults she didn't know was June's worst nightmare. It wasn't that she was shy. She just had a low tolerance for small talk.

Felix turned off the movie and looked around the room, with its familiar pale-pink walls and a long white lacquer dresser with brass handles and a matching mirror. There was a cream chenille armchair and matching ottoman in the corner, over which hung a framed art poster of the word *love*, the red letters a square box with the *O* tipped to one side. An enormous stuffed gray elephant named Ollie stood next to the chair. Felix had spent hours in this room with June, talking, laughing, watching movies. But this was the first time he'd ever been there alone, without her. It made him feel surprisingly lonely, even more so than he did when he was home alone at his own house, in his own room.

For June's sake, Felix tried to pretend that it didn't bother him that her parents had gone from treating him almost like a member of the family to banning him from their house. Or, at least, her father had. June had told him Marlowe had tried to intervene on his behalf but had given in when Mr. Davies insisted.

"That makes me even angrier," June had told him later while they'd sat at one of the long tables in the high school cafeteria. "The way she just lets him roll over her. Like his word is the law and she's some sort of 1950s housewife. I thought the patriarchy was supposed to be dead."

"Well, he is your dad, so technically he is the patriarch of your family," Felix said before he bit into an apple and tried to ignore the anxiety snaking through his stomach.

"That's exactly my point!" June angrily stabbed at her yogurt with a plastic spoon. "That's why I'm so angry!"

Felix knew June was already outraged, and he didn't want to fuel her anger. But the truth was it had made the terrible situation he was in—all thanks to Derrick, his asshole of a cousin—all the worse. Mr. and Mrs. Davies knew him, and yet they'd been so quick to believe the worst of him. It made him feel small, and damaged, and, he had to admit—to himself, if not to June—incredibly angry at the injustice of it all. Angry at Derrick for getting him into trouble, angry at the police and prosecutors for charging him, and, yes, angry at June's parents—or at least her father—for blaming him for something he didn't even do.

Felix stared up at the ceiling, listening to the wind wailing outside. He hoped that whatever it was that had hit the roof—a tree, probably, or maybe another projectile caught up in the wind, like the umbrella that had hit Mick—hadn't caused any structural damage to the house. The loud crash and the way it had caused the house to shake under the impact had scared the crap out of him. And then a few minutes later, he could almost have sworn he heard the front door open and shut at one point, although it must have been his imagination. No one would be crazy enough to go out in this storm.

Wait, Felix wondered. *What was that?*

He sat up and tried to listen. Between the raging storm and how solidly the house was built, it was hard to hear what was going on outside of June's room, especially with her door closed. But it sounded like someone downstairs was shouting.

Felix stood and went to the door, pressing his ear against it. He could definitely hear raised voices, although he couldn't hear who was speaking or what they were saying. Someone was upset, possibly even angry. He wondered uneasily if June's parents had somehow discovered that he was hiding up there. That would definitely cause Mr. Davies to lose his temper. But if that were the case, wouldn't her dad have come upstairs to confront him? Probably. So why else would someone be shouting?

And then a thought occurred to Felix. Maybe the raised voices had something to do with the strangers who'd raced to shore ahead of Hurricane Celeste and docked at the Davieses' house.

Felix stepped back from the door, an uneasy sensation twisting in his stomach. If June or anyone else was in trouble, his first impulse was to go help. But he also knew he couldn't reveal that he was hiding up there. He wasn't worried about himself, but he didn't want to get June in trouble with her parents. Felix turned, went back to the bed, and sat on the edge of it, his long legs bent in front of him.

Zack had been wrong, Felix thought. June's room didn't smell like honeysuckle. It smelled like June, a combination of floral-scented shampoo, laundry detergent, and some unquantifiable essence that was uniquely her. He tried to remind himself that they were just friends, that she viewed him as a second brother. But lately, the pull he felt toward her had become more insistent. It was a bittersweet realization, especially knowing that next year she'd be off to college and he'd be . . .

well, who knew where he'd end up. No matter what happened with his court case, he would be on a different path than the one June was on.

There was a loud thud downstairs.

Felix straightened, and his body tensed as he listened intently. It sounded like someone had dropped something heavy on the wood floors. Was it possible that a window had broken and the storm was knocking over furniture? But no, he would hear the wind howling through in the house, feel the shift in pressure as the storm intruded inside.

Felix deliberated about what he should do. While he thought, he paced around June's room and then back to the door again. Finally, he took a deep breath and cracked open the bedroom door. He peered out the narrow gap and exhaled when he saw the hallway was empty. Felix swung the door open wider and took a few tentative steps out of June's bedroom, hoping that the noise of the storm would cover the sound of his movement.

Now he could hear the voices more clearly. Someone—June, maybe? Mrs. Davies?—was crying. Mr. Davies was shouting, his voice rising up to an anguished cry that Felix could clearly hear.

"What have you done?"

What had they done? And more importantly, Felix wondered, a chill crossing over him, who had they done it to?

CHAPTER EIGHTEEN

MARLOWE

Blood. Why is there so much blood? Marlowe wondered.

She knelt down by Zack. He was lying in an unnatural way, one leg bent over the other, his torso twisted to one side, his arms stretched out to either side. Blood pooled behind his head, spreading out across the french white oak herringbone floor. His eyes were wide open but completely blank.

No, Marlowe thought. *No, no, no.*

How was this happening? Here, in their kitchen, which still smelled of freshly baked brownies and the spiced-orange candle burning on the counter. This was the hub of their family life. It was where they ate dinner and played board games. It was where she'd taught Tom and June how to make chocolate chip cookies while they snuck spoonfuls of the raw batter. She'd make themed dinners—Taco Tuesday, Baked Potato Bar—and line up the serving dishes on the island. And now Zack was lying there, in a pool of his own blood, and he *wasn't moving*.

"Is he . . ." June's words were strangled in her throat. Marlowe could barely hear her over the roaring of the storm. "Is he . . . *dead?*"

"No," Tom said, echoing his mother's thoughts. "He can't be. He's okay. Right, Mom? He's just unconscious, like Mick was earlier."

Marlowe grabbed Zack's wrist, pressing her fingers against his skin, hoping to feel a pulse. She couldn't find the reassuring beat. That didn't mean anything, she told herself. It wasn't like she'd ever had medical training—she could just be missing it. She stared at his chest, willing it to rise with breath, but he remained still.

Zack was not okay. He was very far from being okay.

"What have you done?" Lee shouted, his voice so angry Marlowe didn't recognize it. Lee never raised his voice. He usually retreated to a cold silence when he was upset.

"He attacked me," Jason protested, raising his hands defensively in front of him.

"No," June said, her voice strangled. "You slapped him. I saw you. *We* saw you."

Marlowe looked up and saw Tom and June standing side by side. Tom's face was chalky white, and his eyes looked like pinpricks in his face. June was flushed and had her arms wrapped around herself, tears streaming down her cheeks. Marlowe's children had witnessed violence here, in their home, where they should always be safe. And Zack . . . Marlowe looked back down at the boy she'd known since he was little, when his two front teeth were missing and he'd had perpetually skinned knees. Now his wide brown eyes stared blankly out at . . . nothing.

Marlowe felt the sob before it left her body. The sound that ripped out of her was a loud gasping keen. She wanted to go back in time, back before this moment, back before this storm, back before these people had shown up at their home. Back to when June had rolled her eyes and made sarcastic comments, and Tom had talked about the waves he'd surfed that day, and Zack had chimed in with some outrageous and goofy comment that made them all smile.

He's a sweet kid, but we both know that he's not destined to become a brain surgeon, she had said, just that morning.

No. Zack wasn't destined to become anything other than a statistic. Just one more body to add to Celeste's total count. Although, was that even true? Zack may have died during a hurricane, but it wasn't the storm that had killed him.

Marlowe made another sound, somewhere between a sob and a moan, and she bent over, her eyes closed so that for this one moment, she wouldn't have to look down on Zack's lifeless body. She wrapped her hand around the wrist that she'd just checked for a pulse and was horrified that his skin was already growing cold.

How am I going to tell his parents? Marlowe wondered. Losing a child was the worst thing that could happen to a parent.

"Somebody tell me what happened here," Lee demanded.

"He was touching me." June pointed an accusing finger at Jason. "Zack and Tom came in, and Zack told him to stop. Jason got angry and slapped Zack across the face." She stopped and swallowed, her expression stricken. "They started fighting, and they were grabbing on to each other, and then Jason pushed him. Hard. You saw what happened after that. Zack fell backwards, and he . . . and he . . ." Her voice caught in a sob, and she pointed toward the blood-smeared counter. "He fell and hit his head."

"He started it, not me!" Jason insisted. "He came at me. You saw him. *He* came at *me*."

"You hit him!" June shook her head and wrapped her arms tighter around herself. "Why couldn't you just leave us alone?"

June used her sleeve to wipe the tears from her face, which was red and blotchy, and then shook her head. Tom was silent, clearly overwhelmed by the horror of what was happening. Marlowe could tell that her son was trying not to cry. For a moment, she could see the small children they'd once been. From a young age, June had always been quick to act and to lose her temper, while Tom had been stoic and withdrawn when faced with conflict.

Marlowe turned her gaze back to Zack. "What should we do? We can't just leave him here. Like this, in the middle of the kitchen. Should we move him?"

Lee ignored her question. "I want an explanation for what happened here," he said, his voice like a razor, sharp and full of fury. Clearly,

June's version hadn't been good enough for him. She had explained the details of what had happened but not why a grown man had become violent with a teenage boy.

Marlowe distantly wondered how it was possible that she and Lee were experiencing the same situation—unexpected violence, Zack's lifeless body—and yet reacting so differently. He was rigid and coiled with anger. She felt limp and helpless in her grief.

"What's going on in here?" Bo's voice echoed loudly in the kitchen as he strode in, Isabel and Darcy behind him. When Darcy saw Zack's prone body on the ground, she let out a stifled scream. Isabel stayed silent, hovering in the doorway, her eyes wide and one hand pressed over her mouth.

Lee turned on Bo. "Your brother killed him!"

"That's not what happened!" Jason interjected. "He came at me, Bo! We tussled, and I pushed him, and . . ." He trailed off, flinging a hand at Zack's body. "He just fell. It wasn't my fault!"

Jason looked manic, his eyes wide and wild, the fingers on both hands drumming against his legs, his breathing ragged.

Bo placed his hands gently on his brother's shoulders. "Calm down, bro. Take a deep breath."

"I didn't mean to hurt him! I didn't!"

"I know you didn't," Bo said soothingly. "And everything is going to be okay. Just breathe. Can you do that for me?"

Jason sucked in a breath, but he was still visibly agitated.

"Nothing about this is okay. We took you in. Gave you a safe harbor from the storm. And this is how you repaid us? By killing a young man in our care?" Lee's voice was ragged.

"I don't think getting upset is going to help the situation, Lee. Do you?" Bo asked. He knelt down next to Marlowe, resting his hand lightly on Zack's chest. He waited a moment, then shook his head grimly. "Damn. He seemed like a nice kid."

Marlowe nodded, tears filling her eyes.

Bo patted Marlowe on the shoulder, then stood. "This is not the ideal situation."

Anger slashed through Marlowe's shock. What kind of comment was that? Not ideal? Zack was *dead*. How could Bo be so irreverent now, after what had just happened? She stood, too, turning on him. "Your brother killed Zack. We're going to have to call the police as soon as the storm passes and the phones are working."

"Now, hold on, Marlowe. I agree this is a terrible thing that happened," Bo said. "Someone should get a blanket to put over the boy."

"I'll go get one," Tom said. He turned and moved woodenly out of the kitchen and out of Marlowe's sight.

Lee slammed his hand against the marble countertop. Marlowe flinched at the sound. "This isn't acceptable!"

"Lee, you need to calm down," Bo said. "Bad things happen sometimes. I'm sure Jason didn't mean to hurt Zack. It was just an accident."

Lee turned to him, his expression fierce. "Your brother didn't hurt Zack. He *killed* him. There are going to be consequences. Do you understand that? The police are going to come here. They're going to want answers about what happened here tonight."

Bo sighed, and his head dipped forward. For a moment, Marlowe thought he was absorbing Lee's words, the implied threat. The police would come here, to their home, and demand answers about why a seventeen-year-old boy was dead.

But then, Bo straightened, turned, and went to where he'd left his dark-green backpack in the corner of the kitchen. He picked the bag up and unzipped it. Marlowe watched him, her brow furrowed. Why was he choosing this moment, in the middle of the horror of Zack's death, to rummage through his belongings?

In one swift move, Bo pulled a gun out from his backpack and pointed it steadily at Lee. Marlowe felt a jolt of fear as she watched her husband slowly raise his hands in the air.

"While I would like to thank you folks for your hospitality, the situation here has changed," Bo said. "Now, I'm going to need you all to listen closely. If you follow my instructions, you'll be fine. If you don't." Bo paused and glanced at Zack's body. "Well, let's not think about all of the things that can go wrong in the middle of the storm."

CHAPTER NINETEEN

TOM

Zack was dead.

Tom knew from the cold sliver of horror that shuddered through him that this was true. And yet his mind couldn't make sense of this new reality. He simply couldn't accept a world without Zack in it. His friend was a part of almost every memory, every experience he'd ever had. Zack at the beach, his board tucked under his arm, a huge smile lighting up his face as he looked out at the surf. Zack throwing his head back, laughing deep in his belly, while they sat in the school cafeteria eating peanut butter and jelly sandwiches. Zack talking excitedly while he windmilled his arms around for emphasis. He had always been so alive.

Only now he wasn't.

Tom wandered into the living room, which suddenly seemed larger and emptier now that everyone had relocated to the kitchen. There were half-empty wineglasses on the end tables and napkins crumpled on discarded paper plates, striped beach towels thrown over chairs. His mother would hate this, Tom thought. She liked everything to be neat and tidy. He picked up a plate, planning to clean up a bit, but then set it back down, suddenly overwhelmed by the task of straightening the mess.

He looked around, trying to remember why he'd entered the room. Then it came crashing back to him. He needed a blanket. To cover his best friend's body. Tom heard a raw, jagged sob and realized that it had come from him. He choked back the tears and picked up a gray throw blanket folded neatly on the back of a chair and stared down at it. His mother had wrapped it around Darcy earlier, when the strangers had first come into their house. Would his mom mind if he used this one? The blood might ruin it. Zack's blood . . .

Tom shook his head, trying to dislodge the image of Zack's body lying on the kitchen floor, his head circled by a pool of blood.

His mind kept replaying the scene that had just unfolded in the kitchen. Why had Zack escalated the confrontation with Jason? He could have just walked away. But Tom already knew the answer to that question. Zack had been in love with June for years. He'd wanted to protect her from Jason. He'd always been so brave, so much braver than Tom could ever dream of being. Tom froze when faced with danger or conflict. Just like he had in the kitchen, when he had seen Jason touching his sister's hair in that creepy, predatory way. Zack had charged in, ready to make Jason stop, whatever it took. Tom had just stood there, unable to move or say anything.

Jason had killed Zack. But by not doing or saying anything to help the situation, by staying silent while Zack confronted Jason alone, Tom knew he was complicit in his best friend's death.

Tears were running down his cheeks, and Tom angrily swiped at them with the back of his hand. He turned and headed back toward the kitchen, clutching the gray cashmere blanket. He wondered if they'd move Zack's body or leave him there in the middle of the kitchen floor. It was a crime scene, wasn't it? The police would want to see how it happened, how Zack had fallen.

Only the police wouldn't arrive for hours. Maybe not even until tomorrow. Not until the hurricane had passed, and even then, the roads might be flooded or blocked by trees that had been knocked down. And until they did, they'd all be stuck in the house with the strangers. With Zack's killer.

Tom heard something and froze. He tried to listen to the voices in the kitchen, although the sound was muted by the storm raging outside. When he'd gone to get the blanket, his dad had sounded angry, his mother distraught. But now, even though he couldn't hear the words being said, the tenor of their voices had changed.

They sounded frightened.

CHAPTER TWENTY

MARLOWE

Bo was standing so close to the long oak kitchen table his hip bumped up against one of the upholstered dining chairs. Marlowe froze as she stared at the weapon in his hand. She didn't know anything about guns, except—of course—that they were deadly. Bo was pointing the gun at Lee, his aim steady and straight.

"Jason." Bo looked at his brother, who was across the kitchen, still standing where he had been when he'd pushed Zack. Bo tossed the green backpack to his brother, who caught it easily. "It's time. Let's get going."

"Bo?" Darcy's voice was small and childish. "I don't understand. What's going on?"

She seemed as bewildered as Marlowe felt. But then, to Marlowe's horror, Jason reached into the backpack and pulled out a second gun. He aimed it, with a far less steady hand, right at June. Marlowe felt her horror rise until she saw spots in front of her eyes.

They'd let armed men into their home, she realized. Around their children. And now they were all in danger.

"No," Marlowe said, but no one seemed to be listening to her.

"What are you going to do?" Lee asked, his voice choked in his throat.

"Well, Lee, our plan was to ride out the hurricane and be on our way. And if everyone behaves, that's what we'll do. Once it passes, we'll get back on our boat, and you'll never hear from us again."

"But he killed Zack," June said, pointing at Jason, her voice shrill with outrage.

"June," Marlowe said sharply. "Not now."

Marlowe wanted to go to her daughter, to shield June behind her. But she didn't dare move. She didn't know how Bo or especially Jason, who seemed less clear in the head than his brother, would react. So she stayed still, trying to force herself to breathe. She needed to figure out what they wanted. It sounded like Zack's death had been a terrible accident and not part of a larger plan. Maybe they really would just leave as soon as the storm passed. Although, why had they brought guns into the house with them?

"Darcy, come here," Bo said. The young woman hesitated, and he momentarily took his eyes off Lee to stare at her. "Now, Darcy. Come on."

Darcy walked slowly toward him across the kitchen. She looked unsure, even a little unsteady. "What are you doing, Bo?"

"I want you to go collect everyone's cell phone and bring them to me," Bo told her. When Darcy didn't immediately move, he reached out to touch her arm. "I need you to do that now, sweetheart."

The endearment had an immediate effect on Darcy. Her face softened, and she nodded. Darcy turned to Marlowe first, who was closest, and held out her hand. Marlowe nodded toward the island.

"My phone's there," she said.

Darcy plucked Marlowe's iPhone up off the counter and then went to June, then to Lee, and then finally to Isabel. They each wordlessly handed her their cell phone, and Darcy gathered them in her hands and looked to Bo for further instruction. Marlowe wondered how it was possible that the young woman had fallen so quickly into step when she clearly had no idea what Bo had planned. Yes, he was handsome and charismatic, but he was also holding a group of people hostage at gunpoint.

Bo looked around and frowned. "We're missing someone."

Tom, Marlowe thought. Maybe he'd overheard what was happening in the kitchen and managed to get away. But no. As she heard the wind screaming outside, battering their house, those hopes were immediately doused. That wasn't possible. There was nowhere for him to go.

Bo looked up and smiled. "Tom, thank you for joining us. Please come on in and give your phone to Darcy."

Marlowe turned to see her son, who had just walked into the kitchen. He was clutching a gray throw blanket in front of him as he looked blankly at the two men pointing their guns at his family.

"What's going on?" Tom asked.

"I was just explaining to your family that the situation has changed." Bo smiled, as charming as ever. "Please hand Darcy your phone."

Tom hesitated and turned to look at Lee, who was pale with either fury or terror—Marlowe couldn't tell which. A muscle twitched in his clenched jaw.

"Unless you want me to shoot your father," Bo added in the same pleasant, conversational tone he'd used when he'd complimented the pigs in a blanket earlier that evening. It was chilling how calm he was.

"No! Please," Marlowe said quickly. "Tom, give your phone to Darcy. Now."

Tom stepped toward Darcy, and Bo shifted, aiming his gun at Tom, who froze.

"Hold on there, cowboy. Not so quickly," Bo said.

Darcy darted forward, collected Tom's phone, and then went to stand at Bo's side. She looked up at him, waiting for her next instruction.

"Just set the phones down on the table. Marlowe, do you have a bag?" Bo asked.

"A bag?" Marlowe repeated.

"Any kind will do. A Publix bag, whatever you happen to have on hand."

Marlowe started to step forward and then stopped, staring at Bo's gun. "They're in the cupboard," she said, gesturing at the cabinets to the right of the built-in ovens.

Bo nodded, and Marlowe moved to open the cupboard, where she kept a pile of canvas bags she took with her when she went to the farmers' market on Sunday mornings. She hesitated for a moment as her hand fell on one of the well-worn bags that, in happier days, she'd used to transport locally sourced honey and bunches of peppery arugula.

What is happening? she thought. It felt like her mind was on an endless loop of how to survive, how to keep her family safe, and the sickening knowledge that Zack's body was lying on the kitchen floor.

There were cans of San Marzano tomatoes and cannellini beans in the cupboard. Should she grab a can and use it as a weapon to throw at Bo? But no, that was stupid. Canned goods were no match for a gun. She grabbed a canvas bag, closed the cupboard door, and held the bag out to Darcy. The young woman didn't meet Marlowe's eyes as she took it from her before crossing back to the kitchen table, where she shoved the pile of cell phones into the canvas bag. Task completed, Darcy looked back up at Bo with an unnerving obedience. He smiled and nodded at her, and a flush spread over Darcy's high-boned cheeks.

"Let's move this party back to the living room," Bo said. "I think we'll all be more comfortable in there. Isabel, you go first, and then June, then Marlowe. And before you get any ideas about doing something silly, remember that we have guns pointed at Lee and Tom. And we will not hesitate to shoot them."

CHAPTER TWENTY-ONE

JUNE

June felt like she was living in the middle of a nightmare she couldn't wake up from. Zack was dead. Zack. Funny, goofy, annoying Zack. He'd always been Tom's friend more than hers, but she'd known him for as long as she could remember. They'd grown up together. They'd sat cross-legged on the living room floor playing with Legos and gone trick-or-treating in coordinated costumes, and Zack had gone with them on almost every family vacation they'd taken. And now he was gone. Grief stabbed at her, as sharp and painful as a knife plunging into her chest.

Is it my fault he's dead? June wondered. *Zack died trying to protect me. If I had left the kitchen as soon as I realized I was alone with Jason, or if I'd yelled for help when he touched me, Zack would still be alive.*

Guilt and sorrow washed over her, but the emotions were quickly joined by a hot, rising rage. Maybe she could have stopped the situation from spinning out of control. But she wasn't the one who'd killed Zack. Jason was. He did this. She didn't care if it was an accident. Jason was bigger, and stronger, and older, and should never have gotten into a physical altercation with a younger, slighter boy.

Jason had killed Zack. And June wanted him to pay for what he'd done.

She felt Jason's eyes on her, even as she turned away from him and followed Isabel and her mother out of the kitchen, down the hallway, and into the living room. Even his gaze felt intrusive, like a cockroach crawling over her arm.

And now Jason had a gun.

In her health science class in tenth grade, Mrs. McCurdy had covered the topic of sexual assault. It had been uncomfortable and weird, and everyone had deflected the awkwardness by making jokes. But June remembered that Mrs. McCurdy had issued a somber warning—if you're targeted with sexual violence, fight if you can do so safely. But don't risk your life. You might need to submit to save yourself.

June remembered being deeply offended at this advice. Her first thought had been, *That will never happen to me.* That had quickly been followed by her absolute certainty that if she ever was in danger and a man was threatening her, there was no way she would just submit. She'd claw, hit and scream, and make him stop. She'd even imagined what might happen. A drunken guy pawing her at a frat party, or maybe an unpleasant coworker who'd corner her in a deserted conference room. In these vague scenarios, June would effortlessly know how to defend herself, automatically equipped with martial art skills she'd never bothered to learn. And once she'd repelled her attacker back, the scene would skip forward to the police arriving and taking him away in handcuffs, his head bowed in disgrace, while she looked on with an expression of dignified scorn.

June had never once thought she'd be facing an armed man in her home with a feral, hungry expression on his face.

As soon as she entered the living room, June began to look around for a potential weapon. But they didn't live in the kind of house where there were swords hanging over the fireplace or heavy marble objets d'art or sharp letter openers lying around on tabletops. Their living room was comfortable and cozy, decorated with soft pillows and throw blankets scattered around. June tried to think. There were chef's knives in the kitchen, of course, and silver candlesticks on the table in the dining room, just across the hall from where she now stood.

And then suddenly June remembered. There was a weapon in the house. Her dad had a handgun, which he kept in the drawer of his bedside table. But that was upstairs. How could she possibly get to it?

Felix, she thought and felt a surge of hope.

He was probably still hidden in her room. But her father had shouted, and Zack's body had fallen heavily to the floor. Would that noise have carried upstairs? Would Felix have heard it, all the way up in her room, even behind a closed door? And would he remember her father's gun?

Felix knew where the gun was. She'd shown it to him one afternoon, years ago. She'd put a finger to her lips and beckoned Felix into her parents' bedroom, where she'd slid open the drawer on the mahogany bachelor's chest Lee used as a nightstand. They hadn't touched it but had looked at it for a few moments, their eyes round with awe at the deadly force sitting in front of them, an arm's reach away. But there were so many ifs. If Felix had heard the commotion, if he remembered the gun, if he could get to it.

Please remember, Felix, she thought, trying to send the thought across the house to him.

But even that plan was seriously flawed. If Felix somehow did remember the gun and was able to get it, well, what then? If he came downstairs and confronted Bo and Jason, it would still be two against one. Three, if you counted Darcy, who seemed perfectly happy to do Bo's bidding. And June knew Felix had never held a gun, much less shot one. This obviously wasn't the first time Bo and Jason had handled weapons.

Lee and Tom came into the living room, followed by Bo, Jason, and Darcy. Darcy stood as close to Bo as possible, her body curved toward him.

"Take a seat," Bo said genially, gesturing toward the sofas, as if he were the host. "We might as well get comfortable. We're going to be here for a while."

June's parents sat on one sofa, and Isabel—who looked dazed by what was happening—sat on the opposite one. Tom perched on the round upholstered ottoman between the two sofas.

June didn't want to sit down. She wanted to stay on her feet so she could make a break for it as soon as Bo's attention was diverted. But it wasn't like she had a plan, or at least not one that went beyond finding Felix and going to get help.

"June." When Bo said her name, it was a warning. June couldn't help glancing at Jason and saw that he was staring at her, his eyes brighter and more alert than they'd been earlier.

"Come sit with me, June," Marlowe said, patting the sofa. June walked silently to the sofa and sat next to her mother. Marlowe reached for June's hand, but June pulled it away, out of her mother's reach. She couldn't bear being touched right now. Not after what had just happened. Not when Zack's body was lying on their kitchen floor.

A loud boom of thunder sounded outside, amplifying the already shrieking wind. The storm was effectively also keeping them hostage, June thought. They were completely trapped.

Think, she told herself. She forced herself to breathe calmly while she tried to figure out a plan. There were two plausible scenarios. In one, Bo, Jason, and Darcy would wait out the storm and then escape quickly by boat, as Bo had promised they would do. June wanted to believe this, but she thought it was unlikely. Jason had killed Zack, and now he and his brother, assisted by Darcy, were holding five people hostage at gunpoint. If they left after the hurricane passed over their town, June's parents would contact the police immediately. They would be able to describe their captors in detail, including their names and the make of their boat. She had even overheard Darcy tell Isabel the name of the restaurant where she worked. The two men would be caught and prosecuted and would spend years, maybe even decades, in prison. Darcy would even face a lengthy jail sentence as an accomplice to the brothers' crimes.

The second possible scenario was that Bo and Jason would kill June, Tom, their parents, and Isabel and then disappear back out on the water, without anyone knowing they had ever been at the Davieses' house.

Oh no, June thought, feeling a cold wave of terror.

But there was still Mick, June reminded herself. He had seen their guests and would certainly be able to describe them in detail to law enforcement. Bo knew that.

Unless . . . and suddenly, June felt another shudder of fear pass over her. What if Bo had been lying when he'd told them Mick had decided to drive to his mother's house? They only had Bo's word for it. It had seemed so out of character for Mick, who was smart and capable, to take on the enormous risk of driving in the middle of a Category 5 hurricane. What if Bo had hurt Mick . . . or worse? What if he had killed him?

June twitched, wanting suddenly to stand up, to run away, even if it meant going out in the storm. Because facing the winds and flooding had to be safer than sitting here, waiting to see what Bo and Jason had planned for them.

"We just have to wait for the storm to pass," Marlowe said softly, soothingly. "You heard him. They won't hurt us."

June wondered if her mother could possibly be that naive. She glanced at Bo, who had turned to say something to Darcy in a low voice. June couldn't hear his words, but she could see happiness bloom on Darcy's face, her hips swiveling toward him as she pressed her whole body against the side of his.

"We have to get out of here," June said, her words in such a soft whisper she wasn't sure if her mother would be able to hear her over the sounds of the storm.

Her mother leaned closer, her eyebrows knitting together with concern. "No. We need to stay safe. And that means doing exactly what they tell us."

"They're going to kill us," June hissed.

"Ladies, if you have something to say, say it to the group," Bo said, stepping forward. He was still holding his gun, but now in a relaxed way, as if it were a movie prop. "Don't be shy. Speak up."

"I have to use the bathroom," June said abruptly.

"Be my guest," Bo said, with an exaggerated wave of the hand holding the gun. "Darcy, will you please escort June to the bathroom?"

"You want me to go in with her?" Darcy asked, sounding a little nervous.

"No, just stand outside the door. And make sure she comes back."

June quickly stood. Was this her best chance to break free, to run upstairs and find Felix and grab her father's gun?

"June?" She turned back to see Bo looking at her. "Remember that we're here, with your family. Don't do anything foolish."

June nodded grimly. She walked from the living room to the front hall, past the empty dining room to the downstairs powder room. Once inside, she shut and locked the door behind her. She didn't actually have to pee, so she turned on the faucet and sat on the closed toilet lid, willing her mind to come up with a plan.

The last hurricane she'd experienced had been a few years earlier. That storm had been relatively mild, only a Category 1, but all hurricanes followed the same general pattern. There was the initial stage where the storm arrived on land, with high winds, heavy rain, and electrical storms. Then, as the eye wall approached, the storm intensified temporarily until the eye arrived and everything went suddenly, strangely calm. The authorities always cautioned people not to go outside during the eye, because as soon as it passed, conditions quickly deteriorated again. But that brief period of calm might be their best chance to break free and find help.

Now the only question was, How was she going to pull that off?

After she'd waited a few moments, June flushed the toilet and pulled the door open. Darcy was standing there, one arm wrapped around her torso. Her pretty, fine-boned face was vacant.

"Why are you helping them?" June asked her.

Darcy stared at her out of wide almond-shaped eyes fringed with long dark lashes.

June tried again. "You know they're planning on hurting us, right? And if they do, and you help them, you'll go to jail for the rest of your life. Is that really what you want?"

"Bo won't let anything bad happen to me," Darcy said. "He loves me."

"If he loves you, why would he take you out on a boat with a hurricane coming onshore?"

Darcy's expression hardened. "We're not supposed to be talking. Go back to the living room. Now."

June did as she was instructed. But one thing was clear—Darcy wasn't going to help her or her family survive the night.

CHAPTER TWENTY-TWO

MARLOWE

When June and Darcy returned from their brief trip to the powder room, Marlowe exhaled deeply. Despite the danger she knew they were in, Marlowe felt marginally safer when her family was within her sight. She particularly didn't want June to be separated from the rest of them. She'd seen the way Jason had looked at her daughter.

"Welcome back, ladies," Bo said while June took her seat on the sofa next to her mother. Darcy went to his side. Bo patted her bottom. "Why don't you get us a couple of beers, sweetheart? Would anyone like a refresh on their cocktail of choice? Darcy, bring in a few of those bottles of wine too. We might as well get comfortable. This storm isn't going to end anytime soon."

Darcy obediently set off for the kitchen and returned with bottles of beer, two bottles of wine, and a corkscrew. She handed beers to Bo and Jason and then set the wine on a glass-topped side table. She brandished the corkscrew and deftly opened both bottles of wine with a practiced hand.

Darcy walked around, refilling glasses without bothering to ask anyone if they wanted more to drink. She even poured a healthy slug of wine into Lee's empty highball glass, which had previously been filled with whiskey. He took a long sip from it without complaint. Isabel also picked up her glass and, tipping her head back, drank half the glass in one go. Marlowe ignored her full wineglass. She wanted to keep a clear head.

Bo sat on a low-slung leather side chair, holding his beer in one hand and his gun in the other. Darcy took the matching chair next to him, but Jason remained standing. He seemed even more ill at ease now, turning the bottle in his hands around and around.

"I've always lived a modest life," Bo said. "But I think I could get used to a house like this. It's quite something. The size, the furniture, the view. Well, the view when the hurricane shutters aren't up. It makes me wonder."

"Wonder what?" Lee asked.

"How a man like you"—Bo gestured at Lee with his beer—"ended up in a place like this. While Jason and I live in an apartment smaller than this living room." He turned to Marlowe. "I bet you've never stepped foot in the sort of place I live in. It used to be a shitty hotel. Now they've been converted into what they call *apartments* but which are still just shitty hotel rooms, with shitty hotel room interiors, but they charge by the week instead of by the night."

Marlowe had no idea what to say to this. She'd gone to college and lived first in a dorm and then in a modest apartment near campus that her father had purchased for her. But she knew Bo wasn't talking about student housing with utilitarian furnishings. He meant living in poverty. He was right; she'd never experienced that.

"Do you know I took that test kids take to get into college. What do they call it, June?"

"The SAT?" June asked.

"That's it. The SAT. I took that and got a perfect score. Imagine that. Everyone thought I was just another poor, dumb kid. And then I aced it. That raised a few eyebrows."

"The actual test?" Isabel asked. It was the first time Marlowe had heard her assistant speak since the ordeal had begun, and she was surprised by Isabel's acid tone. The young woman seemed more irritated than frightened by Bo.

"It was a practice test. But no one else got a perfect score like me. But even after that, I didn't have any fancy colleges lining up to let me in."

"You have to take the actual test. The timed one with monitors. And then you have to apply to colleges before you can get in," Isabel said. "They don't come looking for you. That's not how it works."

"I didn't have anyone in my life who encouraged me to apply to college." Bo's tone was now as spiked as Isabel's. "Kids need people to support them. To encourage them. I was smarter than everyone else, but I didn't have a single person in my life who helped me."

Isabel's lips curled derisively, but she didn't reply. Instead, she turned her attention to her glass of wine, which was nearly empty.

"Would you like some more wine?" Darcy asked her eagerly, as if hoping to find an occupation in the middle of this terrifying, surreal gathering.

"Why not?" Isabel held out her glass. Darcy stood and filled it nearly to the brim.

"So what I'm trying to figure out is how it is that a man like you"—Bo nodded in Lee's direction—"ends up here. And another equally smart, or even smarter, man ends up in a one-room efficiency."

"I'm a lawyer," Lee said. "I went to college, then to law school. I worked for years in my profession, first as an associate and then as a partner at my law firm. I've earned what I have."

"That's not quite true, though, is it, Lee? I've met a few lawyers in my time. Some of them do well, but this . . ." Bo raised his beer again and rotated it in a circle. "This is on a different level."

"What kind of law did they practice?" Isabel asked. "Because I've heard criminal defense lawyers make a good living."

Marlowe stared at her assistant, wondering why she was baiting him. Was Isabel drunk? She'd downed quite a few glasses of wine since the storm had descended.

But Bo ignored her pointed question and instead continued to address Lee. "What's a property like this worth? Big house, on the water. I'd guess ten million, if not more."

"We haven't had it appraised recently," Lee said.

Bo's expression hardened. "Don't bullshit me, Lee. You know exactly how much this place is worth. Do you think I'm stupid?"

Lee swallowed. "No. I don't think you're stupid."

"Good. Because you would be wise not to underestimate me. It's a mistake too many people have made." Bo relaxed back in his seat. "I was born with this gift, I guess you'd call it. Although sometimes it feels like a curse. I know people."

"What is that supposed to mean?" June asked.

Marlowe wondered if her daughter was taking Isabel's lead. She hoped not. Nothing would be gained from antagonizing Bo. They needed to do everything they could to keep the situation from becoming even more volatile.

"June." Marlowe put her hand over her daughter's, hoping to silence her. But June pulled her hand away again and looked at Bo attentively, waiting for his answer.

Bo smiled at the teenager, as if he were a teacher and she was his star pupil.

"That's a good question, June. You see, I can read people. I meet someone, and I instantly know everything about them. What motivates them, what embarrasses them, what's important to them."

"You read people," June repeated. "So you think you already know everything there is to know about me? I don't buy that. You don't know anything about me."

"What can I say? It's a gift. It's gotten to the point where I play a game whenever I meet someone new. I make some guesses about them and see how many I get right. I don't mean to brag, but I'm almost never wrong," Bo said. "If I got a job at the local car dealership, I'd be their top salesman within a month. But I don't want to be a salesman, because they're as filthy and corrupt as attorneys. No offense, Lee."

"There's an obvious flaw to your game," June said. "The only way you could win is if the person you're making the guesses about admitted to it. Like, if you guessed my favorite flavor of ice cream was chocolate, I could lie and say it's strawberry. And you wouldn't know the difference."

"It does require a certain amount of honesty from the person playing the game with me. But I always know when someone's lying to me. And I would guess that you don't eat ice cream. That you spend all your time and effort trying not to eat much of anything at all," Bo said.

Marlowe stilled. No one in the family ever directly addressed June's issues surrounding food. She was too prickly about the entire topic. But June just stared back at Bo, her gaze level.

"What does that prove? It's just a conclusion based on observation. I'm thin, so you assume I don't eat. But that doesn't mean you have any insights into my character."

"Why don't you pick someone else for me to play with? How about your dad?"

Bo turned to look at Lee, sitting next to Marlowe on the sofa.

"What about me?" Lee said.

"I've only known you for, what? A few hours? But I think I already know you well."

"I highly doubt that."

"Play the game, Lee." Bo's tone was friendly enough, but this was clearly an order and not a suggestion. Bo tipped his head to one side and regarded Lee for a long moment. "You always think that you're the smartest person in the room. You're a competent but not an exceptional attorney. Your law practice certainly doesn't do well enough to support your standard of living. This all comes from family money, and not yours. It's from your wife's side. That's why you pursued her, why you married her. Not that I blame you. Marlowe is a very attractive woman." Bo smiled at Marlowe. "But the millions that came with her made her even more attractive. Let's see, what else? You like having secrets. They make you feel powerful."

Lee stared back at Bo, and Marlowe felt a shiver of unease pass over her. Did Lee have secrets? And suddenly Marlowe remembered the phone she had found in the safe that morning. She could feel the hard rectangle of plastic still in her pocket. She had completely forgotten she had it when Bo insisted they hand over their cell phones earlier.

Bo continued. "I doubt you've been faithful, but I'd bet you hide that side of your life from Marlowe. She strikes me as the trusting type. And I know that you favor your daughter over your son, probably because she's the smarter of your two children, so you think she's the one who takes after you." Bo leaned forward, his expression avid. "How'd I do? Nailed it, right? Not too shabby for someone you dismissed as a dumbass for taking a boat out in a storm."

His words hit Marlowe like a punch to the stomach. The casual accusations he'd hurled—that Lee didn't love his children equally, that he hadn't been faithful to her, that he had married her only for her money. That Lee kept secrets. She didn't believe that Bo actually had some sort of innate gift to read people. No, he just liked to create chaos and upset people.

And Bo couldn't possibly know that Lee had lied to her back at the very beginning all those years ago.

CHAPTER TWENTY-THREE

MARLOWE

New Year's Eve, 1999

Marlowe hadn't wanted to go to the New Year's Eve party at the Jupiter Island Club. Her parents went every year, and once Marlowe had turned eighteen, her mom had insisted that she accompany them. But by the time she was twenty-one and a junior in college, Marlowe had tired of spending New Year's Eve with her parents' middle-aged friends. When her mother had popped her head in Marlowe's bedroom door and suggested they go dress shopping for the party at the Gardens Mall a few days after Christmas, Marlowe had groaned.

"Please don't make me go to the party," she said. "I just want to stay home, order Chinese takeout, and rent a movie from Blockbuster."

"You can't miss the party!" Katherine exclaimed. "It's Y2K! They're predicting that all of the computers, all around the world, are going to crash at midnight. We might as well be at a party when that happens. Besides, everyone will be there. They'll want to see you!"

"It's all old people," Marlowe said.

"Your father and I are not old. Well," Katherine amended. "We're not *that* old."

"There's never anyone there my age. At least, not anyone I want to talk to. I end up sitting off to the side of the dance floor, by myself, waiting until the clock counts down to midnight and we can finally go home."

Katherine laughed. "You make it sound so tragic. If I remember correctly, you spent last New Year's Eve smooching with Alex Hall on the dance floor."

Marlowe covered her face with a floral sham and groaned again. "Don't remind me! That's another reason I don't want to go. I haven't seen Alex since that night, and I heard he has a new girlfriend. Some random blonde he met at Duke and brought home to meet his family. I don't want to run into them. The whole thing will be humiliating."

Katherine smiled. "All the more reason to get a new dress. Come on—let's go to Saks and see if they have anything nice in stock."

Four days later, Marlowe found herself standing on the country club's outdoor patio, which was lit by candles, luminaries, and Christmas lights wound around every tree and post. Women in gowns and men in tuxedos stood around in loose groups, laughing and talking and drinking. Even though they were outside, the scent of mingling perfumes scented the air. Waiters carrying trays of champagne flutes and canapés circled around while the guests helped themselves to mini crab cakes and bites of tuna tartare.

Marlowe was wearing a black slip dress that had reminded her of Carolyn Bessette-Kennedy's wedding dress when she'd tried it on at Saks Fifth Avenue, and she was sipping a glass of champagne that somehow tasted both too sweet and too dry. The night was chilly, and she regretted refusing the pashmina wrap her mother had tried to insist she bring with her. She rubbed an arm with her free hand, trying to warm up.

"Blini with smoked salmon?" A waiter paused beside her, tray at the ready.

Marlowe smiled. "No, thank you."

The waiter nodded and smoothly moved on.

"You should have tried one. They're pretty good."

Marlowe turned. A tall rangy man with light-brown hair and high cheekbones smiled shyly at her.

"I don't think we've met," he said, holding out his hand. "I'm Lee Davies."

Marlowe transferred her champagne glass to her left hand and then shook his hand. "Marlowe Bond. It's nice to meet you."

She immediately felt awkward and second-guessed if that had been the right thing to do. She didn't normally shake hands with other college kids. This man was in his midtwenties, which made him not a contemporary but close to it.

"Are you a member here?" Lee asked.

Marlowe tipped her head to one side. "I'm not sure. My parents are members. They golf, and sometimes we have dinner here. But I don't know if I'm officially a member. Are you?"

"Definitely not a member. My boss is, and I'm here as his guest." Lee inclined his head across the patio toward a jowly man with thick silver hair and a very red face whom Marlowe vaguely recognized, probably from Sunday-night dinners in the club dining room.

"Your boss is your New Year's Eve date?" Marlowe asked.

"My boss and his wife." Lee laughed. "I think they took pity on me when they heard I was planning on staying home tonight and watching a video."

"That was my plan, too, before it got hijacked."

"By your date?"

Marlowe felt a flutter of anticipation at his inquiry. She realized she was attracted to this handsome, if slightly awkward, man. And he was not-so-subtly asking her if she was romantically attached.

"No, by my mother. She got me here through a lethal combination of maternal guilt and shameless bribery."

"Was the bribe worth it?"

"You tell me. It was this dress." Marlowe grinned. "I should have held out for a pony."

Lee laughed. "It's a very nice dress."

"Thank you." Marlowe flushed. He probably thought she'd been fishing for the compliment. Which she supposed she had been. "So what do you do? For work, I mean."

"I'm an attorney. I finished law school last year and just passed the bar."

"Congratulations!" Marlowe held up her champagne glass, and Lee clinked the edge of his flute against hers.

"Marlowe." Thomas Bond appeared, looking dapper in his tuxedo. Marlowe's father had laughing brown eyes, a warm smile, and dark hair that was slowly being taken over by gray. Thomas wasn't a tall or loud man, but he possessed a quiet authority. He patted Marlowe's bare shoulder affectionately.

"You look cold," he said.

"I'm freezing. But don't tell Mom. She loves to say 'I told you so.' I don't want to give her the satisfaction."

"I won't tell." Thomas smiled at her. "Where is your mother? I lost her about an hour ago."

Marlowe shrugged. "I haven't seen her. Did you check the dance floor? You know what she's like after a few glasses of champagne."

"I was hoping to avoid the dance floor tonight," Thomas said with a sigh. He glanced at Lee and smiled. "Hello. I'm Thomas, Marlowe's father."

Lee held out his hand. "Lee Davies. It's nice to meet you."

"Are you a member here?"

"I've already interrogated him, Dad. He's here with his boss." Marlowe nodded to the red-faced man with the silver hair.

"Ah! You work for David!" Thomas slapped Lee enthusiastically on the back. "He told me he just hired a new, whip-smart associate."

"Whip smart," Marlowe repeated, her eyebrows arched.

"I put it on my résumé, so he had to believe it." Lee smiled. "You know my boss?"

"I've known David for years. He's done quite a bit of work for me." Thomas looked over the crowd of partygoers and brightened. "Ah, there's your mother. I'll see you two around later."

Thomas went to rejoin Katherine, who looked beautiful—and warm, Marlowe thought enviously—in a long-sleeved garnet velvet dress. She'd had her hair styled that day in a French twist, which showed off her long pale neck.

"My parents," Marlowe said fondly, waving her champagne glass in their direction. "If you work for Dad's lawyer, does that make you his lawyer too?"

"I'm not sure. So far, they just have me reading files. It's like training wheels for lawyers. I don't know when I get to actually start meeting clients. What does your dad do?"

"You don't know who my father is?" Marlowe asked and then immediately flushed with embarrassment at how self-important that sounded. It wasn't that Thomas Bond was famous, but here, in the world she'd grown up in, everyone knew exactly who he was.

Lee shook his head apologetically. "I'm sorry. Should I?"

"No, of course not," Marlowe said, adding, "He makes boats."

"Boats?" Lee's brow wrinkled. "He's a carpenter?"

"No." Marlowe laughed at the thought of her father wielding a hammer. "My parents own Bond Marine. They manufacture fiberglass boats. You really haven't heard of them?"

"No, I haven't. But until recently, I was a poor law student. I haven't exactly been in the market to buy a new boat."

"I'm sure you've seen them out on the Intracoastal. Our line of fishing boats is really popular."

"I'll be sure to keep my eye out for one."

"What kind of law do you practice?" Marlowe asked.

"Trusts and estates."

"That sounds boring."

Lee laughed again, the corners of his eyes crinkling. "It is a little, to be honest. Are you really cold?"

"Yes, I'm freezing. But I like standing out here." *And talking to you,* she wanted to add but held back. She was very glad she'd decided to attend the party.

Lee took off his suit jacket. "May I?"

Marlowe nodded, and he draped it over her bare shoulders.

———

Marlowe and Lee went out for dinner a few nights later and then every night after that before she returned to Vanderbilt. Marlowe had never really believed in love at first sight before, but then she experienced it. Marlowe was always desperate to see Lee and felt off kilter during the long stretches when they were apart. Her friends complained that she'd lost interest in going out to parties and bars, and Marlowe knew they had a point. But she preferred to stay at home in her apartment, waiting for Lee's nightly call.

They dated for the next eighteen months, speaking on the phone every night and seeing one another whenever they could get away from work and school. He traveled to Nashville with her parents to attend her college graduation and helped her move her boxes out of her apartment near campus. A month later, Lee asked Marlowe if she wanted to go for a sunset walk on the beach. They strolled down the shore, hand in hand, their bare feet sinking into the wet sand. Suddenly, Lee stopped, stepped in front of Marlowe, and lowered himself to one knee. He looked nervous and excited, and she noticed that his hair was sticking up, as though he'd been running his hands through it.

"Will you marry me?" he asked, the words coming in a rush.

Marlowe burst into tears, nodded, and then knelt down herself. She flung herself into Lee's arms, nearly knocking them both over onto the sand.

In late July, Thomas and Katherine held an engagement party at their home on Jupiter Island. Marlowe was in the living room, standing near the grand piano she'd been forced to take lessons on as a girl. She chatted with the guests, trying to be effusive about how excited she was for the wedding and her future and hide how shy she felt at being the center of attention. She was wearing a floral strapless Lilly Pulitzer sundress, but it was so brutally hot out Marlowe was already perspiring heavily. She kept her arms clamped to her sides to hide the wet patches under her arms.

Her father approached, bringing with him the dapper, silver-haired man whom she remembered from New Year's Eve the previous year, when she and Lee had first met. "Marlowe, this is David Weinstein," Thomas said.

Marlowe smiled at Lee's boss. "Hi, it's nice to meet you."

"The bride-to-be," David said, beaming down at her. "Lee talks about you all the time."

"He talks about you too," Marlowe said. She didn't add that Lee mostly groused about how much work his boss fobbed off on him to free up his time for golf and leisurely lunches. Lee was a hard worker, but Marlowe had the sense that he had an unrealistic expectation of how much success he'd be enjoying after only two years as the most junior associate at the law firm.

"He's coming right along. He's on track at the firm, marrying a lovely young lady." David beamed at her. "Which I like to think I played a minor role in."

"Yes, Lee said he's learned a lot from you," Marlowe said.

"No, I meant in your upcoming nuptials."

Marlowe didn't have any idea what he was talking about. It was the first time she'd met Lee's boss, or at least the first time she could remember having done so. She looked around, wondering where Lee had disappeared to, and hoped he'd be back soon.

But then David continued. "Janet and I brought Lee to the party at the Jupiter Club so that he could meet you."

"So that he could meet me?" Marlowe repeated, confused. How had Lee wanted to meet her? They'd never even seen one another before that night.

"Yes. He knew your father was a client and had heard that he had a charming young daughter. He asked if I could introduce him. Thomas mentioned you'd be at the New Year's Eve party, so I thought it would be a good place to arrange a meeting. And it all worked out perfectly."

Katherine appeared, looking radiant in a turquoise caftan. She glanced at Marlowe's stricken expression and immediately stepped in to relieve her. "David, thank you for coming. You don't seem to have a drink."

"I was just about to track one down when I ran into your daughter," David replied.

"We have the bar set up out on the patio. Come with me, and we'll get you taken care of."

Katherine smoothly led the attorney away, leaving Marlowe to collect herself.

Lee had known who she was—or, more accurately, whose daughter she was—before they had first met? And he'd purposely choreographed the meeting? If that was true, it meant Lee had lied to her. He'd pretended he didn't know who her father was and—Marlowe glanced around at the spacious living room filled with expensive furniture and paintings—just how wealthy her family was.

And for the first time, Marlowe wondered if Lee had proposed because he loved her . . . or if he wanted to become part of the Bond family and all that would bring with it.

CHAPTER TWENTY-FOUR

MARLOWE

The wind screamed as it whipped around the house. Rain poured down ferociously, battering against the storm shutters. Marlowe thought uneasily about how high the river had been even before the hurricane arrived onshore and wondered if the water was right this moment inching its way up the rise of the backyard, toward the house. They'd always reassured themselves that the house had been built too high for water intrusion to be a risk. But this storm was unlike anything they'd ever experienced before.

"None of that is true," Lee sputtered. "I love my wife. And I love both my children equally."

"Sure you do," Bo said with an easy smile. "Marlowe, how did he talk you into marrying him? He must be an even better natural salesman than I am. Although, like I said, I've never been able to stand salesmen. They never stop selling."

"Don't engage, Marlowe," Lee commanded. "He's just trying to stir up trouble."

Marlowe looked back at her husband. She never had confronted him about his lie on the night they met. She hadn't had a chance at the engagement party, where they'd been constantly surrounded by well-wishers. And later, she'd decided it didn't really matter if Lee had set out to meet her. She'd even convinced herself that it was a little romantic, like an old-fashioned knight seeking the hand of a princess he'd never met.

Sometimes, it was infuriating how delusional her younger self had been.

But just because Lee had lied about knowing who Thomas Bond was before he'd approached Marlowe, it didn't mean Bo had any special insight into their marriage. All spouses kept secrets from one another to some degree. Bo certainly didn't know how much Lee loved her or their two children. They were all strangers to him.

Marlowe glanced at Tom, who had been silent ever since they moved to the living room. He was sitting on the sofa, his head bowed and arms braced against his legs, and Marlowe felt a wrench of sadness. She wanted to go to her son, to wrap her arms around him before his grief over Zack's death broke him to pieces.

"What happened to Mick?" June asked, her voice sharp.

"I told you. He drove off." Bo's voice had an edge to it. "He's probably home by now, if the storm didn't blow his car off the road."

"Mick would never drive in a hurricane," June said. "He's too smart for that."

"Are you calling me a liar?"

"I'm stating a fact."

"June, please," Marlowe said. She didn't want her daughter to anger Bo. It would only make this terrible situation even worse. But she wondered if June was right to be suspicious. They had only Bo's word for it that Mick had driven away. At the time, they hadn't had cause to doubt him.

"Don't worry, Marlowe. It's good for young people to ask questions. It's how they learn." Bo's smile didn't reach his eyes. "It's your turn, Marlowe."

Unease snaked through Marlowe. "For what?"

"To play my game. I tell you all about yourself, and then you tell me if I'm right. But you have to follow the rules. Or the one rule. You have to be truthful." Bo leaned forward. "If I guess correctly, you admit it. If you don't, you face the consequences."

"I don't want to play your game," Marlowe said.

"Now that I think about it, Lee broke the rules by lying. I should punish him, but I'll tell you what. If you play, I'll let Lee off the hook. It's your choice."

Marlowe didn't want to even think about what Bo would consider the appropriate consequences for lying or what he would do to Lee if she didn't cooperate.

"You're sick," June said.

"June!" Marlowe said again, this time more sharply.

"No, I'm honest, which is more than can be said for your father," Bo countered. He turned his gaze back to Marlowe. "What do you say, Marlowe? Are you ready to play? If not, I can let Jason take June upstairs to one of the bedrooms for a spell. Maybe that will motivate you."

"Absolutely not!" Lee said, starting to stand. Both Bo and Jason, who were still standing behind the leather chairs where Bo and Darcy were sitting, pointed their guns at him.

Marlowe grabbed Lee's arm, pulling him back down to the sofa. She could feel her pulse race as panic flooded through her. "You said you wouldn't hurt us."

"Jason wouldn't hurt her—would you, brother?" Bo glanced back at Jason, who didn't respond. Jason's gun was still aimed at Lee, but his eyes were on June. "He's gentle as a lamb."

Marlowe's pulse skittered, and her chest was so tight she could barely draw in a breath. She thought of Zack, whose body was lying on the kitchen floor. June had been right. Bo was dangerous, possibly even deadly. And once the storm was over, and before they left the house for good, it was possible, maybe even likely, that Bo and Jason would cover up their presence in the house by killing all of them. June. Tom. Lee. Isabel. Her.

The only option she had now was to keep Bo talking and stall for time while she figured out a way to save her family.

"Fine," Marlowe said. "I'll play."

CHAPTER TWENTY-FIVE

TOM

Everything seemed slightly unreal to Tom, as if the edges of the room where he sat captive with his family and Isabel were blurred and slippery. It seemed like all the events of the day were unfolding at a distance. He could barely track the conversation taking place around him.

Tom remembered watching a documentary with his father about soldiers who suffered from battle fatigue during World War II. Doctors believed their trauma was caused by an overstimulation of the flight-or-fight instinct, and as a result, the soldiers became despondent and disconnected from reality. The men in the photographs looked hollowed out, as if their souls had been stripped away. Tom wasn't a soldier, nor was he at war, but he wondered if he was experiencing something similar, if the violence of the night had fundamentally damaged him.

Zack was dead. His family was in imminent danger. His parents were terrified. June was furious. And yet he felt disengaged from all of it. The only emotion he recognized was a deep, almost overwhelming exhaustion. He wanted to go up to his room, crawl into his bed, pull the covers up over his head, and go to sleep for a very long time. And maybe when he woke up, his life would have returned to normal.

"Excellent!" Bo's voice boomed loudly, startling Tom. He looked up, wondering what he had missed.

His parents looked tense, sitting side by side on the opposite sofa. Marlowe's face was pale, her freckles standing out against the chalky white of her skin. Every muscle in Lee's body was tensed, his lips pressed together, his hands clenched into tight fists on his knees. June, who sat beside them, looked murderous. From the way she was staring down Bo, Tom suddenly felt a flicker of real concern for what she might be planning. Only Isabel, sitting on the sofa opposite from his family, seemed calm—*although no,* he realized. She was drunk. Her eyes were shiny and unfocused, her shoulders slumped forward, and she clutched an empty wineglass in her hands.

Bo was speaking again. Tom tried to force himself to concentrate, to pay attention to what he was saying.

"There are two distinct sides to Marlowe. There's the Marlowe on the surface. The wife, the mom, the nurturer. I bet you never missed one of little June's soccer games," Bo said.

"I didn't play soccer. I was on the swim team," June said.

"And I bet your mom was there in the stands by the side of the pool every time you competed. She probably brought orange slices and cheese sticks for all the little kids to snack on."

He was right about that part, Tom thought. His mom had attended every game of every sport he'd played, and yes, she had always had snacks stored in a cooler bag along with little bottles of cold water. But a lot of moms did that. Not all of them. Zack's mother had never shown up, he remembered with a stab of sorrow for his friend.

"She probably always threw you a big birthday party too. One of those parties with a theme, and you probably each had a separate birthday cake," Bo continued. "She's that kind of mother. Big on family dinners, and vacations where you go swimming with dolphins, and limiting screen time. Marlowe likes everything neat and tidy and taken care of. And everyone always says how nice she is."

"Yeah, our mom is nice. And that's bad, why, exactly?" June asked, a sharp edge to her voice.

"Because that's only one side of your mother. The one she lets the world see." Bo set down his bottle of beer on a side table and wagged a finger in Marlowe's direction. "But there's another layer to Marlowe that she likes to keep hidden. At her core, Marlowe is afraid, and that fear motivates everything she does."

"That's not a secret," Marlowe said. "You're holding us at gunpoint. Anyone would be terrified."

"I'm not talking about just now. You're always afraid, aren't you, Marlowe? And why is that? You were born into money and have never had to struggle to get by. Sure, you might have had a little part-time job when you were a teenager or had some sort of office job out of college. But you never had to worry about having enough food to eat or how you were going to pay the rent or cover a medical bill. You were born with a safety net that meant you've never had to deal with the struggles most people have."

"Everyone has problems," Marlowe said tightly. "You may not believe it, but having money doesn't insulate you from that."

Bo continued as though she hadn't spoken. "And despite this easy, pleasant existence you enjoy, you're absolutely terrified. You're afraid that Lee doesn't love you, not really, and certainly not the way you want to be loved. You're afraid of what's going to happen when your children become adults and don't need you to slice up oranges for them anymore. You're afraid that you're going to get to the end of your life and when you look back, you'll know that however nice the view from your house is, and how many nice things you own, and how nice everyone in town thinks you are, you won't have done a single thing in your life that actually mattered to anyone. That you didn't matter. And as soon as your body is cooling in its grave, everyone will pause for a moment and say 'Oh, how sad' and then immediately move on as though you never even existed."

Marlowe stared at Bo with a naked vulnerability Tom had never seen before. Is that what his mother thought? That she didn't matter? She couldn't possibly believe that, could she?

"That's a terrible thing to say," June said sharply.

"But it's the truth. Isn't it, Marlowe?"

"Everyone experiences that sort of existential concern at some point," Marlowe said. "Everyone wonders if their life has meaning."

"I don't," Isabel said, staring into her empty wineglass.

"You're still young. It's something you start thinking about when you get older," Marlowe said.

Isabel looked up, her eyes narrowed. "It has nothing to do with my age. I don't have the luxury of worrying about whether my life has meaning because I'm too busy worrying about how to pay my rent, which just went up three hundred dollars a month."

Marlowe's face creased with concern. "I'm sorry, Isabel. I didn't know that."

"How would you? He's right." She jutted her chin in Bo's direction. "You've never had to think about paying rent. You probably don't even pay a mortgage, do you? I bet you own this house outright."

"I can help you. We can discuss it after . . ." Marlowe hesitated, stumbling over the words. "After the hurricane passes."

"If I had the kind of money you have, I would live a life of no fucks given," Isabel said, waving her empty glass around drunkenly. "I'd go down to the mall, that really nice one in Boca with all of the expensive stores, and I'd buy *everything*. Then I'd book a trip to Europe and stay there for months, living in five-star hotels. I wouldn't worry about anything or anyone ever again. My life would be one long luxury vacation."

"That's not real life. It's a fairy tale," Marlowe said.

"A fairy tale that you live. Or could, if you wanted to."

"She's right, Marlowe. You could live a bigger, bolder life if you wanted to," Bo said. "But you don't. Now why is that?"

Tom wondered if he should defend his mom, whom he had always loved in a pure, uncomplicated way. She was kind and caring and wanted the best for him and June. She could be overprotective, and definitely overinquisitive, but that was just part of what made her a good mother. But even though he wanted to speak up, he couldn't think of what to say. Or maybe he was just too afraid to speak.

Marlowe pressed her lips together tightly, and her hands were curled into fists. "I've had a fortunate life. I'm well aware of that. But I've had to deal with tragedy in my life too. Money doesn't solve everything."

"Like what?" Bo asked. Tom thought Bo looked eager, leaning forward in his seat, his eyes bright with interest. "What happened to you that was so bad?"

Tom's mother didn't answer right away. Instead, she bowed her head forward, pressing her hands over her face. Tom watched her as she seemed to struggle to decide something. Then she finally straightened, her hands dropping down, and she spoke.

"Lee and I had another baby before Tom and June were born. A baby girl. Her name was Liza, short for Elizabeth."

Tom stared at his mother, stunned. He had another sister? Neither of his parents had ever mentioned having had another child.

Lee interrupted her. "Marlowe, you don't have to—"

She held up a hand to silence him. "Yes, apparently I do. When Liza was six weeks old, she died one night while she was sleeping in her crib. She had a heart defect we didn't know about. There was no warning. One day she was there, and the next—" Marlowe drew in a deep breath and let out a soft sob. "She was dead. Just like that. And I would have spent every last penny I had, every last penny Lee or I could ever earn, to get her back.

"But it doesn't work that way. Money doesn't protect you from losing the people you love. I may not know what it's like to worry about paying the rent, but I do know what it's like to experience pain so intense I couldn't eat, or sleep, or shower. Some days, I couldn't even get out of bed. So yes, Bo, to answer your question, I have spent every day since then terrified. But not of being unimportant or that my life lacks meaning. What I'm afraid of is feeling grief like that again."

When Marlowe stopped speaking, the room was silent for a moment. Lee reached over and took Marlowe's hand in his. Bo nodded slowly.

"Okay, Marlowe. I believe you. You told the truth. Fair play." Bo paused, tipping his head to one side as he regarded Tom's mother. "Now, why don't you tell me where the sketch is?"

Tom wondered if he'd missed something. It kept happening. People talked around him, and he had a hard time following what they were saying. But he hadn't remembered anyone mentioning a sketch. He glanced at the wall, where the Cézanne had been hanging ever since his grandparents' death and realized that it wasn't in its usual place. Where had it gone?

"What are you talking about?" Marlowe asked.

"The Cézanne. Where did you put it?"

Tom tried to remember back to what everyone had been chatting about before Zack's death. His mother had been talking about the architect who'd designed their house, and their father had been joking around with Bo about drunk people in bars. Had anyone mentioned the Cézanne or the Bond Collection? He couldn't be sure, but he didn't think so. So how had Bo known there was a Cézanne in the house?

And then suddenly, Tom's thoughts came into focus, the fuzziness starting to fall away. He realized why his mother's eyes had widened with fear. If Bo knew about the Cézanne, he, Jason, and Darcy hadn't tied up on the dock by accident. They had come here with a purpose. For a reason.

"Where's the sketch, Marlowe?" Bo asked again.

"It's not here. It's at the Norton. I had it moved there ahead of the storm."

Bo let out a mock sigh and hung his head. "Marlowe, we were doing so well. And then you had to go ruin it by lying to me."

"I'm not lying!"

Bo looked up at his brother. "Jason, maybe you should take June upstairs. And after you've had some time alone with her, Marlowe will suddenly remember where she put the sketch."

"No!" Marlowe and Lee shouted the word at the same time. Lee stood abruptly and took a step forward before both Bo and Jason again leveled their guns at him. Tom wondered wildly what he should do. Bo was sitting close enough that Tom could spring forward and tackle him. If he acted quickly, taking Bo by surprise, he might be able to knock the gun out of his hand. It was a risk, but it might be his only chance.

Do it, he told himself. *Now. Do it.*

But Tom didn't do it. His body wouldn't move, as though it was disconnected from his brain. It was like his fear had frozen him in place.

"The sketch is in the safe in Lee's office," Isabel said, setting her glass down on a side table so hard Tom was surprised the delicate stemware didn't break. "It's hidden behind an insipid painting of a sailboat. I'll show you where it is."

Bo smiled, his expression turning almost angelic. "Thank you, Isabel. I appreciate your cooperation."

Isabel nodded uncertainly, her eyes flickering in June's direction. "Please just don't hurt anyone."

Bo began to shake his head slowly, almost regretfully. "I wish that were the case, Isabel. I really do. Unfortunately, Marlowe broke the rules. Well, the only rule. She lied to me."

Bo raised his gun and pointed it. When he pulled the trigger, a deafening explosion ripped through the room.

CHAPTER TWENTY-SIX

FELIX

Felix was crouched at the top of the staircase, trying to hear what was being said downstairs over the sounds of the storm raging outside. He'd been able to only partially follow the conversation taking place down there. But Felix had figured out enough. He knew that the strangers who'd come to the house that day were holding everyone downstairs hostage. And he knew they were armed. Felix tightened his grip on the handgun he'd retrieved from Lee's bedside table. He remembered June showing it to him, all those years ago, and was glad that Mr. Davies hadn't moved it. But the weapon frightened him. He'd never held a gun before, much less shot one. It felt heavy and wrong in his hand, like he was a little kid playing cops and robbers.

Felix was just wondering if he should try to sneak downstairs and find a place closer to the group in the living room—maybe he could make it to Marlowe's office and hide there?—when the gunshot exploded, followed by terrified screaming. Felix flinched so violently he nearly fell over. He grabbed the wooden balustrade to steady himself.

"No," he breathed. His heart was racing, and his senses were on high alert. What had happened? Had someone been shot? Was it June? There was the muffled rush of footsteps across the carpeted floor. He heard someone cry out in anguish, and he thought—although couldn't be sure—that it was Marlowe.

I have to go down there. I have to make sure June's okay, Felix thought. He stared wildly around, trying to figure out what he should do. He couldn't just run down into the living room and confront them directly. He might have a gun, but there were more of them, and they were armed too. And unlike him, they probably knew how to shoot.

I need to get help, Felix thought.

Felix's phone wasn't working, and anyway, the sheriff's deputies had told Tom and Zack that they wouldn't be responding to 911 calls during the storm. But what if he could somehow find a way to tell the police what was happening here in the Davieses' house? Wouldn't they have to come if they found out that armed men were holding the family hostage? That they were shooting them?

Think, he told himself. And gradually, the panic clouding his thoughts started to clear.

Celeste had been raging for hours now. The eye of the storm was going to arrive soon, and when it did, the torrential rain and dangerous winds would stop for a period of time. Felix tried to remember how long the eye of a hurricane lasted for. Twenty minutes? Thirty? The police station was only a few miles away, and most of that was a straight stretch of road that cut through the middle of town. Felix was a fast runner, and he'd probably have enough time to make it there on foot. There was the possible danger that the road between the Davieses' house and the police station could be flooded or blocked by downed trees, but he was going to have to take the risk. It had to be a better option than trying to confront the armed men downstairs on his own.

But first, Felix had to figure out how he was going to get outside without being seen. The stairs to the upper story of the house were visible from the living room. There was no chance he could make it downstairs and out the front door without being seen.

If I can't go out a door, I'll have to go out a window, he thought.

Felix stood and padded back down the hallway to June's room and closed the door behind him. There were hurricane shutters up over the windows, blocking the view to the outside. But if he could figure out how to remove the shutter from the inside and climb out the window, there was only a short drop to the roof that covered the sunroom overlooking the pool and the river beyond. From there, it would still be a one-story drop to the patio, but he might be able to position himself to land on the grass or one of the decorative bushes that skirted the outside of the house. It wouldn't be so bad, he reasoned. What was the worst that could happen? That he'd sprain an ankle? That would make his run to the police station unpleasant but not impossible.

Felix skirted around June's bed and went to the window, moving the stuffed elephant out of the way. He unlocked the window and wished he could open it so he could figure out if it was possible to remove the shutters from inside the house—but he knew it was too risky. The wind was still howling, the house shuddering under the pressure. If the wind blew inside now, it would alert the men downstairs to his presence.

All he could do was wait for Celeste's eye to arrive and be ready to act when it did.

CHAPTER TWENTY-SEVEN

MARLOWE

It all happened at once. The jolting, deafening sound of a gunshot. Tom's ragged cry. Isabel and June both screaming. The flinty scent lingering in the air. Lee crumpling to the ground, a crimson stain spreading on his leg. Marlowe falling to her knees beside her husband, her hands gripping his shoulders. Prickles of black clouded her eyes, and she blinked, trying to see him more clearly.

"Lee," Marlowe attempted to say, although the word caught in her throat.

Lee looked up at her, her horror reflected in his eyes. "He shot me."

Marlowe looked at him, trying to assess the extent of his injury. Lee was still alive, but there was so much blood, and she had no idea what to do to help him. *Pressure,* she thought, remembering a first aid class she'd taken in high school. "A towel. I need a towel."

Darcy appeared beside her, holding out the striped beach towel Marlowe had given her hours earlier to dry off with. Marlowe pressed it down against Lee's leg. "I think I should tie something around his leg. Does anyone have anything I can use?"

"Take this," Isabel said, pulling off her woven leather belt. She handed it to Marlowe.

Lee moaned as Marlowe shifted his leg to slide the belt underneath him.

"I'm sorry, I'm sorry," she said. "I'm not trying to hurt you."

"Let me help," Isabel said, kneeling down on Lee's other side and pressing the towel against his leg while Marlowe pulled the belt tight and fastened the buckle with trembling fingers. Isabel's long nails were polished a dark black, and red blood seeped around her fingers. Marlowe looked down at her own hands and saw that they, too, were covered with blood.

"Mom?" June's voice was a whisper. "Is he okay?"

"He'll live," Bo said dismissively. "I only shot him in the leg. If I wanted to kill him, I would have aimed higher."

Marlowe turned to stare at Bo, who hadn't moved from his seat on the leather chair, the gun held loosely in his hand.

He looked back at her, his expression blank. "I told you not to lie."

The rage that flooded through Marlowe took her by surprise. The intensity of it reminded her of other pivotal moments when she'd experienced powerful emotion. The births of her children. Finding Liza's body in her crib. Seeing Lee as she walked down the aisle toward him on their wedding day. Being notified of her parents' unexpected deaths by a somber sheriff's deputy who'd knocked on their front door. But the hatred she felt in that moment seemed to dwarf all those.

"This isn't a game," she hissed.

"Everything's a game, Marlowe. That's why it's important to always know the rules before you play."

"Fuck off, Bo," Isabel said, practically spitting the words out as she worked to stanch Lee's blood.

"Language," Bo chided her. "That's no way to speak to a guest."

"Mom!" June's voice was insistent. "How's Dad doing?"

"I'm fine," Lee breathed. "Perfectly fine."

"We need to get him to the hospital," Marlowe said. "The eye will arrive soon. I should take him then."

Bo made a dismissive sound, somewhere between a scoff and a laugh. "That's not going to happen, Marlowe."

"Then let June and Tom take him. I'll stay here," Marlowe suggested.

"Five minutes later, the police would be at the front door. I told you we'll leave after the storm. But no one's going anywhere until it passes. And besides, I need your help."

"My help?" Marlowe had no idea what he was talking about. All she could focus on was getting Lee the medical care he needed. "What do you mean?"

"Isabel said the sketch is in a safe. I doubt she knows the combination. I need you to open it."

The safe. Marlowe processed this slowly, as if her brain wasn't working at full speed. He was here to rob them. To take the Cézanne. But none of that mattered right now, not while Lee was moaning in pain. She looked down at her husband's blood-soaked shorts. "Let me get some disinfectant and bandages first."

Bo considered this request. "Where are they?"

"Upstairs in the master bath. In the cupboard under the right-hand sink," Marlowe said, standing on shaky legs. "I'll go get them."

"Not a chance," Bo said. "You're staying here."

"What do you think I'm going to do?" Marlowe turned. "You have my phone. And it's not like I can run away." She gestured vaguely toward the front door and the storm raging beyond. "This isn't a trick. I just need to get medical supplies to help my husband."

"I can get them, Mom." Tom stood up. He looked pale, but when his eyes met hers, his gaze was steady. "I'll go. You stay with Dad."

Marlowe looked at Bo, who shrugged and nodded his assent. "Fine. But come right back down."

Marlowe wondered why Bo hadn't wanted her to go upstairs but didn't mind Tom fetching the medical supplies. Tom was the only uninjured male left in the group of hostages, and he was by far the strongest, lean and muscled from his hours spent surfing. Maybe Bo saw how broken her son was following the death of his best friend. Or maybe he just liked to control everything and everyone. Maybe it was just another game to him. One in which he decided who came and went, who lived and died.

"What should I get?" Tom asked.

"Bandages, gauze, the bottle of bacitracin," Marlowe said. "And anything else you see there that you think might help."

Tom nodded and turned to head upstairs.

"Hurry back down, Tom," Bo said. "If you dawdle, I'll shoot your mother next."

CHAPTER TWENTY-EIGHT

TOM

Tom ran up the stairs, his arms pumping, his breath shallow with panic.

Bandages, gauze, bacitracin, he reminded himself. He wasn't even sure what bacitracin was. Was it the goopy stuff his mom used to smear on his skinned knees or elbows before she stuck on a Band-Aid? He hoped it was labeled.

It was only when he'd reached the top of the stairs and rounded into the upstairs hallway that he suddenly remembered Felix and came to an abrupt stop. Was he still in June's room? Did he know what had happened downstairs?

Tom reached the doorway of his parents' bedroom and glanced inside. Bo's warning was still ringing in his ears. *If you dawdle, I'll shoot your mother next.* But this might be the only chance any of them had to talk to Felix, the one person in the house Bo didn't know about. And Tom couldn't help but think of Zack and the choice his friend would make if he were in this situation. Zack would be brave, even if it was reckless.

Tom hurried past the master bedroom and down to the end of the hallway. He turned the knob and slowly opened the door. Felix was standing by the window, facing the door, his eyes wide with fright. It took Tom a few beats to realize he was holding a gun.

It was pointed straight at Tom.

"Whoa!" Tom said, holding his hands up. "Dude! It's me!"

"Oh, man! Sorry." Felix dropped the hand holding the gun to his side. "I thought you were one of the bad guys!"

Tom pressed a hand to his chest. It was the third time that evening someone had pointed a gun at him, and he wasn't enjoying the experience.

"I almost shot you!"

"Trust me—I noticed." Tom closed the door behind him. "Where'd you get a gun?"

"It's your dad's. June once showed me where he keeps it in his nightstand. I thought we might need it."

"So you know what's going on down there?"

"Sort of. I've been trying to listen, but I can't hear much over the storm. Did they shoot someone? Is June okay?"

"She's fine, but they shot my dad."

"Seriously?"

Tom nodded. "He's alive, but he's hurt. I don't know how bad. My mom sent me up here to get first aid supplies. But they . . ." Tom stopped and swallowed. "They killed Zack. One of the brothers pushed him, and Zack hit his head against the kitchen counter, and he . . . died."

"Oh no," Felix said. He sat down heavily on June's bed, looking dazed. "This is bad. This is very, very bad."

"I think it's going to get worse. Remember how when they docked here, they were claiming that they were just looking for a safe place to tie up?"

Felix nodded. "Yeah. I thought that seemed weird."

"It was all bullshit. They know about the art collection my mom's working on. You know, that our grandparents planned on donating to the museum. They came here to steal one of the paintings, or a sketch, or whatever. This was all planned out in advance."

"Whoa," Felix said. He looked as stunned as Tom felt.

"And that's not even the worst part. No one knows they're here, so chances are they may not be planning on leaving behind witnesses.

June thinks they're planning on killing all of us. I overheard her telling our mom that."

"They don't know I'm here," Felix said.

"Not yet, anyway. Your phone isn't working, is it? They took ours."

"It works; I just haven't been able to get any cell service, and the Wi-Fi has been down since the storm blew in. How long do you think it will take for the cell towers to start working after it passes?"

Tom shrugged. "No way to tell. If the cell towers are damaged, it could be days before they fix them."

"Then I'm going to have to leave and go find help."

"How?" Tom gestured to the window. "You can't go out in that."

"The eye should be arriving soon. It'll be safe to go outside then, at least for a little while."

Tom nodded. It might be their only chance. "How are you going to get outside?"

"Out the window." Felix tipped his head toward the window behind June's bed. "There's a lower roof there, so if I can climb out on there, the drop to the ground shouldn't be too bad. And I think I can make it to the police station on foot before the storm starts again. The only problem is I'm not sure how to get the shutter off the window."

"That's easy. They're slotted on. All you have to do is lift the shutter up off the tabs, and you should be able to push it off. Do you think you can make it there in time? The police station has to be, what, two miles away? Three?"

"I'll run as fast as I can," Felix said. He looked nervous, Tom thought, but resolute. And Felix was a good athlete. Tom had watched him play basketball, and he charged up and down the court so quickly he could usually outrun his guard.

"Do you think the police will come? When they were here earlier, ahead of the storm, they specifically said they won't be responding to 911 calls until the hurricane is over."

"I think finding out your family is being held at gunpoint will motivate them," Felix said grimly.

"Let's hope so." Tom glanced over his shoulder, but the door was still firmly shut. No one had come looking for him. Yet.

"I'd better go. That douchebag threatened to shoot my mom if I didn't hurry back with the first aid supplies. Good luck getting there."

"These guys are bad news." Felix shook his head again. "Just do me a favor. Please keep June safe. Okay?"

Tom nodded but felt a surge of hopelessness. How was he supposed to keep his sister safe if he kept letting his fear immobilize him?

"And take this." Felix held out the gun. "It's loaded. I checked."

Tom stared at it. "What am I supposed to do with that?"

"If you really think they're planning on killing you and your family . . . dude. You may need to shoot them first."

The two teenagers stared at one another for a long moment. Finally, Tom nodded and took the gun. He'd shot it only once when he had gone to the gun range with his dad. He hadn't really enjoyed it—it had been disconcertingly loud, even with ear protection—so he hadn't gone back. But now he wished he had, especially as he gingerly tucked it into the waistband of his shorts. He hoped he didn't shoot himself by accident.

"Can you see the gun?"

Felix looked him over and then pulled off his own oversize hoodie sweatshirt and handed it to Tom. "Put this on. It will cover it up."

Tom slipped on the sweatshirt. It had been baggy on Felix, who was taller and broader than he was, and the material swamped him, falling loosely down to his thighs. Felix nodded approvingly.

"Good luck, man," Felix said, holding out his fist and bumping it against Tom's.

"You too. And, Felix?"

"Yeah?"

"When you get to the police station, please make them understand that these people are really dangerous. I don't know how much time we have."

Felix nodded solemnly and exhaled a shaky breath. "I just hope they believe me."

Tom had been about to open the door so he could slip back out into the hallway. He looked back at Felix. "What do you mean?"

"You know I don't have the greatest history with the police. What if they think I'm making it up? Like, as a prank or something."

This thought hadn't occurred to Tom, probably because it was ridiculous that anyone would think of Felix as a troublemaker. The kid was an honor student and a star athlete. But if they didn't believe Felix . . . Tom could feel panic rising up, threatening to swamp him. He ran a hand over his face, trying to tamp his fear back down.

"You'll have to make them listen," he said. "Make them believe you."

Felix nodded, his expression somber. "I'll do my best."

CHAPTER TWENTY-NINE

JUNE

June knew she should be afraid. These strangers had come into their home under false pretenses. They'd specifically targeted June's family in order to steal the Cézanne sketch. One man had killed Zack; the other had shot her father. And while she recognized the threat the strangers posed and how much danger she and her family were in, June had never been angrier. She could feel the rage building inside her, pulsing and white hot. She had never had a single physical altercation in her life, had never been hit or hit anyone else, but in that moment, June knew she was capable of violence. If she had the ability to do so, she could—and would—kill Bo and Jason without hesitation.

The problem was that they were armed and possibly both insane. Jason was clearly suffering from some sort of mental impairment. Bo seemed more lucid, but he'd shot her father because Marlowe hadn't followed the stupid rules to his stupid game, so he was obviously a psycho.

June watched while her mother dabbed at her father's wound with a cotton ball soaked in bacitracin and then carefully taped a square nonstick bandage over the laceration. That couldn't possibly be an effective remedy for a gunshot wound, June thought. Her father needed real medical care. They had to get him to a hospital.

Marlowe and Isabel had together helped move Lee to the sofa, where he lay reclined, his head cushioned by several throw pillows.

He looked pale, and his khaki shorts were soaked with blood. Bo had denied Marlowe's request for a pair of kitchen shears to cut Lee's shorts off. He was probably worried she'd stab him with them, June thought with another surge of fury. She wasn't sure her mother was capable of that, but June was. She'd love the chance to plunge a sharp blade right into his chest and watch the life bleed slowly out of him.

"Mom, how is he?" June asked.

Marlowe looked up, her expression strained. She didn't say anything, but June knew the situation was dire. Even Isabel, usually so cool and composed, looked distraught as she hovered nearby, ready to assist if needed.

Lee waved weakly in June's direction. "I'm fine," he said. "It's just a flesh wound."

After Tom had returned downstairs and given their mother the medical supplies she'd requested, he'd sat down next to June on the sofa opposite from the one their father was stretched out on. She could now sense the weight of her brother's gaze on her. June looked at him, her eyebrows arched in an unspoken question. And then she noticed that her brother looked different than he had when he'd gone upstairs. He was now wearing Felix's sweatshirt.

June felt a surge of hope. She hadn't even been sure that Felix knew what was going on, although she supposed he must have heard the gunshot. The bullet exploding out of the gun had been so loud her ears were still ringing. But Tom and Felix must have spoken, and for some reason, Felix had given Tom his sweatshirt to wear.

Tom glanced at Bo, who was standing in the corner of the living room, having what looked to be an intense discussion with Jason, although they were speaking too quietly for Tom to be able to overhear what they were saying. Darcy had returned to one of the leather chairs, but she was studying her nails intently. Tom turned back to June, his eyes wide, and his eyebrows raised. June could tell he was searching for a way to communicate something to her.

"The eye of the hurricane should be here soon," Tom said conversationally. "Things will calm down for a while. The wind and rain will stop."

"How long does that usually last for?" June asked.

"I'm not sure. Thirty minutes, maybe?" His eyebrows raised again meaningfully.

June had no idea what her brother was trying to tell her. Did he think the eye would distract Bo from whatever he had planned? That seemed doubtful.

Felix is going to go get help, Tom mouthed.

June felt a jolt of excitement, although she had so many questions. Where was he going to go? And how would he get outside without being seen? He couldn't go out the front door—it was right next to the living room. The back door was covered by the sliding hurricane shutter. There was a door out of the garage, but if he tried to raise one of the garage doors, they would all hear it. Maybe he was planning to go through the french doors in her mother's office, which opened out to the side of the house and a walkway beyond. But to do that, he'd still have to get down the stairs and through the hallway without being seen.

June had to know what he was planning. Because she'd already decided—if Felix was going to run, she was going with him.

There were some obvious problems with this plan. The most immediate was that she would also need to figure out a way to escape. Maybe Tom could create a distraction, allowing her to slip away. Although even if she did manage to get away, she would instantly be missed. As soon as Bo realized she wasn't there, he'd chase after her. And even if she managed to solve both those problems, June wasn't as fast or athletic as Felix. She might slow him down.

But still, she had to try. Sitting there, doing nothing, was intolerable. And she might be able to help. She wasn't sure where Felix was planning to go for help, but she knew the neighborhood better than he did. She knew which of their neighbors might offer aid and which ones wouldn't answer their door if someone knocked in the middle of a storm. And their neighbors had known her since she was a little girl. They'd almost certainly be more willing to help her than they would a tall muscular black teenage male they didn't recognize. June hated that this was true, but she knew it was.

"What are you two talking about?"

June looked up to see Bo striding toward them, closing the distance with an alarming speed.

"No whispering, no secret twin talk," Bo warned.

"We weren't!" June protested, holding up her hands defensively. "We're just talking about what the eye of the storm is going to be like!"

Bo reached down and grabbed June's wrist in his hand with a painful wrench. June let out an involuntary cry of pain as Bo pulled her to her feet.

"Stop!" Marlowe said, rising quickly.

Bo leaned so close to June she could feel his warm breath on her face. His green eyes bore into hers.

"Do you think I'm stupid?" His voice was soft but sharply edged.

"No," June said. She hated the note of panic in her voice.

"Let her go!" Marlowe exclaimed.

Bo ignored June's mother. He continued to stare at June, his fingers still holding her wrist in a viselike grip. Finally, he seemed satisfied with whatever he saw in her expression and released her.

He knows that he scared me, June thought, her anger surging back. She hated that she'd given him that satisfaction.

June stepped back, away from Bo, and sank down onto the sofa. Her legs were trembling, and she could feel the aftershock of adrenaline coursing through her body. Without speaking, Tom reached over and took her hand in his. This act of kindness nearly caused tears to flood June's eyes. She loved her brother, but they were never physically affectionate with one another. But right now, she gripped his hand back, grateful for this small comfort.

But then she felt Tom's hand pull on hers. She glanced at him, but he was watching Bo, who had turned away, back toward Jason. Tom pulled her hand more forcefully, bringing her fingers to brush against the oversize sweatshirt.

And then June felt it. The hard metal object hidden under the borrowed hoodie. She looked at him, startled. Tom's chin dipped in a curt nod. June inhaled sharply; the reality of what he was trying to show her suddenly hit her.

Tom had a gun.

And that, June thought, with a grim satisfaction, *could change everything.*

"Marlowe, it's time," Bo said. "Let's go open the safe."

Marlowe lifted a hand to her throat and glanced down at Lee. June knew her mother didn't want to leave his side, that she feared what would happen if she left him.

"If you'd prefer, I could start shooting your children until you open it," Bo said. "The choice is yours."

He spoke so casually, as if he were asking if anyone would like another round of drinks. June couldn't tell what was more terrifying—his relaxed tone or the fact that she knew without a doubt that he meant every word of his threat.

PART THREE

21:42 update. Southeastern Florida remains under an emergency warning. The eye of Hurricane Celeste is currently making landfall. As the eye moves over the state, wind speed and rain will temporarily abate. However, the storm has already caused catastrophic flooding across southeastern Florida and downed power lines. Once the eye passes over Florida, there is the chance of another life-threatening storm surge along the coastal regions. Everyone in affected areas should continue to shelter in place.

CHAPTER THIRTY

Felix

The wind, rain, and thunder stopped abruptly, almost as if a switch on the hurricane had been flipped off. One moment, Celeste was raging; the next she had gone completely still. Felix wondered what hurricanes had been like for people who lived before there was modern storm tracking and computerized models. First, they'd have been suddenly hit with a monster storm that brought wind speeds that could tear down homes and waters that flooded whole towns. The eye would arrive, and it would finally seem calm and safe to go outside again, only to have the storm suddenly reappear, violent and deadly. It must have been terrifying. Even now, knowing what was happening and having seen what a hurricane looked like on weather maps with its bands circling around the calm inner eye, it was still disconcerting how rapidly the conditions changed.

When everything outside suddenly went quiet, Felix was sitting on June's bed, his head bowed, his elbows resting on his knees, and his hands laced together while he waited. He looked up and listened to the silence.

It's go time, he thought.

Felix stood and moved to the window. He knew he had to act quickly and quietly. Now that the sounds of the storm weren't there to muffle his movements, there was a greater risk that someone downstairs would hear him. Felix unlocked and lifted the window sash and then examined the hurricane shutter. It was silver corrugated metal and fit snugly against the window frame. The shutter was designed to be hung and removed from the outside of the house, but from what Tom had told him, he'd still be able to lift it off the hooks from inside.

But after running his hands over the shutter, it wasn't clear how he was supposed to move it. There wasn't anywhere to grip on to; the surface was smooth. Felix pushed at it—first gingerly, then with more force—but it didn't budge. He crouched down to study it, wondering if there was any way he could put some sort of a lever under the shutter to jimmy it up, but there wasn't enough space. The shutter had been securely installed.

There was a second window on the adjacent wall, behind June's armchair and matching ottoman. Felix picked up the ottoman and set it carefully to one side and then lifted the chair, taking care not to let the wooden legs scrape against the floor. He slid the second window open and examined the storm shutter covering it. It was identical to the first, but it wasn't wedged into place quite as tightly. By pressing his fingertips against the inside of the shutter, he was able to slowly lift the shutter up.

Okay, he thought. *Here goes nothing.*

Felix continued to guide the shutter up until he felt it lift off the L-shaped hooks it was mounted on. He was just about to reach for the bottom edge of the sheet metal so he could pull it safely into June's room when he suddenly lost his grip, and the shutter fell away from the window. It was airborne for just a moment, rising on a light flutter of wind like a metal kite. Then it suddenly fell, disappearing in the darkness until it landed on the patio below with a thunderous clatter.

Felix flinched. The people downstairs had to have heard the noise. Would they go outside to see what had fallen? Or worse, once they saw a shutter had come off, would they realize that someone else was in the house and head upstairs to look for him?

I need to get out of here now, Felix thought, panic flooding through him.

But there was another problem. The shutter he'd managed to take off had been mounted on a window that didn't look out over the roof of the sunroom, as June's other window did. Instead, it was a direct two-story fall in the darkness to the patio below.

"Oh no," Felix breathed, staring down at the impossibly far drop.

Felix hurried back to the other window and tried to lift the storm shutter again, but it was still stuck stubbornly in place.

"Come on," he urged it.

Felix stopped and stood still, his hands on his hips. *What now?* He needed to get out of the house quickly. He had no idea how long the eye would last or how difficult it would be to get to the police station. Every minute counted.

Felix returned to the open window and looked out into the darkness. Most of the exterior lights were out—they must not have been hooked up to the generator—but there were some landscaping lights that ran on solar power that hadn't been blown away in the storm and offered a dull glow. Felix could just make out the ground and the notable lack of shrubbery beneath the window. If he went out this way, he'd fall onto the concrete patio floor.

Not ideal, he thought grimly.

But what other choice did he have? He could try to find a better exit point in one of the other upstairs rooms, one that opened onto the roof of the sunroom or at least had shrubbery below that could break his fall. But for as much time as he'd spent at the Davieses' house over the years, he couldn't remember the architectural layout of the house or the landscaping in the backyard. It wasn't like he'd put any thought into which would be the best spot to jump out of a second-story window and survive the fall. And in the meantime, he could waste precious time going from room to room and taking off storm shutters without any guarantee that he'd find a better escape route. And every minute that ticked by was more time for the intruders downstairs to discover his presence in the house and stop him from leaving.

Felix drew in a deep breath and looked out the window again. An image of June appeared in his mind's eye. She was smiling sardonically, one side of her mouth curved up, her blue eyes dancing with mischief. If he did nothing, risked nothing, June would probably die that night.

I have to try, he thought.

His decision made, Felix took another deep breath and, stooping down to avoid hitting his head, swung one leg out the window. Gripping the windowsill, he swung his other leg out and then lowered his body down until he was hanging out the window. His feet scrabbled around, trying to find purchase against the exterior stucco wall of the house. The air was warm and sticky with humidity, and the brackish smell of the river filled his nostrils. Felix hesitated, his shoulders aching from the effort of holding himself up.

And then he let go.

CHAPTER THIRTY-ONE

MARLOWE

Marlowe stood in front of the safe in Lee's office, the oil painting of the sailboat swung open on its hinges. She and Bo had come to the office alone. On Bo's instructions, Jason and Darcy had stayed behind in the living room to watch over the others.

She was keenly aware of Bo standing behind her, could even hear his calm, steady breath now that the storm had abruptly stopped raging outside. Marlowe was just beginning to twist the dial of the lock to enter the combination when there was a loud metallic clang from somewhere outside that caused her to start, her fingers jerking from the lock.

"What was that?" Bo suddenly demanded. "It sounded like something fell out there. Close to the house."

"I don't know. Maybe the storm knocked something loose. A branch or something."

"That didn't sound like a branch to me."

"It could be another patio umbrella flying around. Or a roof tile, or someone's satellite dish. It could be anything, really, the way the wind was blowing earlier."

Bo nodded toward the safe. "Hurry up. I want to see what's going on out there."

Marlowe turned back to the safe. Her fingers trembled as she spun the dial to reset it, then moved it to the right, then to the left, and then to the right again. She pulled open the door, revealing the contents of the safe. They kept some paperwork there, along with a small amount of cash, Marlowe's jewelry, and Lee's Batman watch, which she'd given him for his forty-fifth birthday. And, of course, the Cézanne sketch. The reason why the strangers were in their home. She took a step back, assuming that Bo would want to rifle through what was inside.

"Is that the sketch?" Bo asked, nodding at the framed sketch still wrapped in brown paper. "Get it out. Let's take a look."

Marlowe lifted the sketch out of the safe and set it down on Lee's desk blotter. She carefully took off the wrapping and then turned the sketch face up so Bo could see it.

Bo stepped forward to study the pencil drawing. "That's it? It's a couple pieces of fruit sitting on a table."

"It's a still life. Cézanne drew hundreds of them. He believed that sketches like this one helped him to see the world more clearly. It was like a practice session for when he painted."

"What's so special about it? It looks like something a kid would draw."

Irritation prickled at Marlowe. "It's valuable because the man who drew it is considered one of the greatest impressionists of that era. But aside from that pedigree, this drawing is special because of the clarity of the perception and the balance of the objects. There's an elegance to its simplicity."

And despite the danger she was in, the danger her whole family was in, Marlowe couldn't help but admire the beautiful sketch that had brought her so much happiness over the years. Was this the last time she'd ever see it? Marlowe had lost enough people she loved that she knew what true grief was, what it felt like. The sketch was a thing, not a being with a soul. But she would miss it. It was a link to her past and future, to her parents, and to their legacy.

Bo shook his head. "No offense, Marlowe, but that sounds like a load of bullshit."

"If you don't want it, I'm happy to put it back in the safe."

"Not a chance." Bo waved the hand still holding his gun at the drawing. "Wrap it back up."

Marlowe pulled the brown paper up around the sketch, then secured it with pieces of tape. "Why are you taking it if you don't even like it?"

"I didn't say I was planning on hanging it on my wall."

"You're stealing it for someone else?"

Marlowe had heard of thieves stealing artwork on commission. It was one of the theories behind the unsolved Isabella Stewart Gardner Museum heist in 1990. The stolen artwork, which had included works by Rembrandt and Degas, was worth hundreds of millions of dollars. The paintings and sketches were never recovered, and there was speculation that a shady collector had hired the thieves to acquire them. Other thieves stole artwork believing they could sell it on the black market, not realizing just how difficult a task that would be. It was nearly impossible to authenticate a stolen piece of art, and even if you managed to accomplish that, it wasn't like you could auction off a stolen Rothko or Jackson Pollock on eBay.

"Don't worry about it," Bo said. "It's not your concern."

Marlowe stared at him. "It's my sketch. My parents have owned it since I was little. Of course I care what happens to it."

"You opened that safe to keep your family safe. Consider it a win-win outcome," Bo said, like he was parroting one of those self-help books that businessmen read.

Wait, Marlowe thought. Something had been sliding at the edges of her consciousness, slipping out of reach before she could think it through. It was probably shock, she knew. Zack's death. Being held at gunpoint. Bo shooting Lee. The fear and panic and grief had overwhelmed her, like a wave swelling up over a small boat at sea. But suddenly she realized what it was that had been bothering her.

She knew that Bo had shown up at their house that day to steal the Cézanne. It wasn't a crime of opportunity. It had been planned.

But *how* had Bo known the Cézanne was here? And perhaps just as importantly, *who* had told him?

It wasn't a secret that her parents had owned the sketch. They'd bought the piece at an established auction house in Paris in the eighties, and that business had almost certainly kept a record of the transaction. The sketch had then hung in the Bonds' living room for decades, where Marlowe's mother, Katherine, had proudly shown it off to various guests over the years. When Katherine and Thomas had died earlier that year, the sketch had been part of the estate left to Marlowe, although she was unclear who exactly would have access to the specifics of her inheritance. Anyone who knew the sketch existed would probably have assumed that its ownership had passed to Marlowe.

But how would Bo have found out about it? And how would he have known that she kept it at the house? Someone had to have told him. Marlowe tried to figure out who, outside the family, would have had this information. It was a relatively small number of people. Beatrize, her liaison from the Norton. A few family friends who had seen the sketch hanging on her wall. And then there was Isabel, her new assistant. Could Isabel be the one who had set this all into motion?

Marlowe's mind whirred, trying to see how this piece of information fit into the puzzle. But no, Isabel had seemed genuinely shocked when she'd found out earlier that day that the Cézanne hadn't been transferred to the Norton ahead of the storm. Marlowe supposed it was possible her assistant had been acting, but she didn't think so. And Isabel had been so angry at Bo and truly concerned about Lee's gunshot wound.

There was another thud outside, this time louder, as if something heavy had fallen to the ground outside. Marlowe and Bo reflexively looked toward the shuttered windows.

"That definitely wasn't a branch. Come on—let's go. I want to find out what's going on out there. Bring the sketch." Bo waited while Marlowe picked up the wrapped Cézanne sketch. He stepped aside so that she could walk in front of him.

Lee's office was located just past the kitchen. Marlowe felt a fresh wave of horror as they passed Zack's body, still splayed on the kitchen floor. Someone had covered him with a gray throw blanket.

Zack, she thought as grief at his loss washed over her again. And as her shock continued to recede, it was replaced with a sharp stab of fury. He'd been only a boy, a sweet, funny boy with his whole life ahead of him. And then they'd allowed these strangers into their home, and now Zack was dead.

Someone will pay for this. Marlowe turned back to look at Bo behind her. Their gazes met, and whatever he saw in her face caused his eyes to shift uneasily.

"Keep going," he said curtly.

Just as they were reaching the arched doorway that opened onto the front hall, there was a loud shout from the living room, followed by yet another sound of something falling heavily onto the floor. Only this time, it was from inside the house.

And then Isabel and Darcy both began to scream.

CHAPTER THIRTY-TWO

TOM

Lee lay crumpled on the ground next to the sofa where he had been resting. Isabel knelt beside him, tentatively touching his arm.

"Lee?" she said.

Tom squatted down next to her, looking anxiously at his father. Lee's eyes were closed, and his breath was ragged and labored. But at least he was breathing.

Please be okay, Tom thought, his chest squeezing with panic.

"What in holy hell is going on in here?" Bo asked, striding into the living room, Tom's mother following behind him. Marlowe was holding a flat package wrapped in brown paper, which she set down on a wing chair.

"Lee!" Marlowe hurried to his side. "Oh my God. Is he okay? How did he fall?"

Isabel stood to make way for Marlowe, who crouched down next to her husband. She rested her hand on his chest, as if—like Tom—she wanted to reassure herself that he was breathing.

"What happened?" Bo demanded.

Isabel glared at Jason, who was hovering behind the leather chairs. Darcy stood next to him, her hands pressed together and her eyes wide with fright.

"Ask your brother," Isabel snapped.

"I didn't do anything," Jason said. His fingers drummed against his legs, and his eyes slid away from Isabel's accusatory glare.

"He thought your temporary absence from the room would be the perfect opportunity to sexually harass June," Isabel said to Bo. "She asked him to stop. He wouldn't. And Lee tried to intervene, but as soon as he stood up and put weight on the leg you shot, he passed out." She waved her hand at Lee, still lying on the ground. "I guess it's lucky he didn't hit his head, the way Zack did."

"I was just trying to talk to her," Jason protested. "What's wrong with that?"

"You put your hands on her." Isabel practically spit out the words. "This is ridiculous. He has no self-control. He was pawing at her like she was working the pole at a strip club. Do you know how sick that is? She's a teenager."

"Calm down," Bo said, although it wasn't clear if he was talking to Isabel or his brother, who was starting to become visibly agitated. "I'm sure Jason didn't mean any harm."

"Stop yelling at me!" Jason shouted, and he took a step toward Isabel, his hands rising up in fists. Tom wondered if he was going to hit her, push her, just as he had hit and pushed Zack earlier, and his head began to buzz with adrenaline and fear.

But then Bo was stepping in front of Jason, speaking in calm, soothing tones.

"It's okay. Take a deep breath. Do your counting."

Tom wasn't sure what that meant, but it seemed to calm Jason a bit. He dropped his hands and began counting silently, his mouth moving with each number.

Marlowe was murmuring to Lee, whose eyes remained closed. Since Jason seemed to be regaining control, Tom turned to his mom, patting her back in support—and so that she would know he was there. He wished he could tell her what had happened, what was happening, but knew it wasn't a safe time to communicate.

When Bo had ordered Tom's mother to go to Lee's office to open the safe, Tom had considered shooting Jason. He'd even reached down, ready to grab the gun. But June had seen what he was planning and stilled his hand. When he had looked over at her next to him on the couch, she had shaken her head almost imperceptibly. At the time, he'd thought she was concerned about their mother's safety. And she would have had a point. If Tom shot Jason, Bo might hurt Marlowe in retaliation.

But that wasn't what June had planned. Instead, she had stood and walked over to where Jason stood in the corner of the living room. He was holding his gun, although his arms were hanging loosely at his sides, like he wasn't sure what to do with himself now that Bo had left the room. Tom watched his sister, wondering why she would deliberately seek out the attention of a man who had already touched her inappropriately. Jason watched her, too, looking startled at her approach.

"Hi," June said brightly. "Do you want another beer?"

"Yeah, but, um, Bo wants everyone to stay here. In this room."

"It will only take a minute. The kitchen's right over there." She lifted her arm languidly, pointing toward the kitchen, just beyond the hall.

"I can go," Darcy offered.

"Thanks." June smiled and tucked her chin down and looked up at Jason under her lashes. Which was *weird*. It was completely unlike June. She'd never been a people pleaser, never been one of those girls who tried to make themselves small so that everyone around them would feel more important. But she had gotten Jason's attention. He didn't take his eyes off her.

"Hold tight; I'll be right back," Darcy said. "Does anyone else want anything?"

"I'll take another glass of wine," Isabel said, holding up her glass. She was cupping it in her hand, the stem between her fingers. "Lee?"

"I could use a whiskey," Lee said, his words almost a groan.

June frowned. "Are you sure that's a good idea, Dad?"

"I don't think I've ever had a better one."

Darcy smiled, nodded, and disappeared off to the kitchen.

"So what do you do, Jason?" June asked. She stroked her hair, curling a lock around her finger. "Are you a boat captain too?"

"No, um . . . no. Bo is the one who usually steers. I just crew." Jason's fingers began drumming against his leg.

"That sounds like fun," June said. "Do you enjoy it?"

"I love boats," Jason said, his voice stuttering over the word. "Our dad worked in a boatyard. He'd take us out fishing on the weekends."

"I like going out in our boat too," June said brightly.

"You do?" Jason looked eager. "What do you like about it?"

"You know, being out on the water and relaxing. Feeling the boat rocking on the waves. Hanging out with my friends at the sandbar. What do you like about it?"

Tom knew that June hated going out on their boat, and thought it was boring and a waste of time. She particularly despised going to the sandbar, where everyone anchored on the weekends, like a floating block party. She always insisted the water there was polluted with beer and pee, and refused to swim in it.

"I feel free when I'm on the water." Jason stepped closer to June. "The rest of the world just goes away, you know?"

"June," Lee said, a note of warning in his voice. "Why don't you come and sit back down over here?"

June ignored her father and instead leaned toward Jason and lowered her voice. "Do you think it would be okay if I ran upstairs and got my sweatshirt? It's freezing down here. I swear—my mom keeps the air-conditioning set so cold you'd think we had pet penguins."

"I don't know," Jason said uneasily. "Bo wouldn't like it."

"I promise I'll be fast. I'll just run upstairs and be right back down. Bo won't even know I was gone."

Jason's hand began drumming a beat against his leg. His eyes slid from side to side before resting on June again. "I don't think that's a good idea."

"But I'm freezing." June wrapped her arms around herself and tipped her head coquettishly.

Tom finally figured out what June was up to. The eye had arrived, and the conditions outside were quiet. Felix was going to make a run for it any minute now, if he hadn't left already. June wanted to go with him. Jason seemed to be weakening, and Tom thought June might just talk him into letting her leave the room.

But then Jason stepped even closer to June, an eager expression on his face.

"I can warm you up," he suggested and reached out and rubbed June's arms with the palms of his hands.

"No thanks. I really just need a sweatshirt." June smiled tightly.

"Hey!" Lee said, stirring on the sofa. "What are you doing?"

Jason ignored Lee, his hands dropping lower to June's waist. He held on to her like they were dancing.

"Please don't touch me," June said, shrinking away from him, trying to dislodge his hands from her waist.

Darcy appeared then, balancing bottles of beer and an unopened bottle of wine in her hands. She stopped abruptly, her eyes widening as she saw Jason looming over June.

"What's going on?" Darcy asked.

"Get your hands off my daughter!" Lee said. He struggled to push himself up off the couch.

"Dad, no!" Tom jumped up, but it was too late.

Lee swung his legs off the sofa and stood, his hands clenched in fists at his sides. But as soon as he put weight on his injured leg, his face went white with pain, and Lee fell heavily to the ground. Both Darcy and Isabel had let out cries of concern, and Isabel and Tom had rushed to Lee's side. A moment later Bo and Marlowe had hurried back into the living room. And when Tom finally looked up and glanced around, he realized that someone was missing.

June was gone.

Tom wasn't sure if she'd gone upstairs to find Felix or if she'd slipped out the front door. But she'd timed it perfectly. Because while Marlowe murmured to Lee, and Isabel told Bo in caustic tones that Jason had been out of line, no one—no one other than him—had yet noticed that June was missing.

Lee stirred, opening his eyes. He looked groggy and disoriented, and he let out a low groan.

"Are you okay?" Marlowe asked.

"I don't think so." Lee winced in pain. "My leg . . . it's bad."

"Do you want us to get you back on the couch?" Marlowe asked.

Lee nodded, and Tom and Marlowe helped hoist him back up. It took some effort, and Lee moaned softly as they moved him, but they finally got him up onto the sofa. Marlowe stroked Lee's hair off his face, and he caught her hand in his and squeezed it.

"I'll be okay," he said.

"You really shouldn't put any weight on that leg," Bo observed.

Isabel turned on him again. "That's very helpful advice, considering you're the one who shot him."

Bo ignored her and instead looked at his brother. "So what happened?"

"I was just talking to June. She said she was cold and wanted to get a sweatshirt, so I rubbed her arms to help warm her up. And he"—Jason flung an arm in Lee's direction—"freaked out and started shouting at me."

"You were touching his daughter," Isabel said flatly.

"I didn't think she'd mind. She was cold. I was helping." Jason fidgeted uncomfortably, looking worriedly at Bo.

Bo sighed wearily and glanced around. Suddenly, his gaze sharpened. "Where is she?"

"Who?" Jason asked.

"June. She's not here." Bo looked directly at Tom. "Where did she go?"

Tom shrugged. "I don't know. I didn't see her leave."

Bo closed his eyes for a moment and rubbed a hand over his face. Then, without warning, he picked a framed photograph of the Davies family up off a side table and threw it against the wall. The picture shattered and fell to the ground, glass flying everywhere.

"What the fuck, Isabel," Bo said furiously through clenched teeth. "You couldn't keep track of a guy with a gimpy leg and a couple of teenagers for ten minutes?"

Wait, Tom thought, horror spreading through him. Bo hadn't been speaking to Darcy or Jason. He'd directed his comment to *Isabel.*

Isabel knew Bo.

Whatever was happening in their house that evening, Isabel was part of it.

CHAPTER THIRTY-THREE

ISABEL

2008

Bo lay on his bed, his head resting on his hands, elbows out to the side. Isabel sat on the end of the bed, leaning against the wall with her bare legs bent over Bo's. Her hand rested on his inner thigh.

The room Bo shared with his brother, Jason, and a boy named Mitchell was utilitarian. There were bunk beds on one side of the room, Bo's narrow twin on the other, and three laminate dressers crammed into the remaining space. Bo's bed had a sky-blue polyester comforter draped over it.

Isabel wasn't technically supposed to be alone with Bo, much less in his room. Mike and Mel Hitchens, their foster parents, had a rule against the three teen boys and two teen girls currently living with them fraternizing without supervision. But it was a rule they never bothered to enforce, and anyway, the Hitchenses were both at work and wouldn't be home for hours.

It was the first foster home Isabel had been placed in. She'd returned home after school one day to the apartment she and her mom had rented in North Miami and found her mother's handbag still sitting on a kitchen chair. At first, Isabel had been confused. Her mom was supposed to be at work, at her job as a receptionist for a dentist. Isabel knocked on her mother's closed bedroom door and had a premonition even before she opened it that something was terribly wrong. Sondra had been a functional addict for years and had a bad habit of mixing pills with booze. She'd had a few close calls over the years. So Isabel was worried and upset but not totally surprised to find her mother in bed, unresponsive, her breath shallow. It had happened before. But this time, the paramedics who arrived weren't able to resuscitate her, and Sondra died in the ambulance on the way to the hospital.

In the week following her mother's death, Isabel's aunts—her mother's sisters—and assorted cousins were around, helping to make the funeral arrangements and stocking the refrigerator with slimy casseroles made from cans of condensed soup. But not one of them mentioned where Isabel was going to live. A few days after the funeral, she overheard the social worker who had been assigned her case file asking one of her aunts if she would take in Isabel, explaining that if the family didn't step up, Isabel would be put into foster care. Her aunt's reply was cold and crisp: "I'm not letting any girl who looks like that live with my husband."

And so, ten days after her mother's death, Isabel had found herself arriving on the Hitchenses' doorstep with all her clothes packed in an old suitcase that had belonged to her mother.

It could have been terrible. The Hitchens had a small house that wasn't very tidy and smelled like wet dog. Mel Hitchens loved watching reality television shows like *The Bachelor* and *The Real Housewives* franchise while her husband spent all his free time playing video games. But neither of them drank, or did drugs, or struck any of the kids in their care, so things could have been worse.

But for Isabel, the best part of having to live with the Hitchenses was that she'd met Bo.

Bo was perfect. He was two years older than Isabel and the most beautiful person she'd ever seen. He had high chiseled cheekbones, slanted green eyes fringed with dark lashes, and full lush lips that Isabel loved kissing. They spent hours every afternoon entwined in each other's arms, tasting and touching one another, and Isabel had never felt more alive. Sometimes she felt guilty for being so happy so soon after her mother's death. But maybe it was meant to be, she thought. Maybe she had been destined to meet Bo, and everything that had led up to that point—her mother's addiction getting worse and worse, the constant worry that Sondra would lose her job and they'd be evicted from their apartment, watching the ambulance racing away—had happened so that she could end up here with him.

"Do you like it here?" Isabel asked, gently stroking Bo's leg.

He shrugged. "It's better than the last place we were at. They were stingy with the food there, and the dad made fun of Jason. Mocked the way he talks."

"That's mean."

"Yeah, well, he stopped after I punched him in his big fat gut." Bo smiled lazily. "After that, they moved us out of that place and into this one."

It wasn't the first time Bo had casually mentioned his past violence, but it always seemed to involve protecting his younger brother, which Isabel decided was sweet. It was hard for kids in the system. Jason was lucky he had Bo to look after him. And now he was looking out for her too.

Isabel lay down on the bed, stretching out and then molding her body against Bo's.

"What are you going to do when you turn eighteen?" she asked. Bo was close to aging out of foster care.

"I'll get a job and get a place of my own. Jason and I will live there," Bo said simply.

Isabel waited for him to say something about her and how she would live with them too.

But Bo continued without mentioning her as part of his plan. "There's this group, this charity, that helps foster kids get set up in their own places. My social worker gave me their brochure."

"You don't want to go to college? Take advantage of the scholarship?" Isabel asked, referencing the program that offered full tuition and housing for all the foster kids in the state of Florida.

"I can't. I have Jason to think about."

"He could go to college too."

Bo looked down at her, his brow furrowing with amusement. "Jason in college? Yeah, I don't see that happening. He'll be lucky to graduate high school. He's failing half of his classes." Bo snaked his arm down and wrapped it around Isabel's waist, pulling her closer against him. "I think I'd like college, though. Especially if all the girls there are as cute as you."

Isabel tried to suppress the immediate surge of jealousy she felt at this. "What would you study if you went?"

"I don't know. Maybe I'd be a lawyer. I think I'd be good at it, don't you?"

Isabel nodded against his chest. She could picture Bo as an attorney, dressed in a sharp suit, arguing in front of a jury. And he was smart enough to go to law school. He got good grades, even though he barely studied. If he applied himself, he could accomplish anything.

"Yeah, well, I don't have time for that. I need to get a job," Bo said.

"What are you going to do?"

Bo shrugged, which jostled Isabel's head. "I don't know. Maybe something with boats."

"Do you know about boats?"

"Yeah, we grew up on the water. I could get a job crewing on some rich guy's yacht. That would make some bank."

It would also take him away from her, Isabel thought with a squeeze of self-pity. She didn't want Bo to go away. She wanted him to stay here, cocooned with her forever. Maybe not here, in the Hitchenses' house, but with her. The two of them together.

"What about me?" Isabel asked, hating how needy she sounded.

"What about you?"

"What's going to happen with us when you leave?"

"Us?" Bo asked.

Isabel could feel her body go rigid. She turned her head to look up at Bo. "Yes, us. You and me. Are we going to stay together?"

Bo smiled at her. She loved his smile, the way his lips curled slowly up, his green eyes glowing with pleasure. "Of course we'll be together. You and I are the same, Izzy. We belong together."

Isabel's face flushed with happiness. She tucked her chin back against Bo's chest and wrapped her arm tightly around his torso. "Good. Because I'd do anything for you."

"I know," Bo said, and he squeezed her arm.

CHAPTER THIRTY-FOUR

FELIX

When Felix hit the ground, his legs crumpled, and he lost his balance, falling heavily onto the rain-drenched patio. For a few long, scary beats, he couldn't move or even breathe. His right ankle throbbed, and he wondered if he'd seriously injured it. Finally, he was able to draw in a deep breath and struggle up to a seated position.

I guess I survived the fall, he thought.

He looked around, but it was dark out, the only light coming from the few landscaping ground lights that hadn't been broken or blown away in the storm. That was one thing he hadn't thought about when making his plan to run to the police station. It was night, and the lights were out. How had he thought he'd be able to see where he was going in the unrelenting darkness?

Felix struggled to his feet, but his ankle pulsated with pain when he tried to put weight on it. He took a few tentative steps and realized with a sinking certainty that running anywhere was completely out of the question. He sighed and wiped his hand over his face. What now? Even if he could find his way in the dark, there was no way he would be able to limp all the way to the police station before the eye passed and the second half of the hurricane blew in.

He looked from right to left. There were houses all along the shore, but he didn't know any of the Davieses' neighbors and had no idea who might be willing to help him. Maybe if he knocked on enough doors, he'd find someone home. The Davieses couldn't be the only ones on the street who had decided to ride out the storm. Getting someone to open their door to a stranger in the middle of a hurricane might be difficult, but he had to at least try.

Felix was in the backyard, so he had to make his way around to the front of the house. It was slow going. He was limping heavily and kept stumbling over things he couldn't see in the darkness—the edges of paving stones, fallen branches, something hard and metallic that felt like a rake or some other gardening tool. Felix placed the flat of his hand against the side of the house every few steps to make sure he was staying on course. Step, step, touch. Step, step, touch.

And then suddenly, his foot hit something large and solid, and before he knew it, Felix was falling again. He sprawled forward, throwing his arms out in front to brace himself as he hit the ground. Luckily, this time he fell on grass, which cushioned his fall somewhat, although the ground was wet, and his clothes were instantly soaked through. Felix sat up and felt around him, trying to figure out what he'd tripped over. His hands touched something solid and covered in fabric.

He fumbled in his pocket and pulled out his phone, hesitating for a moment as he wondered if it was safe to turn on the flashlight. The shutters were up, so no one inside the house would see him. But what if the intruders came outside during the eye to check on their boat? He waited and listened but couldn't hear anything other than the breeze rustling through nearby palm fronds. He drew in a deep breath, exhaled, and then turned on his phone's flashlight, pointing it toward the large solid mass he'd tripped over.

Felix let out a frightened exhalation and promptly dropped his phone.

It wasn't a thing he had tripped over. It was a *body*.

Mick lay face up, his eyes open and unseeing. Felix clapped a hand over his mouth, both to stop the scream in his throat and to keep back the retching that was already convulsing through his body. He grabbed for his phone, which was on the wet grass, and aimed the light back at Mick.

He was dead. Felix could tell without checking for a pulse.

Mick's clothing was soaked through, but Felix could see blood matting Mick's thinning hair. Felix leaned closer with his flashlight and instantly wished he hadn't, because yet another wave of nausea passed over him. Mick's skull was caved in on one side. He remembered what June had told him, that Mick had been hit earlier that afternoon by an umbrella that had flown over from a neighbor's yard. But this looked far worse. It looked like someone had hit him on the head with something hard and deadly.

"Oh, shit," Felix breathed. His heart pounded, and he flexed his hands, unsure of what to do now. It wasn't like he could move Mick on his own, and anyway, he had to keep moving if he was going to find help before the eye passed.

The light from his phone picked up a metallic glint off to one side. Felix looked closer and saw that it was a hammer. He wondered if that was what Mick's killer had used to bash in his head. Even though Felix knew this was a crime scene and the hammer was a potential murder weapon, he picked it up and slid it into his belt loop. He had given the gun to Tom and might need the hammer to defend himself.

What sounded like the front door banged open, and Felix quickly turned off his phone's flashlight. He moved to the side of the house, pressing his back against a wall.

"June!"

Felix didn't recognize the man's voice. It wasn't Lee or Tom. And why was he looking for June? She was supposed to be inside. If she wasn't there, where had she gone?

Footsteps fell heavily on the paved driveway. Felix shrank back, trying to stay as still and quiet as possible.

I need to get out of here before he sees me and before the storm starts back up, he thought. But heading toward the street was now not an option. Felix mentally mapped out the grounds of the Davieses' home in his head. There was the patio and pool and, beyond that, the long sloping lawn and the river beyond it. And then he remembered—the boathouse.

Felix and June had spent hours in the boathouse over the years. It had felt almost like a private clubhouse for their club of two. They'd studied for tests there, watched movies on tablets, read in companionable silence. He needed to get there, away from the man searching for June, and then he'd figure out his next step.

"June!" The voice was calling out again, this time sounding both angrier and closer.

Felix saw a stream of light. The man had a flashlight—or was using his phone as one. He hadn't yet turned the corner of the house, but he would soon. If Felix stayed where he was, the man would see him.

He began limping as fast as he could back in the direction he'd come from. He made it to the back of the house, across the patio, and past the pool and then stumbled down the lawn toward the river. The wind was starting to pick up again, blowing in short strong bursts up off the water. Was the eye ending already? If so, he'd failed. He'd missed his chance to find help.

Felix scrambled down the backyard, toward the river. He could barely see, the only light coming from the occasional flash of lightning over the water. The Davieses' boathouse was just ahead of him. The structure was fully enclosed and elevated off the water on a concrete base. There was a lift that moved the boat up and down off the river and through a large retractable floor that slid open on rollers. As Felix limped toward the boathouse, his feet squelched in mud, and his sneakers were instantly soaked through. The water had risen over the mangrove-lined banks and onto the lawn. He headed over to the wood dock that skirted the boathouse; climbed up a set of metal stairs, his ankle throbbing with every step; and then felt his way to the door.

Felix glanced over his shoulder to see if the man was pursuing him, but he couldn't see anything or, more importantly, anyone chasing after him. His hands shaking, Felix slid the latch on the door of the boathouse open and slipped inside, then closed it behind him.

The boathouse was dark, and in the quiet, Felix could hear his own breath, ragged and shallow. Once the door was shut behind him, he waited for a moment, listening for the sounds of someone following him up the stairs. When he didn't hear anyone coming, he risked turning his flashlight on for a moment. The structure had survived the first half of the hurricane without losing its roof. Mr. Davies's giant boat was there, secured from the storm, and taking up most of the inside space. Felix limped around it and sat down, leaning back against the wall. His ankle throbbed, and when he shone the light on it, he could see it was swollen and discolored. It hurt when he touched it.

I'm such an idiot, Felix thought, turning off the flashlight. *Why didn't I pick a better window to jump from? Why didn't I try to find one that opened up onto the roof of the sunroom so I wouldn't have had to fall so far?*

But he knew why. He'd gotten scared, and he'd panicked. And now, he was stuck in the boathouse, hobbled with what was probably a broken ankle. And it was entirely possible that because he'd screwed up, June and her family would all die.

Felix slumped forward, wrapping his arms around his bent legs. He felt sick to his stomach. Despite all his best intentions, everything he touched continued to go wrong. And this time, the consequences of his failure would be horrifying.

Felix remembered the evening when his cousin and two friends had picked him up from his job at a local golf club in a Lexus sedan Felix hadn't recognized.

"What are you doing here?" Felix had asked Derrick. He'd had to practically shout over the music playing in the car.

"Your mom's working late at the hospital. She asked my mom if I'd give you a ride home," Derrick said.

"Did your mom get a new car?" Felix asked, sliding into the back seat. The leather was soft and buttery, and the car smelled brand new.

"Something like that," Derrick said.

And that was it. Felix didn't ask any more questions. He was coming off a long shift on a particularly hot summer day. His arms were aching from heaving around bags of golf clubs and scrubbing down the carts when they came in from the course. He just wanted to go home and take a nice cool shower and relax for the rest of the evening.

It was only when the police had pulled the car over and advanced with their weapons drawn that he'd realized with dawning horror that he'd made a terrible, life-altering mistake.

And now he was in trouble again. Only this time, June was in danger. She was the only person, other than his mother, whom Felix truly loved, and he had let her down.

He heard a noise and realized that it was coming from him. He had started to cry without even realizing it. His chest was heaving with ragged sobs, and tears streamed down his face, stinging his eyes, his nose filling with snot.

Then he heard another noise, one that caused him to still. He wiped at his face and stared into the darkness, wondering what he was hearing.

Someone was at the door to the boathouse. The man must have seen Felix and followed him there, or maybe he had seen the beam of his flashlight through the windows that were placed high, up near the roof.

Felix tried to shift his weight up, to move into an offensive crouch so he could spring up when needed, but his ankle rebelled. He fell back, his butt hitting the hard floor. The door to the boathouse swung open.

This is it, he thought. *I'm going to die tonight, just like Mick and Zack. I didn't get to go to college or medical school—or ever tell June how I really feel about her. Everything I wanted to be, everything that I could be, is over.*

And then the door burst open, and with a high-pitched scream, the hurricane blew into the boathouse.

CHAPTER THIRTY-FIVE

MARLOWE

Where did June go? Marlowe wondered, staring wildly around the living room. The usually lovely, tranquil space was a mess. Discarded cups and plates littered every surface, beach towels were flung across the backs of chairs, and blood from Lee's gunshot wound was splattered across the patterned taupe rug.

June had been sitting on the sofa next to Tom when Marlowe and Bo had left to retrieve the Cézanne sketch out of the safe. Now she was gone. But where? Was she hiding somewhere in the house? Or had she run for help?

The thought of her daughter outside when the second half of the hurricane was about to descend was so terrifying Marlowe had to sit down before her knees gave out. She perched on the edge of the sofa where Lee was reclined, clasping her hands tightly together. The first half of the storm was unlike anything Marlowe had ever been through before—the winds, the thunder, the torrential rain. At times, it had sounded like the house might blow away. If the second half of the storm was just as intense, it would be deadly outside.

But June was smart. She would know she'd have to get to a neighbor's house quickly. And if she had and they had been able to take her to the police station during the eye, help might already be on its way. True, the sheriff's deputies had told Marlowe they wouldn't be responding to distress calls during the storm, but at the very least, they'd be ready to mobilize once the conditions improved.

As soon as Bo realized June was gone, he ran out of the house, banging open the front door. Marlowe could hear him outside calling for June. He returned a few moments later, slamming the door behind him. When he strode back into the living room, his eyes blazed with anger.

"Where is she?" he demanded, advancing on Tom. "Where did she go?"

Tom shrugged helplessly. "I don't know. I was helping my dad. I didn't see her leave."

"Could she be hiding in the house?"

"How would we know?" Isabel asked. "We told you none of us saw her go."

Marlowe turned to look at her assistant. Bo had been angry at her for letting June out of her sight. Clearly, Isabel was part of whatever was happening in their home.

Marlowe had met Isabel during an exhibit at the Miami gallery where Isabel worked. She'd been struck by the younger woman's poise and professionalism and her keen eye. She'd reached out a few weeks later to offer Isabel a job helping her curate the Bond collection, but it had taken some persuading, including a pay increase and Marlowe's assurance that she would connect Isabel with other people in the art world. And now it turned out she was helping armed robbers steal a Cézanne? Yes, the sketch was valuable, but still, it was crazy. Isabel was risking criminal prosecution and the end of a promising career.

Unless she was sure she'd get away with it and not be caught, Marlowe thought.

The betrayal cut deeply. Marlowe had trusted Isabel. Her assistant sometimes worked remotely on the laptop Marlowe had provided her with. But just as often, Isabel had been here, working in Marlowe's home office. Occasionally, if they worked late, she'd even eaten dinner with the family, chatting with Tom and June over Chinese takeout. They'd even invited her out on the boat one Sunday afternoon. Isabel had ridden in the back, showing off her toned body in a white one-shoulder swimsuit and tipping her head back to enjoy the sun on her face and the salt air breezing past. And all along, she'd been conspiring to bring armed thieves into their home?

Isabel faced off against Bo, her hands on her hips. She didn't seem afraid of him, only irritated by his anger. Her long dark hair that was usually shiny and curled to perfection had deflated and hung limply down her back, and her lip gloss had worn off, leaving behind patches of red.

Bo threw his hands up in the air and let them fall back to his sides in exasperation. "How could you let this happen, Isabel?"

"This was not my fault. You're the one who decided to change the plan without telling me," Isabel snapped back.

Bo turned to Marlowe. "Where do you think June went? To a neighbor's house?"

"I have no idea where she would have gone," Marlowe said. "She knows most of our neighbors, of course, but I don't know whose house she would have gone to. I don't even know who's home. A lot of people evacuated for the storm."

"Does she have any friends from school in the neighborhood? Does she hang out at any of the houses?" Bo pressed.

"No." Marlowe shook her head. "She doesn't have any friends nearby. We're not particularly close with anyone who lives on this street."

Bo was studying her, and Marlowe knew he was trying to figure out if she was lying. But everything she'd said was true. The most they socialized with their neighbors was attending the DiMarcos' annual Christmas party. She had no idea whose house June would flee to.

"Will your answer change if I shoot your son?" Bo asked, raising his gun in Tom's direction.

Marlowe's heart lurched. "No! Please. I don't know where she went. How could I? I was with you in Lee's office when she left."

Bo shook his head in disgust and lowered his gun. "This is great. Just great. We talked about this, Isabel. About how important it was to keep everyone together."

Isabel shook her head dismissively. "Did we talk about you bringing your ditzy girlfriend along? Or Jason killing a teenager? Because I don't remember any of that being part of the plan."

"That was an accident!" Jason protested.

"This has been fucked from the beginning. And it's not my fault," Isabel said, pointing a finger at Bo. "You're the one with the impulse-control problem."

"Wait . . . you know each other?" Darcy asked, looking from Bo to Isabel.

Isabel rolled her eyes and gave an exaggerated golf clap. "Way to keep up, genius."

Bo continued to glare at Isabel. His facial stubble, which had been scruffy when he'd first arrived at the dock, had grown in even thicker as the evening had progressed.

"Darcy got us into the house," Bo said.

"With her teeny-tiny bikini?" Isabel shot back.

"Because she's a girl. Two men on their own are a threat. Two men accompanied by a woman are less threatening," he said.

"I don't understand what's going on," Darcy said plaintively.

Marlowe almost felt sorry for her. Almost. But any pity she might have felt for Darcy's naivete had ended when Darcy had been so quick to go along with Bo's violent plan. She had willingly become a part of this, just to please him.

"We'll talk about it later, Darcy." Bo's tone had a warning note. "We need to focus on finding June."

"We could go door to door," Jason suggested. "See if anyone's seen her."

"Good idea, bro. That way we can make sure all the neighbors who stuck around can get a good look at us," Bo said sarcastically.

Tom started suddenly and lifted his head, looking up as though he'd heard something.

June? Marlowe wondered wildly. *Maybe she's in the house, and Tom heard her footsteps.* But then she heard it too. The wind had started whistling again, gusting up off the river. The house seemed to shudder in response, as if waiting for the next onslaught.

If June had left on foot to find help, she'd run out of time. Celeste was back.

PART FOUR

22:13 update. Southeastern Florida remains under an emergency warning. The eye wall has passed over the coast, and conditions will continue to deteriorate. Be prepared for severe storm conditions, and wind in excess of one hundred miles per hour. This is a life-threatening storm with the possibility of fatalities. Continue to shelter in place.

CHAPTER THIRTY-SIX

JUNE

A gust of wind picked up June's thick curly hair, lifting it up off her neck. Rain began to patter down, a steady drizzle quickly turning into a heavy downfall. Thunder rumbled nearby, and lightning crackled down over the river, lighting up the backyard.

It's too late, June realized. She shouldn't have wasted time trying to find Felix outside in the dark. She should have run for help, tried to find a neighbor who would take her in and help her contact the police. She should have made sure that someone in the outside world knew what was happening inside her home.

Instead, she was stranded in her backyard, back pressed against the soggy trunk of a palm tree, listening for Bo. She thought he'd gone back inside—the beam from his flashlight had disappeared—but she wanted to be sure before she moved out into the open. But now that the winds were picking up, she knew she'd have to get going. She couldn't be outside when the full ferocity of the storm descended again.

June crept down the sloping yard, toward the elevated boathouse. It was the only nearby shelter, other than her house, that she could get to quickly. The river had risen so high she had to wade through water in order to reach the stairs that led from the ground floor up to the second-story entrance to the boathouse. She thought she saw a light for a moment, but maybe it was just another flash of lightning.

June reached out with her hand and blindly felt for the railing. As she climbed up, the wind began gusting so hard it nearly knocked her over. June's bare feet slipped on the slick stairs, and she grabbed the railing to stay upright, half climbing and half hoisting herself up the stairs. When she finally reached the second-story deck, she was out of breath and chilled, her clothes wet against her skin.

June pushed the door open, and the wind screamed by her into the boathouse. June rushed inside, struggling to close the door against the storm. Her feet scrabbled against the floor as she tried to find purchase, and it was only when she threw her body weight against the door that she was able to shut it. June paused, gasping at the effort, listening to the rain sleeting outside, hammering against the metal roof.

Then June heard another sound. A sound coming from inside the boathouse.

She wasn't alone.

A cold dread filled her. Who would be here? Was it Bo? He would have spotted the boathouse when they docked their boat that afternoon. Was it possible he had passed her in the dark and come down here looking for her? The idea of being alone in the dark with that psycho made June want to run back out into the storm. She reached back behind her, her hand fumbling for the door latch.

"Who's there?" a frightened voice said from the darkness.

Panic flared up through June, and she was about to bolt when suddenly she realized she recognized the voice. "Felix?"

"June?"

"Yes, it's me! Where are you?"

"Hold on—I'll turn on a light."

Felix turned on the flashlight on his phone, temporarily blinding June. She held her hands up in front of her eyes.

"Sorry," Felix said, turning his phone so the light shone away from June.

She hurried across the boathouse, past her father's boat, and knelt down next to Felix, who sat leaning against the wall.

"Hi!" she said. "Thank God it's you!"

"Hi." Felix reached out and took June's hand in his.

She gripped his hand back, relief overwhelming her. "What are you doing here?"

Felix smiled weakly. "Same thing as you, probably. Well, sort of. I was going to run for help, but I hurt my ankle when I jumped out of your bedroom window. This was as far as I got."

June blinked in the darkness. "Wait. Did you just say you jumped out my window?"

"Well, sort of. I climbed out, and dangled, and then sort of dropped onto the patio. I'm pretty sure I broke my ankle."

"What did you think was going to happen? Did you think you'd suddenly turn into Spider-Man on your way down? That you'd be able to shoot webs out of your wrists and swing to safety?"

Felix snorted. "No, but that would have been pretty cool. Better than falling two stories onto concrete. Which, by the way, really freaking hurt. It still hurts." He reached down and grabbed at his ankle.

"Tom told me you were planning to run for help. I didn't realize that plan included throwing yourself out a window."

"Again, it was more of a drop. I was hoping I'd land on some bushes or something to break my fall, but it was so dark outside I couldn't really judge it. And I was going to run for help, but then I couldn't put any weight on my ankle. I barely made it down here. That guy almost saw me."

"Bo?"

"Is that his name? He was looking for you."

"I know—I heard him." June shivered, both from fear and from the sudden drop in temperature Celeste had ushered in. Her clothes were soaked through from the rain. "What are we going to do now?"

"I think we're stuck here for the duration. I don't have any cell service, but we might eventually get through to someone." Felix held up his phone. "Although I should probably turn this off, to save power."

"We can turn the lights on."

"The lights work in here?"

"They should. The whole boathouse is wired to a generator, so the boat lift will work even if the main power is out." June hesitated. "The only problem is that if anyone is outside, they'll see the lights through the windows."

"No one's going to still be outside now that the storm has started again," Felix said.

June stood and went back toward the door. A moment later the room was filled with light, and she and Felix blinked at one another as their eyes adjusted.

"Wow," Felix said, staring up at the boat. "It looks so much bigger out of the water."

June also looked up at the *Dreamweaver*. It was a glossy white forty-four-foot fiberglass fishing boat with navy-blue stripes and had been built by Bond Marine, the company her grandparents had owned. She had no idea how high it was, but it did look bigger here on dry dock, towering up over them. She wondered for a moment if they could use the boat to escape but immediately dismissed the idea. The keys were back inside the house, and anyway, it would be deadly to go out on the water with Celeste bearing back down. The *Dreamweaver* was useless to them.

"I wonder if Mick made it home. He might come back to check on us," June said hopefully as she sat back down next to Felix. "He might even let the police know that there are strangers in the house. He thought they were sus."

Felix hesitated, and June suddenly knew that whatever he was about to tell her was going to be terrible. He reached out and took June's hand, folding it into his.

"Mick's dead," he said quietly.

The words hit June like a physical blow. She'd suspected something had happened to him—or, more accurately, that Bo had done something to Mick. But that was different than knowing for sure.

Felix continued. "His body is out in the yard, by the side of the house. I tripped over him while I was trying to get away."

"Are you sure he wasn't just hurt? I mean, how do you know he's dead?"

"I'm sure. I looked at him closely, and . . . he was definitely dead. I think someone hit him on the head with a hammer." Felix lifted his T-shirt so June could see a hammer tucked there in the belt loop on his shorts.

"You took the hammer?"

"I thought I might need a weapon."

June closed her eyes as the horror of this washed over. She couldn't remember a time when Mick hadn't been in her life. She'd always been fond of him. He could be gruff, but he had a kind heart, and he'd always looked out for her and Tom. He'd kept an eye on them when they were younger and out playing in the yard or swimming in the pool, and he had probably still been watching over them even as they had gotten older. His presence had always made her feel safe. And now he was gone, just like Zack. And Bo had obviously killed him.

Which meant . . . oh no. June's eyes flew open. She had already suspected that Bo had no intention of letting any of them live, that he would make sure there were no witnesses left behind. But this proved it. If Bo had killed Mick, he was planning on killing all of them.

She let go of Felix's hand and jumped to her feet.

"What are you doing?" he asked.

"I have to go get help."

"June, stop. You can't go out in the storm!"

"I don't have a choice. You can't walk, so it has to be me."

"Listen to the wind blowing out there. No one could survive being outside in this storm. It will knock you over before you get halfway up the yard."

"I don't know how much Tom told you, but it's not an accident those people are here. They planned it. They came to steal the Cézanne. And if they killed Mick, that means they're planning on killing everyone. We're all witnesses. They need to get rid of us so we can't tell the police who they are."

"You're not going to help anyone if you get hurt."

"I can't just sit here while they kill my family! And I'm sure once the storm passes, Bo will come looking for me too."

"Maybe he won't find us here." Felix didn't sound very hopeful.

"This is probably the first place he'll look," June pointed out. "I'm going to have to try and make it to one of our neighbors' houses."

"Do you know which ones are home? And anyway, who's going to answer their door in the middle of a hurricane?" Felix shook his head. "No. We need to think about this. We need to make a plan."

"The last plan didn't work out so well."

"So we'll figure out one that does. Come on." Felix patted the ground next to him. "Sit down."

A gust of wind shook the boathouse so violently June almost fell back next to Felix.

"Do you think it's safe in here?" she asked.

"It was built to protect your dad's boat, which is his favorite thing in the world."

June smiled weakly. "That's true. He loves it more than he loves me."

"No way. Your dad doesn't love anything more than you."

"Bo said that too. Well, he said my dad loves me more than he loves Tom."

"That's a weird thing to say."

"I thought so too. But I don't think it was about me or Tom. It had something to do with my mom. The whole time we were sitting there, he was taunting her. Trying to upset her."

"Why would he want to do that?"

"I have no idea. It's possible he's just an asshole. But it seemed personal. Like this wasn't just about stealing the Cézanne sketch."

"It's kind of weird that your family has this, like, priceless work of art just hanging in your house."

June shrugged. "It's not like my mom bought it. She inherited it from her parents, and anyway, she's donating it to the museum, along with all of their other artwork. But it was almost like Bo hates her. He was picking at her, trying to upset her. Isn't that weird? Oh!" June suddenly remembered her mother's story, the one that she had never heard before. "I had a sister. She died before Tom and I were born. Bo basically manipulated my mom into telling him about it."

"You had a sister? What happened to her?"

"She died when she was a baby. Actually, it sort of makes sense, now that I think about it. My mom's always gotten weepy at big events. Our birthdays, holidays, things like that. I thought she was just being hormonal or whatever, but now . . . I think she was remembering Liza. That was her name. I think that all along she's been sad Liza wasn't there with us. I wonder why they never told Tom and me about her."

"Maybe it was too hard for them to talk about."

"Maybe."

They fell into silence, listening to the wind howling outside, the rain sheeting against the boathouse. Felix shifted beside her and then winced.

"Your ankle?"

"Yeah." Felix let out a disgusted snort. "I actually thought I could run all the way to the police station. I figured I could make it there in twenty minutes or less, unless I got to a road that had been blocked or flooded. But it was such a stupid idea. Even if I hadn't jumped—or dropped—out of a window and hurt my ankle, it's so dark outside I wouldn't have been able to see where I was going." He shrugged helplessly. "So much for my big plan to save everyone."

This time, June took his hand in hers and squeezed it. "Thank you for trying to save us."

"What now? What do we do?"

June hesitated. She knew what they needed to do. But she also knew how dramatic it was going to sound, and she wanted Felix to take her seriously.

"I think we might have to kill them before they kill us," she said.

CHAPTER THIRTY-SEVEN

MARLOWE

Marlowe sat on the edge of the sofa, holding Lee's hand in hers. He was still reclining back, cushions propping up his head. He occasionally let out a groan of pain when he shifted his weight. Tom sat opposite them. All three were silent, bracing for whatever was coming next. Isabel had stepped away from the family and was standing off to one side of the living room with Bo, talking to him in low, urgent whispers. Jason and Darcy lingered nearby, but neither one was included in the conversation. Bo was angry, his handsome face fixed in a scowl, but Isabel looked worried.

She should be worried, Marlowe thought bitterly. Isabel had brought the intruders here, into their home. That made her just as culpable for what had taken place there that evening as Bo and Jason were. There was a direct connection between Isabel's plotting and Lee's gunshot wound and Zack's death.

"Stop worrying!" Bo said to Isabel, his voice rising with irritation. "We'll find her. Even if June made it outside, she can't have gotten that far before the storm started back up again."

"What if she went for help?" Isabel asked. "What if she's already at the police station right now, filing a report?"

"There's no way she made it to the police station. And the roads will be flooded and undrivable for hours."

"You don't know that. She could have made it there. And the police could be at that door as soon as the storm lets up." Isabel pointed toward the front entrance of the house.

"Trust me—we'll be long gone before they arrive."

"Bo." Darcy took a tentative step forward. "What's going on? How do you two know each other?"

"Not now, Darcy," Bo said sharply, holding up a hand. "I'm trying to think."

Darcy recoiled, and she bit her lower lip. But instead of backing down, she took another step forward. "I deserve to know the truth. Are you involved with her?"

"Oh, for God's sake." Isabel sighed and threw an exasperated look at Bo. "This is what I was talking about. Bringing her along was a serious lapse of judgment."

"I already told you why I did that. And I don't have to run every decision I make by you first."

"Every person who knows what happened here tonight is a liability. It was supposed to be just you, me, and Jason. And now she knows, and they know." Isabel waved in the direction of Marlowe and her family, and Bo turned to look at them.

"You let me worry about them."

Bo's words spent a spike of fear through Marlowe.

"Bo!" Darcy crossed her arms and stared at him. "Are you two involved? Are you cheating on me?"

He closed his eyes and breathed out a long, measured breath. "No, Darcy. We used to date when we were teenagers. But that was a long time ago."

"Oh. So you were, like, childhood sweethearts?" Darcy's expression softened, but there was still suspicion lurking in her large brown eyes.

"Something like that," Isabel said, glancing at Bo under lowered lashes.

And then Marlowe saw it. She recognized the look in Isabel's eyes. Isabel was in love with Bo. Marlowe didn't know if Bo was aware of her feelings but thought he probably was. Bo was handsome, charming, and engaging, and, perhaps most importantly, he had a sexual energy that was hard to miss. But Marlowe thought that while it might be easy for him to manipulate sweet, stupid Darcy, Isabel would be harder for him to control.

The wind was blowing fiercely again, howling against the house, and large booms of thunder began sounding at regular intervals. The house shuddered, but something had changed, Marlowe thought. The air felt different, as though the storm was coming right through the walls, making its way inside. A loud crash sounded from upstairs.

"Did you hear that?" Jason asked, looking up at the ceiling.

Bo nodded. "She's upstairs."

Marlowe's heart lurched with dread. June was still in the house? She'd allowed herself to hope that her daughter had escaped and was safely at one of their neighbors' houses by now.

Isabel looked up too. "We should go upstairs and see what's going on."

"The last time I left this room, someone escaped." Bo looked over at his brother. "Jason, you go check it out. She must be hiding up there somewhere. Take Darcy with you. Check the closets and under the beds and anywhere else she could be hiding."

Jason nodded and slouched out of the room. Darcy followed him, glancing back over her shoulder at Bo and Isabel.

Lee's grip on her hand tightened, and Marlowe gazed down at him. He was pale but conscious, although his breathing was shallow.

"She'll be okay," Lee murmured. "June's a fighter."

"Unlike me," Tom muttered, so softly it took Marlowe a moment to realize he'd spoken.

"Tom, no," Marlowe said, immediately wanting to smooth over whatever it was he was feeling. It was ridiculous for Tom to think that he could have stopped what had happened here. Bo and the others had obviously planned this, taking care to target them when they were most vulnerable. She wondered if Bo's ugly claim that Lee loved June more had hurt Tom, and she hoped he hadn't taken it to heart. But Tom just shook his head and glanced away.

They all looked up again, this time alerted by footsteps running on the floor above and then Jason pounding the stairs. He burst back into the living room, breathless and his face flushed, Darcy just behind him.

"She's not up there," Jason said.

"Are you sure? You didn't look for very long," Bo said.

"There was a window open in one of the bedrooms. She must have jumped out of it."

Jumped? Marlowe thought numbly. *June jumped out of a second-story window?* Was that the sound she and Bo had heard while they were in Lee's office? But the windows upstairs were so high off the ground. There was no way she could have jumped out of one and not seriously injured herself. And *why* would she have done that? If June's plan was to head outside, why wouldn't she have just left through the front door? The thought of her daughter hurt and outside facing the hurricane-force winds and rain caused Marlowe's stomach to tighten and lurch. She had to force herself to breathe.

"I wouldn't be surprised if she broke both her legs. But hey, at least she won't get very far," Bo said. "She's probably out there now, getting blown away by the storm. What was the noise up there?"

"The window was still open, and the wind knocked a picture off the wall. I closed it," Darcy said. "But it's a mess up there. The wind was tearing through the room. It was wild."

Bo shrugged this off but began to pace around, clearly trying to figure out his next course of action. June disappearing hadn't been part of his plan. Which meant . . . Marlowe swallowed. June had been right. Bo didn't want to leave behind any witnesses. She wasn't sure if this had always been his plan or if that had changed once Jason had killed Zack.

Even if it had been an accident, it was still a death that had taken place during the course of a crime. Marlowe had watched enough old *Law & Order* episodes to know that would classify Zack's death as a felony murder, and Bo, Jason, and even Darcy would all be held accountable.

If they were caught.

But now that June was gone, and Bo didn't know where she'd gone, things had changed. He wouldn't be able to simply vanish. There was a witness out there on the loose. Two, if Mick had really driven away, although Marlowe doubted that Bo's story about Mick driving off in the middle of the hurricane was true. For someone who professed to hate liars, Bo had no compunction against lying himself.

And despite her terror, Marlowe felt another glimmer of hope. June had survived the drop from the window. She might be hurt, but she must have gotten away, or Bo would have seen her when he had gone outside to investigate. Marlowe wished she'd had the foresight to give June the mysterious cell phone, which was still nestled in her pocket. Cell service wasn't working now, but maybe it would be once the winds died down.

"What now?" Isabel asked, turning to Bo. "We can't go out and look for her in the storm."

"As soon as it's safe to go outside, we'll find her," Bo said grimly.

Isabel threw up her arms. "We have to get out of here as soon as possible. For all we know, June could have already found help. The police could be here any minute."

But Bo was shaking his head slowly. "I don't think so. The police aren't going to risk their necks going out in the middle of a hurricane. We've got a little time." He turned his head to look at Marlowe. "How do you think we should pass the time, Marlowe? Maybe we should play my game again."

"Bo! No!" Isabel stepped in front of him. "We don't have time for this."

"Don't tell me what to do, Isabel," Bo said. His voice was calm, but there was an ugly undercurrent to it that chilled Marlowe. He stared at Isabel for a long moment. Marlowe thought that the young woman would bend under the force of his gaze, but Isabel surprised her. She drew herself up, squared her shoulders, and stared right back at him.

"Your current plan isn't working. We need to make a new one."

Bo nodded, as if considering her words. He rotated his head, cracking a joint in his neck. His hand went to the spot he'd cracked, and he rubbed it gently.

"We could do that," he agreed. "Or you could tell Marlowe all about how you've been fucking her husband for the past six months."

CHAPTER THIRTY-EIGHT

FELIX

Felix and June sat together, leaning back against the wall of the boat-house, listening to Celeste rage outside. Felix's ankle was throbbing. He shifted, trying to find a more comfortable position, but the movement caused him to flinch with pain.

"Your ankle is bad, isn't it?" June asked.

Felix nodded, and June leaned forward to examine it.

"I think it's swollen," she said. "And the skin is darker. That probably isn't good. Hold on."

June hopped up and went over to the cupboards that were built in along the opposite wall.

"Is there any food in there?" Felix asked hopefully. "I'm starving."

"How can you be hungry at a time like this? But I wouldn't be surprised if my dad has something stashed in here. Always be prepared, as he likes to say. What do I see here?" June pulled out a bottle of whiskey and held it up for Felix to see. "My dad hid some booze in here. Do you want some alcohol to dull your pain?"

"No thanks. It would probably just make me puke."

"Probably." June put the whiskey back and then pulled out a few more items. "I have no idea why, but there are granola bars and cans of Vienna sausages in here. What do you think went into that deci-sion-making process? Do you think my dad is out on the boat and suddenly thinks, 'You know what I'd love right now? A Vienna sausage. Washed down with some whiskey.'"

"No idea, but hand them over," Felix said.

June skirted back around the boat and handed Felix a box of unopened granola bars and two small cans of sausages, along with a couple of bottles of room-temperature water. Felix used the built-in tab to pop the top of one of the cans, pulled out a few sausages, and shoved them in his mouth. He chewed thoughtfully.

"These are weirdly gross and good at the same time," he said.

June went back to the cupboard and then returned with her arms full of life jackets.

"What are those for?"

"I'm going to stack them up, and you can rest your ankle on them."

She piled the orange life jackets in front of Felix. He gingerly shifted his leg up onto them, although it hurt like hell to move.

"Ouch," he said. "Why am I doing this?"

"You're elevating it."

"I don't know that elevation will do much to fix a broken ankle."

"Huh. I thought you were supposed to elevate injured limbs. It can't hurt, can it? Hold on—let me grab a blanket out of the cupboard."

June joined Felix on the floor and wrapped a soft plaid blanket around their shoulders. Between the wind and their damp clothes, they were both chilled. The storm was blowing at full throttle, and every time the wind gusted up from the water, the whole structure shook under the force. Felix wondered if the storm would rip the roof right off but decided it was probably better not to think about it. And it was sort of cozy to be here, tucked under a blanket with June by his side.

"I have an idea," June said. "But you're going to think it's crazy."

Felix popped another Vienna sausage into his mouth, and after he'd chewed and swallowed, he said, "Tell me."

June outlined her plan. She was animated, her eyes bright, her hands gesturing as she spoke.

Once she'd finished, Felix nodded. "You're right—that's insane."

"Do you have a better idea?"

"Not at the moment. But if you give me a few minutes, I can probably come up with one that doesn't involve us going outside in a Category 5 hurricane, running up the lawn to your house—ignoring the fact that my ankle is broken, so I can barely walk—and then what? Oh, right, taking off a storm shutter and breaking a window to distract the psychos who are holding your family hostage. And all in the hopes that Tom takes that opportunity to shoot all of them," Felix said. "Solid plan. Except for the part that this isn't a movie and your brother isn't a superhero, and we'll probably all just die."

"You don't have to be so negative."

"Okay." Felix nodded, although he knew June couldn't see him in the dark. "Why don't you tell me the positives?"

"We'd be doing something," June said. "Not just sitting here waiting for something bad to happen."

"So far, our doing something hasn't gotten us anywhere. Well." Felix shrugged. "I guess it got us to the boathouse. But now I can't walk, and we didn't make it to the police station, and we're stuck here until the storm passes."

"My family's in danger. I need to help them."

"I know." He squeezed June's hand. This was a new thing, their holding hands. He liked it, although he was trying not to read too much into it. "But our getting killed trying to save them isn't going to help. Do you hear the wind?"

Celeste had picked up her previous strength. The wind was shrieking, rain sheeted down, and there were frequent loud booms of thunder. Felix wondered if the second half of a hurricane was more intense than the first half. It sounded like it.

"This boathouse is built to withstand a hurricane, right?" he asked.

"I assume so," June said. "Mick built it. Well, he designed it. But he knows what he's doing." She hesitated. "Knew what he was doing. It's weird talking about him in the past tense."

"Zack too," Felix said but then wished he hadn't. June was already frightened enough without reminding her of the peril her family was facing.

"I know. That was awful. Poor Zack. He was just trying to protect me."

"He was?"

"Yeah, the guy who pushed him—Jason—was all over me. He was touching my hair." June made a face. "It was gross. Zack was trying to make him stop."

"Good for Zack," Felix said, wishing that he had been there and that he had been the one to protect June. He was taller and stronger than Zack had been. That Jason creep wouldn't have been able to push him around so easily. Felix would have shoved him right back.

June shifted, and her arm brushed against his. He was suddenly hyperaware of how close she was and how good she smelled. He wanted to wrap his arms around her and pull her closer but decided against it. It wasn't exactly great timing, considering her family was being held hostage. Instead, Felix grabbed the box of granola bars. He offered one to June. She hesitated.

Felix had noticed when June stopped eating. They used to order pizzas and split them down the middle, pop huge bowls of buttery popcorn to eat while they watched movies, and bike down to Jinxy Cones for strawberry sundaes on hot summer days. That had all changed a year ago. The most he ever saw her consume these days was a Greek yogurt for lunch. June was skinnier than she'd ever been, and he knew she liked being thin. But it worried him, the way her face had hollowed out and her bones protruded. He wanted to tell her that she was pretty no matter what she weighed, but he had never figured out the right words.

"You'll need the energy if you have to run for help," he pointed out.

June finally shrugged and nodded.

"That's true," she said, unwrapping one. "And it's the s'mores flavor. That's my favorite."

"Mine too," Felix said.

They unwrapped their granola bars, and June nudged him with her shoulder. "So what's your plan?"

"The same as before. We keep checking my phone to see if service has been restored and call the police as soon as it has."

June shook her head. "I like my plan better. It's more proactive."

"Maybe, but mine is better if we want to stay alive."

Felix could picture the men waiting for the storm to die down and then heading outside to hunt for June. They would have flashlights and guns and were probably bigger and stronger. June might get lucky and slip away. But if they found her, they would kill her.

Another gust of wind hit the boathouse, and it shook under the force.

June slumped back against the wall. "I really hate them."

Felix squeezed her hand and said, "I hate them too."

"It's more than that." June turned to look at him, her expression serious. "I meant what I said before. I think we might have to kill them. But the part I didn't tell you is that I want to kill them. I want to make them pay for what they did to Zack and Mick."

Felix felt another flicker of fear. But this time, it wasn't over what the guests would do if they found them hidden here. June had always had a quick temper, but he'd never seen her like this. She was so angry she might act without thinking through the consequences. And that could very possibly get them all killed.

CHAPTER THIRTY-NINE

MARLOWE

As Marlowe absorbed Bo's words, she slowly withdrew her hand from Lee's and folded her hands in her lap. She sat very still, her posture straight. The shuttered room was dark, but the light on the side table seemed too bright, like it was a spotlight shining in her face. Thunder boomed outside, close to the house, and Darcy flinched at the noise. The soda Tom had been drinking was sweating beads of water, the droplets running down the side of the can and pooling on the glass-topped table.

Marlowe turned her head to look at Bo. He was watching her, his unusual green eyes bright with interest to see how his latest strike had landed.

He had been targeting her all night, almost like he was trying to break her down, slowly ripping shreds of skin off her bones. All his blows had been carefully aimed at Marlowe's most sensitive spots. Her family's safety. Her husband's love. And now, his fidelity.

It seemed oddly personal for what was otherwise a simple plan to steal a painting. Well, maybe not such a simple plan, considering Bo and his accomplices had timed the theft to take place during a hurricane. But even that had been clever, Marlowe had to admit. They were cut off from the police and from anyone stopping by unexpectedly while the crime took place. And yet stealing the Cézanne was transactional to Bo. He didn't even like the sketch. Exposing her husband's infidelity was meant to hurt her.

"Aren't you going to say anything?" Bo asked.

Marlowe slowly shook her head. She wasn't going to play his truth game anymore. Besides, Lee's and Isabel's shocked silence told her all she needed to know. Neither one was denying it. She just wished Tom wasn't there, sitting across from her, listening. Her son had been through enough that night.

"Come on, Marlowe. You must have questions. How long has it been going on for? How did they meet? Remember how you just happened to run into Isabel at the gallery where she worked and decided to hire her to be your assistant? Whose idea was that, I wonder."

Marlowe's brain turned, and the memory clicked into place. It had been Lee's idea. Of course it had. He'd brought it up over dinner one night at their favorite local Italian restaurant, after Marlowe had admitted how daunting she was finding the task of curating the Bond collection.

"I think it would be different if it wasn't my parents' artwork," she'd said, tearing off a piece of warm bread and dunking it in a dish of olive oil. "Almost every painting has a memory attached to it. Of when they bought it, or why my mother loved it, or even just as a backdrop to my childhood. A painting I'd pass by in the hallway every morning or that hung next to our Christmas tree. It's impossible to remain detached."

Lee twirled a length of pasta around his fork. "Why don't you hire someone to help you? An assistant. Someone who can help you evaluate which pieces should be included."

It was the perfect solution. The more Marlowe thought about it, the more she decided Lee was right. She did need help. Now she just needed to find the right person to hire.

A few weeks later, Lee had suggested they attend the opening of an exhibit at the Mercer Gallery in Miami. The collection on display that night was a series of paintings of oversize flowers in jewel tones, and they were charmingly offbeat. Lee went off to get them drinks, leaving Marlowe to admire an abstract painting of a bright-red poppy on her own.

Marlowe sensed Isabel behind her before she spoke. The younger woman's overpowering perfume wafted toward her, a heavy mixture of roses and musk.

"That's my favorite piece in the exhibit," Isabel said.

Marlowe nodded and turned to look at the younger woman. "I like how joyful and playful it is."

"Yes, joyful. That's the exact word for it." Isabel smiled at Marlowe and then held out a hand. "I'm Isabel Sargent. I'm an assistant here at the gallery."

Marlowe clasped her hand in greeting. "Marlowe Davies. It's nice to meet you."

"And you as well."

Isabel's dress was cut like a men's tuxedo jacket with a neckline so low it was obvious she wasn't wearing a bra. She wore red lipstick, and her long dark hair was pulled back in a low ponytail. Marlowe was a little intimidated by her poise and beauty.

The two women chatted about the collection, and Marlowe was impressed with Isabel's extensive knowledge of the artist and the inspiration for the paintings—and the ease with which she conversed about how it compared to other shows the gallery had hosted that year. When Lee returned, carrying two glasses of white wine, Isabel smiled pleasantly and walked away, leaving behind a trail of her musky perfume. Marlowe had found the young woman before they left and asked for her business card.

Had Lee first suggested she hire Isabel? Marlowe didn't remember it that way. But he probably had found a way to influence her decision. Lee knew her better than anyone, and all spouses learn how to manipulate one another to some extent. Even those with good intentions.

She looked at her husband, reclined next to her on the couch. He had shrunk back into himself. Maybe it was the pain of his injury, or maybe the revelation of his infidelity had diminished him. And for what may have been the first time, Marlowe really saw her husband. Not the man whom she had wanted to be with so badly she had allowed herself to pretend that he hadn't married her for her family's influence and money. She studied his familiar face—his pale eyes, high cheekbones, and thin lips, the lines that fanned out next to his eyes, the crepey texture of his neck.

And even though she didn't want to think about it, she found herself picturing him touching Isabel, pulling her into his arms, bending his head to press his lips against hers, holding Isabel the way he had held her. In that moment, Marlowe felt her heart break.

She'd always thought they had a true love story, the kind that endured even their grief over losing Liza. But she'd been wrong. It had never been real. Their entire marriage had been based on greed.

Lee never loved me, she thought. *Not the way I loved him.*

"I'm sorry. You weren't supposed to find out like this," Lee said.

She nodded stiffly. "I'm sure."

"It's not what you think."

"What do I think, Lee?" Marlowe asked. She remembered the day they'd invited Isabel out on their boat. Marlowe had suggested it, but Lee had enthusiastically gone along with the idea. Of course he had. It was a chance to spend time with Isabel.

Who does that? she wondered. *Who brings their girlfriend along on a family outing?*

"It isn't just . . . it's not a physical thing," Lee continued. "Well, it's not just that. Isabel and I fell in love. We didn't mean for it to happen; it just did."

"You could have come to me. You could have told me you were unhappy."

"I wasn't unhappy. Not exactly."

When did they meet? Marlowe wondered. *And where?* It was hard to imagine where their lives had overlapped. Lee went to his office in downtown Shoreham during the week and spent his weekends with their family or out on his boat. Before Isabel took the job with Marlowe and relocated to Shoreham, she had lived two hours away in Miami. Presumably, her social life had consisted of doing whatever single, glamorous women in the city did. Going to clubs, and gallery openings, and chic restaurants that specialized in fusion food.

Had Lee sought her out? Had he downloaded a dating app onto his phone in order to meet women? And then she remembered her discovery that afternoon.

"That phone I found in the safe was yours." She said the words aloud without thinking. The phone was still in her pocket, and she didn't want Bo to know she had it. But she still looked at Lee for confirmation. He wouldn't meet her eyes. Of course that was what it was. Not that Marlowe had ever been in the habit of tracking who Lee spoke to or texted. But she had occasionally checked up on the twins' phone usage, especially when they were younger and had their first phones. She knew how to access those records on their wireless account. The cheap pay-as-you-go phone had been his workaround in case she got suspicious and checked up on him.

"It's all starting to come back, isn't it?" Bo said. He sounded delighted. "How Lee encouraged you to hire an assistant and then arranged for you to meet Isabel. And she did her homework. Isabel has always been an excellent student. She would have known just what to say to make you want to hire her."

"What's the point of this? Why are you telling her?" Isabel asked Bo, her voice flat.

"Because I want to," Bo said.

"This wasn't part of the plan. You and Jason were supposed to come in, take the sketch, and leave. No one was supposed to get hurt. No one was supposed to find out I was involved. You weren't supposed to bring along a friend." Isabel waved a hand in Darcy's direction. "And Marlowe wasn't supposed to find out about . . ." She stopped without completing the sentence.

"About you and Lee? I think Marlowe might have noticed Lee packing his suitcase and walking out the door," Bo said. "And you two lovebirds running off into the sunset together."

"Shut up, Bo," Isabel said irritably.

Is that what Lee had planned? Marlowe wondered numbly. The twins would be off to college in less than a year. Had he decided that this transition would be the perfect time for him to leave and start an exciting new life with Isabel? How had he planned to explain his abandonment of their marriage to their children and friends? But that was probably the easy part. People always found a way to justify their own bad behavior.

"Why did you want her to work for your wife?" Darcy asked.

Marlowe had underestimated Darcy, who she'd assumed over the course of the evening was not very bright. But Darcy's question was astute. Why would her husband want his mistress to work for his wife? It made no practical sense. It wasn't a convenient way for them to spend time together. Lee was at his office during the workweek, when she and Isabel worked on the Bond collection. Isabel was rarely at the house at the same time as Lee. Maybe it was just that the job allowed Isabel to move to Shoreham, to make it easier for Lee and Isabel to spend time together.

And then her brain turned and clicked once more.

The only reason, the only possible reason, Lee would have wanted to install Isabel as Marlowe's assistant . . . was that he was somehow a part of what was happening in their home that night. He had conspired with her to bring these people into their home that day.

It was worse than an affair, worse than simple, sordid infidelity. Lee had arranged for strangers to invade their home, to endanger their family, to kill Zack. Lee might not have been the one holding a gun or the one who had pushed Zack to his death, but his culpability was even worse. He was a father, a husband. He was supposed to protect his family. And instead, he had put them squarely in harm's way.

But why? That was the part Marlowe couldn't figure out. For money? They had money, more money than they could spend. They had a beautiful home, late-model cars, a boat, nice vacations. Except . . . that money was hers. Lee had signed a prenuptial agreement. And her parents had put the money Marlowe inherited from them into a trust. If she and Lee divorced, he wouldn't be able to touch the capital. He wouldn't be penniless, of course. He made a nice income, and they'd made good investments over the years that were marital property, including their house. If they divorced, Lee would be comfortable. But he was used to a different level of wealth and all that it brought.

Lee didn't just want to leave Marlowe. He wanted to leave with his lifestyle intact. Even if that meant taking things that didn't belong to him. And putting his family in danger.

Marlowe stared at Lee. "You son of a bitch."

Bo let out an amused laugh. "And she finally worked it all out. I knew you'd get there eventually. Lee decided to rob you on his way out the door. With Isabel's help."

"Don't act like you're not involved." Isabel put her hands on her hips, her elbows jutting out.

Bo raised an eyebrow. "Does Lee know just how involved I am?"

"What's that supposed to mean?" Lee asked, an edge to his voice.

"That's the interesting thing, Marlowe," Bo said, ignoring Lee's question. "You'd think that a man who married for money would have been a little wiser when a young woman showed up in her tight little outfits, showering him with attention. It never occurred to him that she was playing him the same way he'd played you."

CHAPTER FORTY

ISABEL

Six Months Earlier

Isabel walked in the front door of her Miami apartment and immediately dropped her heavy leather shoulder bag and kicked off her high-heeled pumps. Her feet and back were killing her after a long day of work at the Mercer Gallery. The current show on display was a series of black-and-white photographs of Miami's Art Deco District. Isabel thought they were dull and pedestrian, like what you'd find in a calendar given out by the chamber of commerce, but the show had been surprisingly successful. Half the pieces had sold at the opening the week earlier, and she'd just had a full day of private viewings.

"I made three sales today," Isabel told Bo and Jason, who were sitting on the white leather sofa that Isabel had bought secondhand off Facebook Marketplace. They were drinking beers, their legs sprawled out in front of them. Neither one of them looked like they'd taken a shower after work that day at a local boatyard, power washing boats in dry dock. Isabel wondered if their sweat would stain the leather.

"Can you guys put some towels down so you don't ruin the leather? And, Jason, please get your feet off the table," she said irritably.

"Someone's in a mood," Bo commented, taking a swig from his bottle of beer.

"I'm exhausted. I've been on my feet all day." Isabel sat down on a yellow slipper chair, which was wedged in a corner of the tiny living room. The apartment was claustrophobically small. One of Isabel's favorite fantasies was imagining that she'd one day live in a sprawling house, where she'd be able to walk across her living room without banging her hip against a side table.

Bo set down his beer and stood. "Put your shoes back on. I'm taking you out to dinner."

"Where are we going?" Jason asked. "How about Schooner's? I'm in the mood for one of their burgers."

"Sorry, little bro, but you're not invited. I'm taking my girl on a date."

Isabel was too tired to go out. All she wanted to do was take a nice long shower, put on her pajamas, and zone out to something mindless on TV. But she and Bo never went on dates. They always just hung out at her apartment, which was nicer than the crappy efficiency Bo shared with Jason. And if they went out somewhere, Jason usually tagged along. She couldn't pass up the chance to sit in a restaurant with Bo, just the two of them, maybe holding hands across the table. Isabel could feel herself soften at the idea.

"Where are we going?" she asked.

———

"Wait . . . where are we going?" Isabel asked an hour later. Bo had gotten on I-95, and they'd been driving north out of Miami, already heading past Fort Lauderdale.

"Capital Grille. It's nice. You'll like it. You can get a steak."

"There are steak houses in Miami. Ones that are closer to where we live."

Bo hesitated. Isabel knew him well enough to know he was trying to decide what to tell her. It wasn't exactly that he lied to her. He just heavily edited what he chose to share.

"You know how you've been wanting us to get a place together?" he finally said.

"Only for the past ten or so years," Isabel said and then wished she could swallow the words back. She didn't want to piss him off and ruin the evening.

"I figured out a way for us to do that."

"We can do that now. Between what I pay in rent and what you pay for that shitty place with Jason, we could afford a two-bedroom apartment." This wasn't a new conversation. They'd had it many times. Bo had always been resistant to the idea of them cohabitating.

"I want more for us than that," Bo said. "I want us to have a house. And yeah, Jason might need to live with us. At least for a bit while he gets his shit figured out. But I want us to have a real home. Not just a crappy rental."

And Isabel experienced what she always did with Bo when he talked about their future. That softening, the loosening of her jaw and core, all the places where she held her tension. They understood one another, knew what it was like to struggle, and shared a strong physical attraction. But sometimes, usually late at night when she couldn't sleep, Isabel wondered if he was really the right man for her. Maybe she'd be better off if she found someone who might be a little less attractive, a little less exciting, but more steady and solid. Someone she could build a real life with.

"What's your plan?" she asked, because with Bo, there was always a plan. It was the way his mind worked.

There was another beat of hesitation. "You're going to think this sounds crazy," he said.

"Try me."

"You need to get married." Bo raised a hand to stop Isabel before she had a chance to respond to this. "And then get divorced. And we'll get a nice settlement and be able to set up our own home. Have a future that's not just working sixty-hour weeks and still scrambling for the rent."

Isabel turned to watch the cars pass by on the highway. The sun was starting to set, and everyone's low beams were on. A Dodge Charger raced past them, weaving dangerously in and out of traffic, and Bo swore softly.

"What an idiot," he said.

Isabel had fantasized about Bo proposing marriage before. Of course she had. They'd been together, off and on, for fifteen years. She'd just never imagined he'd suggest she marry someone else.

When Isabel was a sophomore at Florida State University, she and Bo had had one of their breakups. That particular one—and there were many—had occurred after Isabel suggested Bo look into getting licensed as a heating, ventilating, and air-conditioning technician.

"You can make great money, and it will give you stability," she'd said with a peppy enthusiasm that wasn't at all like her. It had felt forced and almost manipulative. Like she was trying to mold him into something he wasn't. But even knowing that, she'd been surprised by his vitriol.

"That is not the life I have planned for myself. And if you knew me at all, you would never even suggest I take a job like that," he'd said through gritted teeth before hanging the phone up and blocking her texts.

Isabel had been devastated, the way she always was when Bo deserted her. She hadn't even understood his anger about her HVAC technician idea. What was wrong with doing HVAC work? It paid well and was in high demand in South Florida. And at that time, Bo had been working odd jobs—a shift at a boatyard here or occasionally crewing on a boat. He always talked about the life he was going to have, where he was successful and admired, but he always spoke of it in vague terms. As though one day everyone would suddenly recognize his genius and hand him the life he thought he was entitled to.

When first days and then weeks had passed without hearing from Bo, Isabel had eventually moved on. She'd even started dating a guy she met in her American history class. James had been good looking, with an easy laugh and a sweet nature. He'd brought Isabel roses on Valentine's Day, and made her a playlist of her favorite songs, and rubbed her shoulders when she was stressed during midterms. And Isabel, who knew she could be remote and prickly, had found herself relaxing into the relationship. James was planning to go on to veterinarian school after he graduated.

"I just want to help animals," he'd said one afternoon when they were lounging in Isabel's dorm room.

Isabel had known in the back of her mind that Bo would pop up again one day, and probably at the least convenient time. And that was exactly what happened. It was James's birthday, and his friends had arranged an impromptu party at a local pizza-and-wings place. Isabel had just left her dorm to head there when Bo appeared in the courtyard outside.

"Hi, beautiful," he'd said.

And then he'd spun his story, as he always did. He'd told her how he had been going through a hard time when she'd made the HVAC pitch, and he knew he'd lashed out at her unfairly. He had been apologetic and sweet and told her that she was an angel. He'd told her he'd been in love with her from the first moment he'd laid eyes on her—and that going forward, everything would be different. He'd take care of her, cherish what they had together. And Isabel had gone right back to him, even though it meant breaking up with a tearful James on his birthday.

James had gone on to veterinarian school and gotten married to a classmate he met there shortly after they graduated. Isabel had seen the photos of the wedding on his Facebook page, bile rising in her throat at the sight of the happy couple, their perfectly photographed faces highlighted like models in a magazine spread.

"You want me to get married. To someone else," Isabel now repeated, the words tasting like ashes in her mouth.

"That's right. It'll go by quick. You'll get the guy's attention, he'll salivate over you, and he'll be hooked."

"So you want me to go fuck some guy for his money. And then take that money and give it to you. Like a prostitute."

"Isabel." Bo's voice was light and full of love. "Of course that's not what I want. But look at how the world is set up. There are people with money, and then there are people like us who do all of the work and never get ahead. We need to change that. To balance the scales."

"But that's ridiculous. Rich men don't just marry young women without having a prenup agreement."

"You'll talk him out of that. I know for a fact that you're very persuasive."

And the worst part was she felt a stab of pride in that moment. That she had the sort of looks and body that would make Bo confident she could get any man she crooked a finger at.

"It sounds like you have someone specific in mind."

"Oh, I do, sweetheart."

And Bo then told her the rest of his plan, which was so ridiculous, so over the top, that Isabel started to feel better. It would never work. She'd go along with it for that one night, and when Bo saw how silly and pointless it was, he would drop the entire silly scheme.

———

Isabel and Bo sat at the bar at the Capital Grille on PGA Boulevard in Palm Beach Gardens. The room was meant to evoke an old-fashioned men's club, with white tablecloths and oil paintings covering the walls, hung in a gallery style. Isabel was sipping a delicious pineapple cocktail and just starting to relax when a group of men entered the bar.

"Game time," Bo said, his voice low in her ear.

The men were all middle aged and were wearing sports coats over open-necked button-down shirts. They looked as if they'd all had a few cocktails already—talking too loudly, one of them stumbling as he approached the bar.

"That's him there. Green-checked shirt, blue sports coat," Bo said. "He has dinner here every second Thursday of the month with the same alumni group."

Isabel scanned the group until she saw him. He was tall with an angular face and high cheekbones, and he looked fitter than the other men he'd come in with. She supposed that was something. But he was also much older than Isabel, with graying hair and a lightly lined face. He looked like someone's dad. The man seemed to sense her eyes on him, because he glanced back at her, his expression curious. Isabel smiled at him, and he smiled back.

"That was fast," Bo said, impressed.

Isabel turned back to her boyfriend, irritation flaring. "I know how to get a man's attention in a bar."

"I know you do. You look really hot tonight."

Most guys get jealous if a man's checking out their girlfriend, thought Isabel. *Mine just wants to pimp me out.*

"Please stop." Isabel raised a hand, palm out. "I'm not doing this."

"At least talk to him and see how it goes. You don't have to sleep with him tonight. In fact, it's probably better that you don't. You should make him work for it."

"Bo!" Isabel set down her empty martini glass on the glossy wooden bar. "I want to go home. I've had a long day, and I'm not in the mood for this."

Bo's expression darkened. "Just do what we talked about. See how it goes."

"I don't want to."

"That's it!" Bo stood suddenly, scraping the barstool back from beneath him. "I've had enough of your shit. All you ever think about is yourself. What about me? What about what I want?" Bo threw down the crumpled cocktail napkin he'd been holding. "Find your own damn way home. I'm leaving."

Bo stormed out of the bar. Isabel watched him go, frozen with shock and embarrassment. Everyone in the bar had heard Bo shout, and their heads swiveled to stare at her, sitting abandoned at the bar. Why had he gotten so angry? And how could he say she only thought about herself? Their entire relationship was on his terms—how he wanted to live, how he didn't feel ready to commit. Isabel had even stayed with Bo when he had gone to jail for six months, convicted of stealing equipment from a boatyard. She'd helped pay for his attorney's fee, even though she couldn't afford it. Didn't her loyalty count for anything?

The bartender appeared in front of Isabel, a practiced smile in place. "Would you like another cocktail?"

Oh my God, Isabel thought. *How much is the bill going to be?* She couldn't afford drinks in a place like this, not when she had next month's rent to worry about. Surely Bo would know that and would come back.

But he didn't return. He had brought her all the way to Palm Beach Gardens, made a scene, and then deserted her. Bo had hurt her in countless ways over the years. But this was inexcusable. It had to be the end. Isabel looked down at her hands and realized they were shaking.

"I'll have one more," she said.

The bartender made an elaborate show of shaking the drink exuberantly in a silver cocktail shaker. When he poured it into a freshly chilled martini glass, it was frothy and a pale lemon color. He placed the drink in front of her on a white cocktail napkin.

"Thank you," Isabel murmured. She picked up the drink and took a sip. It tasted like pineapple and vanilla, and she had to stop herself from gulping it down.

She sensed the man's presence at her side before he spoke.

"Are you okay?" he asked in a warm, solicitous tone.

It was the man Bo had pointed out, the one whom she'd smiled at. *It can't possibly be this easy, can it?* she wondered.

"I'm not sure," she said truthfully. She didn't have to fake the emotional tremor in her voice.

"Do you mind if I sit?" he asked, gesturing toward the stool Bo had just vacated.

"Go ahead." Isabel took another sip of her drink.

"What are you drinking?"

"It's a pineapple martini. The bartender said it's their signature drink. It's good."

He sat and signaled for the bartender. "I'll have what the lady is drinking. And please put her tab on my bill."

Isabel felt her face flush. "You don't have to do that."

"I know, but I want to. I'm hoping I'll be able to talk you into staying for another drink. I can't listen to any more golfing anecdotes." He tipped his head toward his group of rowdy friends at the end of the bar. One of the red-faced men was shouting boisterously, his voice rising up over the crowd. "And hopefully your friend will be long gone by the time you leave." The man held out his hand. "I'm Lee, by the way."

Isabel took his hand.

"Hi, Lee. I'm Isabel. It's nice to meet you."

———

An hour and a half later, Isabel emerged from the restaurant, looking around. She'd told Lee she'd get an Uber home. But then she saw Bo flash the headlights of his pickup across the parking lot and stopped abruptly. He'd waited for her. Had the scene at the bar just been an act? Isabel checked over her shoulder to make sure Lee hadn't followed her out of the restaurant and then headed for his truck.

She opened up the passenger door and stared at Bo. "You fucking asshole."

"What? Come on, Iz—get in the car. We'll talk about it on the way home."

Isabel wanted to slam the door, spin around, and walk away in a grand *fuck you* gesture, one middle finger raised in a salute. But an Uber home would cost a lot, more than she could afford. She deliberated for a moment and then finally climbed into the truck and fastened the seat belt across her shoulder.

"I gather that went well," Bo said.

Isabel crossed her arms. "Just take me home."

Bo was silent as he pulled out of the parking lot and headed toward I-95. He merged onto the highway, and Isabel stared at the window, her head still buzzing from the potent cocktails.

"You talked to him," Bo said. It was a statement, rather than a question, and Isabel turned sharply to look at him.

"You saw us?"

"I went back inside to use the restroom. I poked my head in the bar while I was passing by."

"What if he'd seen you? He thought that after you screamed at me and humiliated me in front of everyone in the bar, you'd left and stuck me with the check. Which you did, you asshole."

"I assumed he'd pick up the tab. Didn't he?"

Isabel dipped her head in acknowledgment. Not only had Lee paid for the cocktails; he had also insisted on buying her dinner. They'd had steaks, creamed spinach, and potatoes au gratin and eaten at the bar. Everything had been delicious—decadent, even. It had somehow, after Bo's scene and her own agitation, turned out to be a lovely evening.

"Did he like you?" Bo asked.

"It doesn't matter. He's married," Isabel said flatly.

"He's married for now. That doesn't mean he'll stay married."

Isabel let out a disgusted snort. "So I'm supposed to break up his marriage? No thanks."

"If he was interested in staying married, he wouldn't be buying you drinks in a bar." Bo drummed his fingers on the steering wheel.

He seemed oddly upbeat for a man who had just sat in a parking lot while another man bought his girlfriend dinner, Isabel thought. If the positions were reversed, she'd have been wildly jealous.

"Why are you doing this?" Isabel asked.

"Because I want us to be together," Bo said simply.

"We can be together without me throwing myself at a married man!"

Bo pulled the car over onto the shoulder and rolled to a stop next to a battered guardrail, the top bent from a past impact. *Someone might have died here,* Isabel thought. The traffic passing them on the highway seemed faster than normal, the cars blurs as they sped by. Bo turned to look at Isabel, and her anger and frustration turned into something else. Fear. Isabel loved Bo, had been in love with him for fifteen years. He was charming, and funny, and so incredibly sexy. But he could also be unpredictable and even dangerous, if pushed.

"What are you doing?" Isabel asked, trying not to sound as nervous as she felt.

"What kind of a life do you think we'd have, Isabel? Let's say we ran down to city hall tomorrow and got married. What would happen then? Do you want to know? Because I can tell you. We'd work at our shitty low-paying jobs for years, you at the gallery, me at the boatyard. Or maybe we'd move on to other shitty low-paying jobs. We'd spend nearly every penny we made renting some crappy apartment with paper-thin walls and cockroaches running around the kitchen. If we were very lucky and didn't have any emergency expenses—like one of the cars breaking down or an unexpected pregnancy—we might save up a little bit of money to buy some shitty little house on a shitty street with shitty neighbors. The kind of neighbors who play the music too loud at night and break in to steal your television when you're not at home. And then maybe we'd have kids who would go to the same shitty school that the shitty neighbors' kids attend. And every day we'd struggle and skimp and worry about the power bill and the cost of groceries, and we'd never get ahead, not one single day of our lives. Maybe for our twentieth anniversary, we'd save up to take a cheap weekend cruise that we booked at a discount.

"Is that what you want in life? Because I don't think you do. Hell, you work in an art gallery surrounded by rich people and their nice things. And you want all of those things for yourself, don't you? You love expensive clothes, and shoes, and handbags. You want to walk into one of those fancy boutiques where the clerks work on commission and have them swarm all over you. You want a nice house in a good neighborhood, where everyone's got a designer dog and the kids all get a new car on their sixteenth birthday."

Isabel suddenly felt very tired and chilled by the air-conditioning in the truck. She pressed her fingers at the bridge of her nose, willing herself not to cry. Because she did want all those things—the house, the clothes, everything. When she was younger, she had thought it was only a matter of time and hard work. But somewhere around her thirtieth birthday, Isabel had started to realize that not everyone got to have the future they dreamed about.

"It's not bad to want things," she said. "It's not bad to want a better life for yourself."

"No, it's not. And you deserve to have everything you want. We both do. And I've figured out a way for us to have the life we want."

"There has to be another way. One that doesn't involve me trying to seduce a married man away from his wife. We'll get better jobs. You can go to college and get your degree."

Isabel didn't know why she was trying to talk him into it. She already knew he wouldn't go to college, wouldn't work hard to improve his life. Bo had already proved, time and time again, that he wasn't interested in hard work. And she also knew that he wasn't good for her. Thinking that someday they'd share a normal life together was just another fantasy, in a life that had already been poisoned by fantasies.

"There isn't another way." Bo turned his signal indicator on and began to accelerate, merging his truck back onto the highway. "Some people are born into wealth and status. And then there are those of us who have to reach up and take it."

She considered Lee, who had been kind and even attractive for an older man. He'd also had impeccable manners. He hadn't pretended to accidentally graze the side of her breast with his arm or pressed his leg against hers underneath the bar. He'd asked her questions, and listened to her answers, and laughed at her jokes. He had told her he was married but also that he wasn't happily married. He'd waved his hand thoughtfully as he'd said it, adding that he and his wife had grown apart over the years and that it was sad but not a tragedy, that these things happened. Some relationships just naturally wound down over time.

After they had eaten, Isabel had thanked him for dinner and stood to leave. Lee had reached out, touched her wrist, and asked her almost shyly if he could have her number. There had been a spark there, in that moment when his fingers lightly stroked her skin. Isabel had a feeling she'd hear from him soon.

As they sped south toward Miami, Isabel finally looked at Bo, his handsome profile dimly lit by the high-mast lights that stretched over the highway.

"Why Lee? Why are you so fixated on him? This entire plan is ridiculous, but even if I was going to go through with it—which I'm not—why not find someone who isn't already married?"

Bo was silent for so long Isabel thought he was ignoring her question.

"Because it has to be him," Bo finally said. "That's why."

CHAPTER FORTY-ONE

FELIX

Felix and June looked up at the same time, staring at the ceiling of the boathouse.

"Did you hear that?" June asked.

Felix nodded. "It sounds like the wind is letting up."

"The hurricane must be passing. It's finally over!"

"There's no way to know that for sure without looking at a weather map. This could just be temporary. Another band of the storm could still blow through." Felix pulled out his phone and tapped on the weather-map app, but it didn't load. There still wasn't any service. He cursed silently. Felix wanted evidence that the swirling circle of the storm had moved past Shoreham before June even thought about going outside.

She had already hopped to her feet and was pacing around like a caged animal. She looked like Felix felt before a basketball game, revved up on adrenaline.

"You can't go outside yet," he said, even though he knew she wouldn't listen. He wasn't sure what the right course of action was. Stay, go, pursue, hide. He just wanted her safe.

"It's time," June said. "I'm going to go try to find help."

"Just wait a little longer, until we know for sure."

But she was already shaking her head. "I can't wait. I need to get going."

Thunder boomed outside, followed by a flash of lightning at the windows. Felix jumped.

"That sounded like it was still close by."

"It's passing. The thunder sounds further away than it did before. I'll be fine." June stopped and looked down at Felix, who was still sitting on the floor, his ankle propped up on the stack of orange life vests. "But you can't stay here."

"Why not?"

"Bo or Jason might come in here looking for me. If they find you sitting there, they'll shoot you."

Felix felt a chill pass over him. Normally, when people spoke like this, it was hyperbole. *You're dead* or *He's going to kill you*, said jokingly. But he knew June wasn't exaggerating. The intruders had already killed two people. They wouldn't hesitate to kill him too. Felix glanced down at his ankle, which was throbbing, the skin mottled black.

"I can't go with you," he said. "I'll just slow you down."

"I know. You're going to have to hide until I get back. They don't know you exist. But if you're hidden, you'll be safe."

Felix looked around the one-room boathouse, most of which was taken up by the *Dreamweaver*. "Where am I supposed to hide? I don't think I'll fit in the cupboards where you found the Vienna sausages."

"Probably not," June agreed. Then her face brightened, the way it always did when she had a new idea. "I know! You can hide in the head!"

"What's that?"

"The bathroom onboard the boat."

"The boat has a bathroom?" Felix looked up at the enormous boat skeptically. Although the Davieses had invited him many times, he'd never stepped foot on the *Dreamweaver*.

"Yes, of course. There's a galley and living quarters belowdecks." June patted the side of the boat. "What did you think? That we jump off the boat every time we have to pee?"

"I have literally never wondered how people pee when they're on a boat."

Felix had been terrified of the water his entire life, or for as long as he could remember. He couldn't even sit at the side of June's pool and dangle his feet into the tranquil aqua-blue water. It was an unfortunate phobia to have, considering that he lived in Florida, just a few miles from the beach. Half his friends practically lived at the beach, surfing the waves or playing volleyball at the nets the city had set up. And he didn't even know why it frightened him so much. His mom had assured him that he'd never had any traumatic water-based incidents when he was little. All he knew was that whenever he got near the water, his chest tightened, his pulse accelerated, and he felt an overwhelming urge to run as far away from it as possible.

"We pee in the head. And it's the perfect place for you to hide." She tilted her head, considering. "You'd probably be more comfortable in the living room, but there isn't a door to the cabin, so if Bo or Jason looked down there, they'd see you right away. I think the head would be safer."

"No thanks. I'm good. I'll be fine here." Felix patted the floor. "And it hurts too much to move."

"It will hurt more to be shot. Come on—don't worry. The boat isn't going to float away. It's just sitting in dry dock. But come on. We have to hurry."

June reached down, and, clasping Felix's hand, she helped pull him to his feet. Or foot, rather, since he couldn't put any weight on his right ankle. They moved slowly, Felix's arm around June's shoulders, as he hop-walked toward the ladder on the side of the boat. Felix used his upper-body strength to haul himself up the short ladder and onto the deck. He looked around unhappily. Even if the boat was in dry dock, it was still a boat.

"Down here," June said.

She helped Felix navigate down a flight of stairs that led below-decks. They passed through a narrow galley, a living room with a sectional couch and a dining table, and then into a bedroom. A small bathroom was off to one side. With each step, Felix felt a fresh stab of pain in his ankle. He hoped June couldn't see the tears in his eyes.

"I don't like this," he said, once he was sitting on the toilet.

June hesitated, peering at him. "You're not going to puke, are you?"

"I wasn't planning on it." This was not how Felix wanted June to think of him. "Don't worry. I'll be fine."

"I'm going to turn off the lights when I leave, so it's going to get dark in here."

"Wait. Take my phone with you," Felix said, handing it to her. "You may need it. And here—take the hammer too."

"In case I find a random loose nail that needs hammering?"

"No. In case you need to hit someone over the head with it."

"Or break a window," June said, looking down at the hammer clasped in her hand.

"No! You said you were going for help. Promise me you're not going to do that stupid thing where you try to cause a distraction that you were talking about earlier."

"It's not that stupid."

"Promise me," Felix insisted.

"Okay, okay. I promise." June turned to go.

"June?" Felix said. He suddenly felt anxious at her departure. "You won't forget that I'm here, right?"

She smiled at him, that closed-lip, catlike smile he loved. "Not a chance."

CHAPTER FORTY-TWO

Tom

Tom sat hunched forward on the sofa, trying to process what was happening around him.

Marlowe stood abruptly and moved to sit beside him on the sofa, her posture stiff, her shoulders tensed. Lee still lay on the opposite sofa, staring up at the ceiling, occasionally wincing when he moved. Jason and Darcy occupied the pair of leather chairs next to the sofas. Jason's shoulders were slumped, his arms resting on his legs, and his eyes unfocused. Darcy kept glancing over to where Bo and Isabel stood in the arched doorway that led into the front hallway, having another heated whispered conversation.

Tom wondered where June and Felix were and if they'd managed to find someone to help them—and, if they had, how long it would be until that help arrived. He could feel the cold weight of the gun tucked into his shorts, the metal digging into his skin.

If help doesn't come soon, I'm going to have to do something, he thought.

Tom had never had an affinity for violence. He knew kids who did. When they were in the sixth grade, Aiden Powell had invited him over to his house once to hang out. While Tom was there, Aiden had trapped one of the little green lizards that ran wild on his patio and used a pocketknife to cut off its tail, holding the squirming body up with a look of fascinated pleasure on his face. The casual cruelty had so sickened Tom he'd called his mother and asked her to pick him up early. He'd told her he wasn't feeling well, which wasn't a lie, and he'd kept his distance from Aiden after that. But even normal, nonpsycho kids liked playing first-person-shooter games, like *Call of Duty* and *Doom*, and would laugh when they blew out the brains of a bad guy. Tom had never gotten into those games, never thought it was fun to shoot imaginary characters on a virtual platform.

The idea of shooting real people inside his home was even less appealing.

But he knew he could do it. Or he knew he would have to do it. Even though he couldn't hear what they were saying, he could tell by the way Isabel was whisper-shouting at Bo that she was arguing against more violence. And Bo, who had his arms crossed and his eyes narrowed, his expression intractable, was clearly refusing to agree to Isabel's demand. Tom and his parents—and possibly his sister and Felix, too, if they hadn't gotten safely away—were all in danger. It wasn't *if* it would happen . . . it was *when*.

At some point, before the night was over, there was going to be more violence. And Tom was going to have to pull the gun out of his shorts and shoot one or both of the men. Although he didn't think he'd be able to shoot both before they returned fire. But maybe he could take out one. Jason was closer, and since he was staring blankly into space, Tom was pretty sure he could shoot him right now, killing Jason before anyone had a chance to react.

But Bo was the more dangerous of the two. And he probably had excellent reflexes. If Tom shot Jason, Bo would shoot him. The better plan would be to shoot Bo first and then worry about Jason. Tom didn't love his odds of success. If you counted Darcy and Isabel, it was four against three, and his father was too injured to be any help.

Or is it five against two? Tom suddenly wondered.

He looked at Lee lying on the sofa. He still loved his father, of course, but it was no longer the pure and uncomplicated emotion it had been before the storm. It was now mixed with something that felt like hatred. Lee had had an affair with Isabel and betrayed Tom's mom, which would have been bad enough on its own. But that selfish act had also led to these people being in their home—and all the violence that had spun out from there. It had led to Zack's death. And that was unforgivable.

Tom glanced at his mom, who was pale and still. He wondered if she was in shock.

"Are you okay?" Tom asked softly.

Marlowe started and then nodded.

"What's that sound?" Bo asked, his voice cutting across the room.

Tom listened but couldn't hear anything. And then he realized that was what Bo was hearing . . . nothing. Well, not nothing, but the sounds of the storm were abating. The wind was still whistling, but the gusts were losing strength and were no longer shaking the house. The rain was heavy but not torrential. How long had it been since the eye had passed? He had no idea. It could have been thirty minutes or two hours. The weirdness of the night and the shock of everything that had happened had made time soft and flexible, instead of the usual steady, reliable march he was used to. And Tom didn't have his phone with him, so he couldn't check to see what time it was. He thought of the wristwatch sitting in his dresser drawer upstairs, the one his grandparents had given him for his sixteenth birthday. He hadn't worn it since the day they had given it to him, and he'd put it on because he hadn't wanted to hurt their feelings.

If I make it through tonight, I'm going to wear that damn watch every day for the rest of my life, Tom thought grimly.

"The storm's letting up," Bo said. "We need to be ready to go."

Jason jumped up from his chair and went to stand by his brother, waiting for further instruction. Tom wondered if he had just missed his last best chance to take out one of the two men.

"What's the plan?" Jason asked.

"We need to go look for the girl. I bet she's hiding out there some-where. This might be our best chance to find her."

"We need to get on the boat and get out of here before the police show up," Isabel insisted.

Tom wondered if their boat had even survived the storm. It wasn't uncommon for hurricanes to scatter boats, like a toddler throwing a handful of Legos across the room.

"We have some time. The wind's just now letting up." Bo looked at Jason. "Go outside and see if she's hiding out there somewhere. I saw a boathouse down by the shore. She might be in there."

Jason nodded. "What do I do if I find her?"

Bo looked at his brother, his gaze steady and level. "Bring her back here."

Jason nodded once and turned to go.

Tom's heart began to beat wildly. This was it. This was his chance. When Jason went outside, he would shoot Bo. He forced himself to draw in a deep breath, trying to calm his nervous system. There was a trick his surfing instructor had taught him years ago. Instead of wasting energy wondering if you could do something, you pictured yourself doing it. And so Tom did just that. He remembered how to shoot from the afternoon he'd spent at the gun range with his dad. He imagined standing and pulling the gun from his shorts. He thought of how the weight of the gun would feel in his hand, his fingers wrapped around the grip. He pictured pointing it at Bo and then squeezing the trigger back until a bullet exploded out of the gun. And he'd continue to fire until Bo was on the ground, not moving.

Suddenly, there was a loud crash from somewhere in the house. It sounded like glass shattering, and the pressure inside the house shifted as the wind blew down the hallways and into the living room.

"What was that?" Jason asked from across the room.

"June," Bo said. A smile spread over his face. "She decided to save you a trip outside, little brother. Go get her and bring her in here."

"Where is she?" Jason asked, looking around him, as if June would just pop out.

"I don't know. Go look around. Take Tom with you." Bo gestured at Tom with his gun. "Go on—get up and go with him."

Tom felt his mouth opening and closing as he tried to think of a good reason why he should stay where he was. If he left with Jason, he would lose the chance to shoot Bo.

"I said get up," Bo said, pointing his gun at Tom, who immediately put up his hands.

Tom stood, trying to decide what to do. If he and Jason were alone in the house, he'd have to take the chance to shoot him instead. He knew it was more important to neutralize Bo, but he was out of options, and they were running out of time. Tom drew in another deep breath and followed Jason out of the living room. The wind was stronger there, and there were papers blowing everywhere.

"Where is it coming from?" Jason asked.

"I'm not sure. My mom's office, maybe?"

"Go on." Jason lifted his chin. "You first."

Not ideal, Tom thought, but he turned left and walked down the hallway, into the wind. The doorway to his mother's office was off to the right, just before the kitchen, and Tom stepped inside.

Marlowe's office had windows along the back wall that looked out onto the river, which Tom and Zack had covered with hurricane shutters earlier that day. But now, one of the shutters was off, and a window had shattered. The wind was gusting inside, scattering papers off Marlowe's desk and swirling them around the room. The storm was losing strength, but the wind was still forceful enough to knock over several of the large glossy art books on the built-in bookshelves. A collection of nautical-themed paintings rattled on their hooks.

Tom went to the window, wondering how it had broken. Fragments of glass were scattered across the floor. June or Felix, or the two of them together, must have removed the storm shutter and broken the window,

Tom thought, his heart starting to beat a little faster. But why? To cause a distraction?

"What the hell?" Jason asked, walking by Tom to examine the window. He lifted a hand, as if that would ward off the wind whistling into the room, and leaned toward the window. "How did it break?"

This is it, Tom thought. The moment had arrived for him to act. He reached down to his shorts, his shaking fingers closing on the grip of the gun. Just as he was pulling out the gun and preparing himself to shoot the man in front of him, something at the window caught his eye. It was dark outside, and the office was lit, so it took Tom a few beats to realize that June was standing there, her hair blowing around her pale face as she peered into the house. She looked like a ghost.

"Jesus Christ," Jason said, startled by her sudden appearance.

June lifted her arm, and Tom saw that she was holding a hammer. She slammed it into another pane. The window cracked, jagged lines spreading out across the glass. June raised the hammer, and this time she threw her arm back and then stepped forward as she swung it as hard as she could against the window. The pane shattered with a loud crash, and the wind sprayed fragments of glass into the room.

Jason let out a shout and raised his arms up to protect his face from getting cut by the glass blowing toward him.

Now, Tom told himself, and he raised his arm, his finger finding the trigger.

Jason made a strange gurgling noise, his hands going to his neck. He staggered back a few steps, and Tom had to jump out of his way to avoid Jason colliding with him.

What happened? Tom wondered.

And then he saw it. A large, jagged shard of glass was stuck in Jason's throat. Blood spurted from the wound, more blood than Tom would have thought possible from a cut that size. It was everywhere, running down Jason's neck, soaking his T-shirt, splattering on the basket weave sisal rug. Still clutching his neck, Jason sat heavily on the ground, his fingers fumbling at the glass, trying to pull it out. But there was too much blood, or maybe he was too panicked, because he couldn't get ahold of it.

Jason looked up at Tom, his eyes wide with shock.

"Help me," he said. The words were so strangled Tom wondered if Jason was choking. But on what? His own blood? Tom realized the shard of glass must have cut into an artery in Jason's throat.

Jason's hands were still scrabbling at his neck, frantically trying to dislodge the glass. He coughed, a horrible wet sound that made Tom's skin crawl. His breathing became labored as he fought against the life draining away from him. And then it was suddenly over, faster than Tom would have thought possible. Jason suddenly went still and fell backward, his head hitting the carpeted floor, blood still seeping from his neck.

Tom took a tentative step forward to look. Jason stared up with blank, open eyes. He looked dead. Tom wondered if he should check his pulse to be sure.

A banging noise on the window made Tom startle and look up. June stood just outside, waving at Tom to get his attention. When their eyes met, she waved her hands toward herself.

"Come on," she mouthed.

Tom hesitated, not sure what to do. This was his chance to escape. He could join June, and hopefully Felix, and the three of them could run for help. But he still had the gun. Shouldn't he go back and try to shoot Bo before he hurt their parents? But then June slapped the palm of her hand on one of the still intact windowpanes and this time yelled, "Come on! Hurry!"

There was no way Bo and the others in the living room hadn't heard her raised voice. Tom glanced back, wondering if Bo would come storming into the office at any moment. He hurried toward the window, his feet crunching on the glass scattered over the floor. Tom unlocked it and slid it up. More glass fragments rained down, and he could feel them nicking his hands and arms, drawing blood. Tom sat on the windowsill, the wind stinging his face and blowing back his hair. Then he swung his legs over the sill and dropped into the darkness, landing on the grass next to where his sister stood. She hugged him briefly.

"Is Jason dead?" she asked.

Tom nodded, still feeling dazed by what he'd just witnessed.

June's lips curved up in a grim smile. "Good," she said. "One down. But come on—we have to get out of here before Bo comes to look for you."

"Where's Felix? Did you find him?" Tom was hoping their friend had been able to run for help during the eye and that the police had already been alerted to their dire situation.

"He's in the boathouse. He broke his ankle jumping out of the window, and he can barely walk."

"Damn it." Tom ran a hand over his face. "What about Mom and Dad? We can't just leave them in there."

"Dad can't walk. We're going to have to go get help."

"I can go back and shoot Bo." Tom held up the gun he was still clutching in his right hand.

June hesitated, deliberating. Tom knew she was weighing the odds of success against the price of failure. She reluctantly shook her head. "It's too risky. If you miss, he could shoot you. He's planning on killing all of us. You know that, right?"

Tom nodded. "Yeah, I figured. He doesn't want to leave any witnesses behind."

"Let's go. We'll go from house to house until we find someone who's home. We can't be the only idiots who stayed in town for the storm."

CHAPTER FORTY-THREE

ISABEL

Isabel stood in Marlowe's office, the wind gusting in through the broken windows, and stared down at Jason's body, her hands pressed over her mouth to stop herself from screaming. She had known Jason since he was a scrawny and awkward thirteen-year-old who'd stuttered and been unable to make eye contact—and the only person who cared about him had been his older brother.

Bo. She looked back over her shoulder, toward the door of the home office, wondering how she was going to go back to the living room and tell the man she had spent half her life in love with that his younger brother was dead.

Isabel didn't want to look any closer, but she forced herself to. There was a large shard of glass stuck into Jason's neck. From the amount of blood that covered him, soaking through his shirt and onto the carpet beneath him, Isabel guessed that the glass had cut into an artery. His eyes—green like Bo's but less intense, as if the color had been diluted—stared up in lifeless surprise.

It was just one more fucked-up thing to happen on this completely fucked-up day.

She wasn't sure if Jason's death was an accident or if he'd been killed intentionally. But Tom was gone, and wind gusted in through the open window he'd obviously left through. It was only a matter of time before he found help and the police arrived. And if she and Bo were still here, in this house, they would spend the rest of their lives in jail.

Isabel put her hand over her face, absorbing this stark reality. And perhaps the worst part was this was all her fault. She was the one who had set the events of that evening into motion.

At first, she had pretended to go along with Bo's original plan. She didn't know why, because she hadn't wanted to. But Bo had always held this power over her, had gotten her to do things she didn't want to do. It just used to be small things, like when Bo would get her to flirt with the clerk at the 7-Eleven while he stole a six-pack of beer out of the cooler.

Lee had called her the night after they'd met at the Capital Grille and invited her out for another dinner, this time at Café Boulud in the Brazilian Court Hotel in Palm Beach. Over the assortment of petits fours, Lee casually mentioned that he'd booked a room upstairs, and Isabel, by then pleasantly drunk on a nice French pinot noir, accepted his invitation to join him there. By their third date, Lee told her he was in love with her. By the fifth, he announced he was planning on leaving Marlowe. And within a few months, he had arranged for Isabel to take the job with Marlowe so that Isabel could relocate to Shoreham and be closer to him. He rented an oceanfront apartment for her near his office and visited her there as often as he could.

But Lee didn't leave Marlowe. At first, he made excuses—it wasn't the right time, he wanted to wait until the twins left for college. But eventually, he admitted that the money was Marlowe's. He made a decent living, but once he left her, he wouldn't be able to access any of the substantial capital he and Marlowe lived on.

And Isabel didn't really mind. She'd already decided during those months when she worked with Marlowe and then fucked her husband in the apartment he paid for—she had made up the story about her rent increase, just because she was feeling spiteful—that she couldn't marry Lee. She liked him more than she thought she would. He was smart, and erudite, and a more skillful lover than she would have guessed. But it occurred to her, like a creeping rot, that Bo simply wasn't worth it. She had built up this idea of him, of being with him, into some sort of ultimate life goal. But did she really want to end up with a man who had no ambition or work ethic and was happy to pimp out his girlfriend for financial gain? No, she did not.

She told Bo she needed to see him, planning to tell him that she was done. She'd get her old job back at the gallery, or another one like it, and move on with her life. It would be hard work, but she was used to that. At least it would be honest, and she would be free to have a future that wasn't entangled with Bo's. They arranged for him to come up to visit her in Shoreham one weekend when Lee would be out of town with his family. The Davieses were going on a road trip to look at prospective colleges the twins might apply to.

The day before he left on the trip, Lee came by the apartment to see her. Isabel needed to end her relationship with him, too, but she also needed a place to live until she found somewhere else to rent. As they were lying in bed together, the afternoon sunlight streaming in and the gentle roar of the waves rolling onto shore outside, Lee said, "I have an idea."

Isabel looked up at him, her hair falling around her bare shoulders. She knew he loved her like this, tousled and naked next to him. "What's your idea?"

"Would you know how to sell a painting on the black market?" Lee asked. "Or is that just something I've seen in movies?"

"No, it happens more than you think. There are lots of buyers and sellers who prefer to sell under the table. It avoids all those pesky taxes."

"And you know dealers who would handle that kind of transaction?"

Isabel considered the question. "Probably. Why are you asking?"

"Because I think we should sell the Cézanne sketch," Lee said.

Isabel sat up, stretching her back. "What are you talking about?"

Isabel knew all about the sketch through her work with Marlowe. The Cézanne was going to be the jewel of the Bond collection. Isabel had already suggested that they hang it on its own wall in the new wing of the museum, to amplify its presence.

"The sketch is worth millions," Lee said, his hand cupping the curve of her waist. "A similar one sold at auction for over fourteen, and that was five years ago. We could get more for it today. If you could find someone to sell it."

"That's not the problem." Isabel was already shaking her head as she lay back down. "Marlowe would obviously notice it was missing, and I'm the first person the police would look at. There's no way I'd get away with it."

"I've thought about that too. We'd need to make the theft look like a break-in. And we'd have to make sure you had an alibi for when it was stolen. Do you know anyone who could help us pull that off?"

Isabel hesitated. "I might know someone. Do you remember the man I was with at the Capital Grille the night we met?"

"The jerk who left you there with the unpaid tab?"

Isabel nodded. "You're right—he is a jerk. But this might fall within his skill set."

"Can you trust him?" Lee asked, looking down at her. His face was close to hers, and she could see the faint outline of a scar on his cheek. She reached out and ran the tips of her fingers over the scar. Lee shivered at her touch.

"We can trust him," she said, knowing that the words were a lie as soon as they left her lips.

Isabel wasn't immediately sold on Lee's idea, but she promised him she'd think about it. And she did. She thought about what stealing a valuable piece of artwork would involve—how they could remove the sketch from the house, whom she would contact about selling it, what sort of price they could realistically get for it. Once she started running through all the details and all the potential problems that would arise, she found she couldn't stop thinking about it. She started to envision a different life for herself—one where she would be in charge of her own destiny, free of Bo. And she thought about all that money.

When Bo arrived at her apartment that weekend, she made them sautéed red snapper for dinner, which they ate with a chilled bottle of Sancerre on her little patio that faced out toward the ocean. Over dinner, Isabel told Bo about Lee's idea. The one where they would steal the Cézanne, and sell it through her contacts, and divide the money between them. Isabel kept a few key points to herself. She'd already decided she would let Lee continue to believe that they would use the money to start a new life together, and she would also let Bo believe that she still wanted a future with him. But Isabel planned to take her cut and use it to seed a new life for herself. She'd buy herself a condo, maybe eventually even open her own gallery.

At first, it was hard to convince Bo, who was still set on his plan of Isabel marrying Lee for profit. Bo had always been stubborn, and once set on a course, he liked to see it out. But he gradually came around, especially when she told him how much the Cézanne sketch was worth and how much they could get for it in a private sale. And then, as the sun set and the sky turned pink over the ocean, they made a new plan.

The timing of the theft was Lee's idea. There was a hurricane circling over the Atlantic Ocean, which was expected to make landfall in Florida the following week. At that point, the hurricane was forecast to be a Category 2 storm, and Lee didn't think he'd have any problem convincing his family to stay home instead of evacuating. Isabel would also be there. Lee told her to drop hints to Marlowe that she was uncomfortable being on her own during a hurricane, and if that didn't secure her an invitation to ride out the storm with the family, Lee would suggest it to Marlowe himself. That way Isabel couldn't be blamed for the crime, and she'd be on hand if Bo had any trouble finding the Cézanne. Bo and Jason would dock at the Davieses' house ahead of the storm, pretending to be boaters in distress. While they were in the house, Bo and Jason would wait until a time when Marlowe was distracted and then take the sketch and immediately leave on the boat they'd arrived on. This was the part Isabel was the most worried about, since this would mean Bo and Jason would be heading back out when the marine conditions were still hazardous. But Bo waved away her concerns. He insisted he knew how to navigate a boat in stormy conditions. Isabel knew an art dealer in Miami who would probably be willing to sell the Cézanne privately and discreetly in return for a hefty cut of the proceeds. The family would be able to give a description of Bo and Jason to the police, but the two of them would hide out for a bit, perhaps even leaving the state until things had calmed down.

"We'll go to New Orleans," Bo said. "No one will be looking for us there."

But nothing had gone according to plan. First the storm had intensified into a deadly Category 5 storm. Then Marlowe had unexpectedly put the Cézanne in the safe, and Isabel had no clue how they would get it out of there. It meant sneaking it out of the house was impossible. And then Bo had brought Darcy along, whom Isabel hadn't even known about and whom she was pretty sure he was fucking. Every time the girl was near him, she looked like she'd turned into one of those heart-eyed emoji. It shouldn't have bothered Isabel, who had already decided she was going to part ways with Bo, but it still stung. And then Bo had clearly done something to Mick while they were outside. She didn't know what exactly, but she doubted the man was still alive. And finally, Jason had shoved Zack, and he'd hit his head and died, and everything had spiraled completely out of Isabel's control.

Or had it ever been in her control? Because Isabel now suspected that Bo's plan had always differed from the one the two of them had hatched over dinner that night on her patio. He had picked Lee for a reason. And he'd taken a perverse pleasure in tormenting Marlowe that night.

And now Jason was dead, too, and Isabel was going to have to tell Bo. She wasn't sure what their next step would be. They needed to get out of the house, and quickly. Selling the Cézanne would be more difficult with the notoriety the home invasion was sure to bring, but they could still try. And maybe Isabel would have enough money that she could disappear. She could move to South America or somewhere else where the authorities here couldn't reach her.

"Isabel?"

Bo's shout from the living room was both a question and an order. Isabel straightened and ran a hand through her disheveled hair. She was going to have to pull herself together, because the night wasn't over yet. Not even close. And then she turned away from Jason's body and walked slowly back to the living room.

CHAPTER FORTY-FOUR

MARLOWE

Where is Tom? Marlowe wondered, her body stiff with dread. He'd left with Jason to explore the cause of the crash from the other room, and neither had returned. Instead, there'd been another series of crashes, and then it had sounded like someone was shouting outside the house.

Was that June? Marlowe wondered. Or was the storm causing her to hear things that weren't there?

After the last crash, even more wind began blowing through the house. Papers were still skittering down the hallways, and a half-empty wineglass tipped over, the white wine splattering on the carpet. Bo had sent Isabel off to find out what was happening, and now she hadn't come back either.

What's going on? Marlowe wondered. *And where are my children?*

Although they weren't children, not anymore. But it was hard for her to think of Tom and June as anything other than the two bright-eyed, freckle-faced toddlers they'd once been. Before they'd built this house, they'd lived in a cute little bungalow with a kidney-shaped pool in the back, and she'd spent hours in the water with them, watching them giggle and paddle around with floaties on their arms, and then she'd served them Goldfish crackers and halved grapes in little dishes shaped like Mickey Mouse's head. Marlowe wished she could push a button and be whisked back to that happier, easier time.

Isabel walked back into the living room. She was alone. At the sight of her assistant, Marlowe felt what was quickly becoming a familiar surge of rage over what Lee and Isabel had done. What they had plotted. How they had betrayed her.

Why is it some people are allowed to go through the world, hurting whomever they please, and never face the consequences? she wondered. Although it was hard to believe that would be true this time. There would have to be a reckoning for Zack's death.

Isabel was pale, her expression haunted. She had her arms wrapped around herself, as if she were cold.

"What's wrong?" Bo frowned when he saw Isabel. "Where did Jason go? Did he find June?"

Isabel bowed her head, her long dark hair falling forward. When she looked back up, tears were glistening in the younger woman's eyes. Marlowe's heart started to pound. Something had happened.

"I need to tell you something." Isabel closed her eyes for a moment. "He's dead."

"Who's dead?" Marlowe stood abruptly, thinking, *Not Tom, not Tom, not Tom, please, not Tom.*

Understanding flashed across Isabel's face, and she quickly shook her head at Marlowe.

"Not Tom," Isabel said, her words echoing Marlowe's thoughts.

Relief washed over Marlowe, and she sat back down, clutching her hands together. Tom wasn't dead. At least she knew that.

Bo stared at Isabel. "What the hell are you talking about? Where's Jason?"

"Bo, listen to me. Jason is dead," Isabel said softly. "I don't know exactly what happened, but . . . a piece of glass sliced an artery in his neck. I think it was from a broken window in Marlowe's office. There's a lot of blood, and . . ." She stopped and swallowed and then reached out to touch his arm. "Jason didn't make it."

Bo stared at her for several long beats, as if he couldn't comprehend what she was saying. Isabel looked at him intently, and finally the impact of her words seemed to hit him. Grief broke across his face. Bo lifted a hand to his forehead, touching it, and his body shuddered. Marlowe thought he was crying, but no. His eyes were dry.

"I'm so sorry," Isabel said.

Darcy stood and hurried to Bo's side, but he held out an arm, stopping her before she could wrap her arms around him.

"No." The word was harsh, almost guttural. Darcy froze as if she'd been slapped and then took a step back, wrapping her arms around her slim torso.

"I want to see him," Bo said.

"We need to talk first. Because there's more," Isabel said. "Tom is gone. I don't know where he went, but the window in Marlowe's office is open, so it's pretty clear he escaped. The storm is passing. Tom, or June, or both of them together will have gone for help by now. We need to leave before the police arrive. We need to go now."

"Do not tell me what we need to do." Bo bit the words out one by one. "Do not *ever* tell me what to do. I am going to see my brother." The tone of his voice rose steadily, and Darcy took a step back, as if she were afraid of what he would do.

Isabel looked like she wanted to argue, but something in Bo's expression stopped her. She nodded and pointed toward the back of the house. "Marlowe's office is down the hall and off to the right."

"Stay here," Bo ordered her. "Watch them."

Bo turned and strode out of the room. Darcy returned to sit in the leather chair. Marlowe wondered if Isabel would join Lee on the couch, but no. She hovered by the doorway and didn't even glance in the direction of her injured lover.

"Isabel," Lee said. "We need to go. We'll take my car. I don't know if the roads are drivable, but we have to try."

Isabel finally looked at Lee, her expression a mixture of fear and pity. "We're not going anywhere together."

Lee's eyes widened, and he shook his head. "But . . . I did all of this for you. For the two of us. So we could be together."

"That was never going to happen. You were always just the means to an end." Isabel's words were crisp and final.

It was strange how quickly love could shift to revulsion, Marlowe mused as she looked at her husband's stunned expression. Just a few short hours ago, she'd thought she would spend the rest of her life with this man. Now she'd happily never lay eyes on him again. She wondered if she should feel some satisfaction that Isabel was discarding him as easily as he had discarded her. But Marlowe was too consumed with worry for her children to care about Lee.

Bo strode back into the room, his face alight with rage. His cheeks were flushed, and his green eyes were too bright. A muscle twitched in his jaw. Marlowe felt a thrill of fear. Bo was scary when he was calm. Angry, he was terrifying.

"This isn't how this was supposed to go, Isabel!" Bo shouted. "Jason dying was not part of the plan!"

Isabel shrugged helplessly. "None of this has gone according to plan. But we have to leave now. If we don't, we're going to spend the rest of our lives in prison. Is that what you want?"

"I want my brother! And I want her"—Bo raised his gun and swung it wildly in Marlowe's direction—"to pay for what her family did to mine."

Marlowe flinched. She stared at Bo, at the gun he was pointing at her. She had no idea what he was talking about. Did he think Tom had killed Jason? She supposed it was possible, since Jason was dead and Tom was gone. But she didn't think so. Tom wasn't capable of killing anyone. It wasn't in his nature.

"What are you talking about?" Isabel stilled. "What did Marlowe do to you?"

"She didn't do anything. I never even met her before tonight," Bo said. He stopped and shook his head. "But her father is a different story."

"You knew my father?" Marlowe asked.

"My dad knew him. He worked at your parents' company. At Bond Marine. He was a welder at the factory. Your father blamed him for a fire, even though it wasn't his fault."

There was another turning and clicking in Marlowe's memory. "I remember my parents talking about that. Someone showed up drunk for his shift and caused the accident."

She'd been a teenager, eating dinner with her family in the kitchen. She remembered being ravenous after track practice, stuffing herself on lasagna and garlic bread while her parents picked at their food and discussed the terrible accident that had happened on the factory floor that day. One of the welders had had a few beers on his lunch break and mistakenly ignited some gasoline that had pooled on the floor. Two men had been hurt in the fire, one badly enough that he had to be taken to the hospital in an ambulance.

"He wasn't drunk!" Bo said. "He was just going through a hard time. My mom died—he was a single parent. It was a lot for a man to deal with."

"They fired him," Marlowe said. Her father had been conflicted about the decision, but her mother had been adamant it was the right choice.

"He made the choice to drink while he was working. And someone was badly hurt because of that choice," Katherine had said, setting her fork down on her plate. "The next time, he might get someone killed."

"My father never bounced back from that," Bo said. "He came home from work that night and fell into a bottle that he never climbed out of. He died a couple of years later, and Jason and I ended up bouncing around from one foster home to another. We never had a chance."

Marlowe was ashamed to realize that the incident had barely been a blip on her consciousness. She'd been more focused on her calculus test the next day and her upcoming track meet. But somewhere out there in the world that day, a domino had fallen over and set off a chain reaction, leaving the life of a man and his two young sons in ruins. Those dominoes had continued to fall, one after another, right up until this moment.

The room seemed to recede, as if Lee, Isabel, and Darcy were no longer there. It was just Marlowe and Bo, staring at one another. Her dark-blue eyes met his rageful green ones, which were now wet with tears.

"You think my parents hurt your family, so you decided to hurt mine as payback?" she asked.

"I wanted to take something from them, the way they took everything from me. But then they died before I could. So I decided to go for the next best thing."

"I had nothing to do with your father being fired. I was a teenager when that happened."

"You've lived a life of privilege and obscene wealth off the backs of my father and men like him. Men who were lucky to make it to retirement, much less have two nickels to show for their efforts."

"My parents paid their employees well," Marlowe countered.

Bo ignored her. "And you live here, in this big house on the water, and spend your time debating which expensive painting you should keep and which you should donate to some stupid museum. As if that matters in a world where kids have to sleep under the roofs of strangers who wake them up in the middle of the night touching them in places where little kids shouldn't be touched."

Marlowe tried to swallow, but her mouth had gone dry. "I'm very sorry that happened to you."

"Not me. Jason. I did my best to keep him safe, but . . ." Bo stopped and shook his head. His hand holding the gun dropped down, and tears suddenly flooded his eyes. "What happened to us wasn't right. Someone needs to pay for that."

"You're right. Someone should pay for it." *But not us,* she wanted to add. *Not my children. This is not our debt.*

There was the distant sound of sirens. Marlowe looked up, and for a moment she felt hope. Maybe the sirens meant Tom and June were safe. That they'd found someone to help them. It was all that mattered now.

"Bo! We need to get out of here. Now!" Isabel exclaimed.

Bo looked a little startled, as if he—like Marlowe—had forgotten for a moment that the others were there. Isabel, determined, insistent. Lee, unable to move from the couch. Darcy, looking like she wasn't sure what she should do with herself. Bo wiped at his cheeks and then straightened, his eyes growing cold.

"No. I'm going to finish what I started," he said. And then he raised the gun again and pointed it at Marlowe.

And she knew then that he was going to kill her. That had been the plan all along. From the moment their unexpected guests had arrived at the dock, they had been leading up to this moment. Bo saw this, killing her, as a blood debt. And he wanted that debt paid, even if it meant spending the rest of his life in prison.

Marlowe drew in a breath, knowing it could be her last one. She wondered what it would feel like to be shot. She knew it would hurt when the bullet penetrated her skin, slicing through her body. But how much pain would she feel before oblivion?

The next moments flicked by like stills from a movie, Marlowe's eyes widening as she watched. Bo steadying the gun, his finger firm on the trigger.

Isabel stepping in front of him, both hands up in front of her, palms facing out. "Stop," she said.

The sound of the gun exploding, filling the room with noise and smoke and a metallic smell that filled Marlowe's nostrils. Darcy's mouth falling open, a scream ripping out of her.

And finally, Isabel staggered back a few steps, a shocked expression on her beautiful face, before she collapsed to the ground.

CHAPTER FORTY-FIVE

JUNE

Tom and June were hammering their fists on their next-door neighbor's door when they heard sirens in the distance. June's eyes widened as she looked at her brother.

"Do you think that's the police?" she asked.

He shook his head and shrugged. "There's no way to be sure. It could be an ambulance or a fire truck. The sirens all sound the same to me." He dropped his hand. "I don't think anyone's home."

"Maybe we should try to figure out where the siren is coming from. We could try to wave them down," June suggested.

Tom shook his head. "We don't know what direction they're coming from or where they're headed. We could lose a lot of time trying to find them and end up missing them altogether. But those sirens mean that they're responding to emergency calls now, right?"

June put her hands on her hips, trying to regain her breath. She was still winded from their run. "Which of our neighbors do you think would most likely have stayed?"

Tom considered this. "The Coopers definitely left. They stopped to talk to Dad on their way out of town yesterday afternoon. I heard Mr. Cooper say that Mrs. Gold left a few days ago to go stay with her daughter in Tampa. Those people across the street"—Tom pointed into the darkness—"are snowbirds. I don't even remember their names, but they're only down for a few months every year, so they won't be home."

June struggled to maintain her patience. "Do you know anyone who is in town?"

"The O'Donnells' car was parked in their driveway earlier. I noticed it when Zack and I were putting up the storm shutters. They must have decided to stay, because it was too late to evacuate at that point."

"Okay, let's go try their house."

The twins hurried down the curving paved driveway and out to the road. The worst of Celeste was passing, but remnants remained. It was still raining heavily, although not sheeting down as hard as it had been at the height of the storm. June's hair and clothes were completely soaked through, and the pavement was rough under her bare feet. An occasional slash of lightning appeared in the sky, followed by a rumble of thunder. The wind was still blowing in intermittent gusts that they had to brace against as they made their way to the next neighbor's house. On a normal night, it would have been faster to cross the lawn, but the grass was swampy and waterlogged, sucking their bare feet into the mud. At least the road, which ran parallel to the river, wasn't flooded.

But they also weren't alone. When June raised the flashlight app on Felix's phone to illuminate the path in front of them, red eyes peered back from both sides of the road.

"Alligators," Tom said. They both stopped abruptly. The animals normally stuck to shallow bodies of water, where you would occasionally see the tops of their heads and torsos floating near the surface. They didn't usually venture up to the street. Although, June thought with a twinge of panic, there was the occasional story of one going after a pet dog.

"This is creepy. I feel like I'm a walking cheeseburger," she said.

"They're just confused and displaced from the storm. Watch out for coral snakes too. The water will have driven them out of their nests. They'll bite if you step on one, and their venom can be deadly."

"Thank you. That makes me feel so much better." June rolled her eyes. "We're basically walking through a nature documentary where all of the animals want to kill us."

"If we don't bother them, they won't bother us."

"Let's just hope they're not in the mood for a snack. Come on—let's go this way."

June turned right and aimed the flashlight in front of her. They hurried up the O'Donnells' driveway. The house was dark. "There aren't any lights on," June said. "They might have gone to the emergency shelter."

"They have shutters up. And it's late. They could just be asleep."

"Let's see if we can wake them up."

They walked up the steps to the O'Donnells' front porch and began pounding on the door. June wondered if it was wise to make so much noise. With the storm letting up, Bo might have left the house by now to look for them. But if they were going to save their parents, they didn't have a choice. They needed to get help, and quickly.

"Hello!" Tom yelled, continuing to knock. "Mr. and Mrs. O'Donnell, are you in there? Is anyone home?"

Several minutes passed of them pounding on the door and yelling, and nothing happened. June could feel her anxiety swelling, and then she thought she heard something. Had it come from inside the house or outside? June looked around, using Felix's phone to illuminate the front yard of the O'Donnells' house. She couldn't see anyone, but that didn't mean they weren't there. She turned and began hitting the door with the flat of her hand so hard it stung from the impact.

"Please! We need help!" she called out.

Just as she was lifting her hand to knock again, the door suddenly swung open. June blinked up at Mrs. O'Donnell surrounded by light flooding out from the front-hall chandelier. She was in her sixties; had a sleek gray bob, deeply tanned skin, and bright-blue eyes; and had a bright-pink satin floral robe wrapped around her thin frame. Mrs.

O'Donnell looked down at them and crossed her arms, her expression stern, as if she suspected June and Tom were playing a practical joke.

"What are you two doing out here? It's the middle of the night," she said. "And I don't know if you've noticed, but we're in the middle of a hurricane!"

"Thank God you're home," June said. She could feel tears of relief flooding her eyes. "Our parents are being held at gunpoint. We need to go to the police station."

CHAPTER FORTY-SIX

MARLOWE

"Isabel! No!" Lee's voice was so anguished that despite her shock, Marlowe had what was becoming a familiar stab of pain and anger at her husband's infidelities.

Isabel lay on her side, her arms extended in front of her, one leg tangled under the other, her long hair covering her face. All around her body, the taupe carpet was soaked with her blood.

As Marlowe looked down at Isabel's body, she felt an unexpected rush of loss. Maybe not for the woman who had betrayed her. But instead for the potential Isabel had. She had been smart and savvy, and she could have had a different life. She could have run her own art gallery one day or risen to a prominent position at a museum. She certainly had the talent. But instead she'd fallen in love with the wrong man, and it had led to her death. And, after all, her last act had been to save Marlowe's life.

Bo was also staring down at Isabel, his anger replaced by an expression of shock and grief. He lowered the gun and ran his other hand over his face. He looked up at Marlowe. "They were all I had. Jason and Isabel. They were my family."

Marlowe stared back at him, speechless. She knew he hadn't meant to kill Isabel. He'd meant to kill *her*. She wondered if he would try again.

The sirens outside sounded as if they were getting closer.

"Bo," Darcy said. "I think that's the police. We need to go."

Bo turned to her, looking almost confused by her presence.

"Check her pulse," Lee said from the couch, struggling to push himself up. "Maybe she's just hurt. We can call an ambulance, get her to the hospital."

"She's dead," Bo said flatly.

"Why? Why did you shoot her?" Lee asked. He sounded almost childlike in his anger and confusion.

Bo closed his eyes and drew in a deep breath. Then he slowly raised the gun and pointed it at Lee, who cowered back, holding his hands in front of his face.

"This is all your fault. If you had been a good man, a decent man, we wouldn't be here," Bo said through gritted teeth. "You married Marlowe for her money. You cheated on her with Isabel. And then you came up with the plan to rob your wife so you and your girlfriend could run away with that money. If you hadn't done that, made all of those choices, none of this would have happened. Isabel would still be alive."

"I loved her," Lee said, bracing his elbows to rise up into a seated position. "Everything I did, I did for her. So we could be together."

Bo let out a sound that could have been a laugh or a sigh. "You never even knew her. You only knew the person she pretended to be." Bo swung the gun in Marlowe's direction. "Come on. It's time to go."

Marlowe froze, unsure of what he was asking her to do.

"Come on," Bo said, his voice rising. He gestured at Marlowe to stand up. "Let's go!"

She stood, slowly, wondering what he was intending to do. Was this the moment he was going to shoot her? But Bo stepped forward and wrapped one hand viselike around her wrist. He pulled her roughly, and Marlowe stumbled toward him.

"What are we doing?" Darcy asked. "Are we going to leave on the boat? Or should we take one of the cars?"

"You're staying here," Bo said. "Marlowe and I are going."

"What?" Darcy stepped forward, her face morphing between confusion and outrage. "You can't leave me here. You have to take me with you."

"Lee, where are the keys to your boat?" Bo asked.

"What? Why do you need my boat?" Lee asked.

Bo lifted his gun and put the end of it against Marlowe's head. She felt the cold metal pressing against her temple and closed her eyes, bracing herself for the explosion and the pain that would follow.

"I'll ask you again. Where are the keys to your boat?" Bo repeated.

"They're in the laundry room, on a hook next to the garage door," Lee said. "Please don't hurt Marlowe. Please."

"Bo!" Darcy stood in front of him. "You can't just leave me here!" She grabbed for his arm, wrapping hers around it, as if she could anchor him in place.

Bo easily shook her off. "Darcy, I've enjoyed our time together, but consider this our official breakup. You can tell the police you had nothing to do with any of this. They'll probably let you off with a slap on the hands."

"What?" Darcy shrieked. "They're going to arrest me?"

Bo ignored her and roughly pulled Marlowe forward. She staggered as he dragged her with him out of the living room, down the hallway, and into the kitchen. He was so strong Marlowe couldn't fight against him. She just had time to focus on the shock of seeing Zack's body again, still sprawled on the floor near the sink, shrouded under the gray blanket, when Bo said, "Where's the laundry room?"

"Just leave me here," Marlowe said. "You'll move faster without me."

"Not a chance. Come on." Bo pulled her forward again.

Lee had always teased Marlowe that she treated their laundry room like a temple. It was neat and organized, all the detergents put away in cupboards, the machines gleaming and glossy. There was a rack of hooks next to the door to the garage, where the family hung their house and car keys.

"Where are the keys to the boat?" Bo demanded.

Marlowe reached forward and plucked the key off the hook. The key chain had a miniature hot-pink surfboard on it, which Tom had gotten from his favorite surf shop. She handed it to him.

"Why don't you take your boat?" she asked.

"Technically speaking, it's not my boat. I borrowed it from the boatyard where I work. Or worked. But I don't know what condition it will be in after that storm," he said. "Do you know how to work the lift in the boathouse?"

Marlowe nodded reluctantly, and Bo tightened his grip on her wrist. Together, they went into the dark garage, where the cars were surrounded by the piled-up patio furniture. Marlowe stumbled against one of the chairs, its leg sticking out, and it skinned her shin.

"Just take the boat and go," she tried again. "You don't need me. There's no point in taking me."

"You, Marlowe, are the entire point."

And Marlowe knew then that she was going to die. She didn't know what Bo had planned—she was pretty sure that all his plans were in ruins at this point—but he was going to make sure that she didn't survive the night. He hadn't even bothered to take the Cézanne in the end. The sketch was back in the living room, sitting on an ivory wing chair, still wrapped in its brown paper. But it had never been about the Cézanne, Marlowe realized. This night had been about seeking vengeance. Bo raised the garage door, and together, they stumbled outside.

It was calmer out than she had expected. It was still raining and thundering, but the worst of the hurricane had passed. And yet there was no way to know what the conditions would be like out on the water. The swirling tail of the hurricane was almost certainly still affecting marine conditions.

"Why don't you take my car?" Marlowe suggested. "It will be safer than going out on the boat."

Bo laughed, although it was more like a humorless bark. "Safer? I don't care about what's safer, Marlowe. I've lost everything. All of the people I cared about are gone. All of our plans for the future are finished. But if I'm going to go down, I want it to be on the water. I want the last thing I see to be the ocean all around me."

Marlowe hadn't thought it was possible for her to be even more frightened. But Bo's words filled her with cold terror. "This is a suicide mission?"

"This is about righting a wrong."

The light from the garage shone onto the driveway. Marlowe saw that Mick's truck was still parked there and let out a strangled sob. He hadn't driven off into the storm, after all. Bo must have killed him when they had gone outside. So many people had died that night. And she was going to be next.

Still holding her wrist, Bo forced Marlowe to stumble along with him, around the house, past the pool and patio, and down the sloping backyard toward the boathouse, their way lit by the occasional flashes of lightning over the water. As one strike of lightning hit nearby, illuminating the backyard, Marlowe gasped. The fishing boat Bo and the others had arrived on was lying upside down on the rain-drenched grass.

"I guess it's a good thing we can take your boat," Bo commented as they passed by the beached vessel. "Mine appears to be out of commission."

Ahead, the river was dark and churning, and Marlowe could only imagine how much worse the open water of the ocean would be.

Please let Tom and June be safe, she thought.

And then something else occurred to her. *What if they're hiding in the boathouse?* It was the most logical place for one or both of them to have fled to for shelter. Bo had even mentioned the possibility earlier. She didn't want to think about what he'd do if he found them there.

She looked warily up at the boathouse. She could see through the hurricane-impact windows that the lights were off inside, but that didn't necessarily mean it wasn't occupied.

Marlowe's feet squelched through the mud, and one of her flip-flops got stuck. She was trying to free it when Bo tugged her forward, and she was forced to go with him, leaving the sandal behind. As they got closer to the river, the water rose up to her ankles. Even Bo was forced to slow his pace as they picked their way through the swampy ground to the base of the boathouse. Bo pulled out his phone and used the flashlight function to light the path up to the second story.

"Nice boathouse," Bo commented, raising his voice to be heard over the gusts of wind. "But only the best for you, right, Marlowe?"

"It's Lee's. I had nothing to do with it."

"Except that your money paid for it. I bet you feel pretty foolish right about now."

Marlowe pulled her arm away from him, her anger overriding her fear. Bo pushed her forward toward the spiral metal staircase. "Ladies first."

The stairs were slick with mud and water, and Marlowe slipped going up them. She took each step one at a time, pulling herself up the banister as she went. Bo was right behind her, his hand pressed firmly on the small of her back. Marlowe wondered if she should turn around and try to push him down the stairs. What was he going to do, shoot her? Going out on the boat into the storm was already a death sentence, which was apparently the whole point. But when she looked back, the flashlight blinded her, and then Bo was urging her forward again, and the moment to act had passed.

Marlowe swung open the door of the boathouse, and together, they stumbled inside. Bo flipped on the light switch, illuminating the space, which was empty, except for the *Dreamweaver*. Marlowe noticed a plaid blanket crumpled on the floor and a pile of orange life vests stacked near the wall.

"Where are the controls for the lift?" Bo asked. Marlowe pointed at a panel on the wall. "Well, go on—get it started."

"Me?" Marlowe had never operated the lift by herself before. Lee was the boater in the family, and the rest of them just humored him when he wanted them to join him out on the boat for the day. But she'd seen him operate the lift enough times that she thought she could do it. But why should she help him? He had already made it clear that he was planning on both of them dying out on the water.

"Yes, you. I'll be right here, with a gun pointed at you. And before you think about coming up with some sort of plan to stop me, consider this—we either leave here by boat together, or we go look for Tom and June instead. It's your choice."

CHAPTER FORTY-SEVEN

FELIX

Felix wasn't sure how long he'd been sitting on the closed fiberglass toilet aboard the *Dreamweaver*. Although calling it a bathroom was an overstatement. It was basically a closet equipped with the chemical toilet and a tiny sink and shower. Felix's ankle throbbed, and he shifted miserably. June had shut off the lights when she'd left, and he'd been sitting in complete darkness ever since.

He suddenly heard a noise, and he stilled, wondering if he'd imagined it. No, he definitely heard something. Footsteps up on the deck above.

June, he thought.

Felix sat up straight, flexing his neck, so relieved that June had finally returned he almost called out to her. But he stopped himself. What if it wasn't June, or what if she wasn't alone? And then he heard things that didn't make sense. The squeaking, rolling sound of the retractable floor opening on its wheels. The electrical hum of the hydraulic lift being turned on. A man calling out, "Get on board. Now."

Felix froze. He recognized the voice from earlier that evening. It was Bo, and he was here on the boat. There were footsteps again, heavy on the deck above. Felix tried to figure out how many people were up there. Two? Three?

And then, the boat began to *move*.

Felix threw out his arms to brace himself against the walls on either side of him as the boat started to lower down toward the water. What were they doing? How could they plan on taking the boat out? The roaring of the storm had been gradually fading, but it would still be treacherous out on the water. And Felix was terrified of the water on a calm day. As the boat moved down, down, down, he began sweating, and his heart pounded in his chest. He wondered if this was what a heart attack felt like.

Part of Felix wanted to rush out of the bathroom and up the stairs to the deck, to insist they let him off right now. But even if his ankle wasn't broken, he couldn't let them know he was there. Bo and his accomplices had already killed at least two people that night, and they were armed. Felix just hoped that Bo and whoever was with him didn't have to use the bathroom.

The boat continued to descend on its hydraulic lift. He knew when they reached the water because the boat immediately began to bob up and down on the waves. Felix clamped his hands over his mouth. The engines started, and the boat began to move forward, dipping queasily on what must have been massive waves.

The next moments were the longest and scariest of Felix's life. It made the day the police had arrested him and put him in the back seat of the police cruiser pale in comparison. All he could do was cower on the toilet, his arms wrapped around himself, willing himself not to be sick. Or die. Or be sick, *then* die. Out on the water, the sounds of the storm were louder, the wind shrieking again, and the boat pitched and rolled.

But then he lifted his head, not quite believing what he was hearing. A man and a woman were shouting, and he was pretty sure the woman sounded like June's mother. But that didn't make any sense. Why would she be leaving on a boat with the strangers?

But he knew there was only one reason. Bo must have forced her to get on the boat. Marlowe was still a hostage.

CHAPTER FORTY-EIGHT

MARLOWE

As the boat sped away from shore, Marlowe sat huddled in the back on a molded bench. Bo stood in the partially enclosed cockpit, protected from the elements on three sides, steering them down the river. The *Dreamweaver* was dipping up and down so violently Marlowe thought she might vomit. She'd never suffered from seasickness, but she'd also never been out on water this choppy.

When they reached the point where the river opened into the ocean, Bo turned the boat north and steered them out onto the open sea. The waves there were even larger, towering over the boat like moving walls of water. Rain poured down, and lightning struck the water all around them, each bolt accompanied by a loud boom of thunder. Celeste's swirling mass was still over the water.

This is it, Marlowe thought, terror rising up into her throat. *We're going to die out here.*

Conditions deteriorated quickly. The wind picked up again, stinging Marlowe's skin and whipping her hair into her face. She dropped onto the deck, wrapping her arms over her head, but it did little to protect her from the storm. Marlowe's clothes were soaked through with the salt water, and she began to shiver uncontrollably as the wind cut across the boat. Bo was already struggling to steer the boat out onto the ocean.

"Damn it!" Bo said, wrestling with the wheel.

"We need to go back!" Marlowe yelled.

Bo ignored her and continued to push the boat forward. A wave rose up and crashed over the boat, drenching Marlowe again. One of the engines cut out, and then another. There were four engines in total, but Marlowe had to imagine the other two would eventually break down too. A recreational fishing boat wasn't built to withstand these conditions.

The *Dreamweaver* lurched up and then back down so violently it knocked Marlowe sideways, and she hit her head against the base of the fiberglass bench. Her head throbbed, and for a moment, her vision went fuzzy around the edges. Water poured over her, filling her lungs and nose, and she coughed uncontrollably. When she was finally able to focus, Marlowe pushed herself up into a seated position. She knew she didn't have much time left.

Marlowe had never really thought about why they named hurricanes, but now she knew. Celeste was alive, a monster that was planning to consume everyone in her path.

Another engine died, and Bo swore again, hitting his hand against the wheel.

"Come on!" he shouted at it.

She wondered what he was hoping to accomplish. He had told her he wanted to die at sea. So why was he fighting to keep pushing the boat forward? Maybe his self-preservation instinct had kicked in. Maybe he'd realized he'd made a terrible mistake taking them out here.

Marlowe watched as the heavy Yeti cooler Lee stored at the end of the boat to keep cold drinks in tumbled off and disappeared into the ocean. She wondered who would be thrown into the water first, her or Bo. It was just a matter of time now.

The final engine cut out, and the boat died. They were still moving, the boat pitching up and down, but they were no longer propelling forward. Bo slumped forward and covered his face with his hands.

This is it, Marlowe thought. *This is the end.*

Marlowe wasn't ready to die. She didn't know if anyone ever was, but she certainly wasn't. She wanted to see her children graduate from high school and go on to college and their lives beyond. She wanted to meet her grandchildren and take them to run around in the fountains at the water park. She wanted to watch her body change over time as she grew older and hopefully wiser. She wanted to live a full life, a complete one.

But instead, she was going to die that night, out on the ocean, in the middle of a terrible storm.

Marlowe thought that she saw something move by the stairs that led down to the living quarters. She squinted, trying to make out what it was. Maybe it was the water swelling up again or something else tumbling out of the boat. Bo must have seen it, too, because he stood and turned.

"What was that?" he asked.

Marlowe blinked, not quite believing what she saw. Someone was standing at the top of the stairs. Her heart lurched in panic. Was it Tom or June? Was one of her children here on this death mission to nowhere?

Lightning crackled across the sky, illuminating the deck, and suddenly Marlowe recognized who was standing there.

"Felix?" she said, confused. What was Felix doing here?

Before Marlowe could process what was happening, Felix threw himself forward, ramming his body into Bo's, knocking him off balance. Bo was flung back against the metal guardrail along the side of the boat and teetered there for a moment, struggling to stand back up. Marlowe gasped, hoping that he would fall over the side.

Felix staggered back, trying to regain his balance. Bo managed to right himself and rushed toward Felix.

"Watch out!" Marlowe screamed.

Bo raised his hands into fists, drew one arm back, and uncoiled all his weight forward. His knuckles connected with Felix's jaw. The blow

281

seemed to stun Felix, who staggered back and fell against the built-in bench, landing next to where Marlowe sat huddled in terror.

She wondered if he'd been knocked out. But no, Felix was pushing himself back up, trying to stand. There was something stilted about his gait, almost like he was limping, unable to put weight on his right foot. Felix lurched forward, his arms stretched out in front of him, and slammed into Bo with the full force of his body. Bo stumbled back again and this time hit the side of the boat just as yet another crashing wave tipped the boat nearly onto its side.

As the floor below her tilted, Marlowe grabbed at the side railing behind her. But her fingers were grasping at air, and suddenly, she was falling, her body sliding across the smooth fiberglass deck. The boat careened even farther to one side, and she saw the black swirling water of the Atlantic Ocean churning below her. Marlowe braced her legs against the bench, but she knew it wouldn't be enough to keep her onboard for long.

She was going to fall into the sea.

"Grab the rope!" Felix yelled.

Marlowe looked up. Felix was holding on to a rope that snaked across the deck, the end of it uncoiling near her. She reached for it, just managing to grab hold of it as she felt herself starting to fall. Marlowe clung on desperately.

Lightning slashed through the sky, illuminating the deck of the boat. Bo was still at the guardrail, struggling to hold on to it. He stared back at Marlowe, and when their eyes met, she saw the terror etched on his face. An enormous wave suddenly rose up and washed over the ship. Marlowe heard Bo scream as he lost his grip and tumbled into the dark water.

Marlowe looked down at the churning swell of the sea, but even when another flash of lightning lit up the water, she couldn't see Bo among the white-capped waves. It was as though the ocean had already swallowed him whole.

The boat rocked back, finally righting itself. Marlowe fell onto the deck, still gripping the rope in her hands. Felix stumbled forward, landing hard on the deck next to Marlowe.

"Are you okay?" she asked him. She remembered that Felix was terrified of the water, that he'd never wanted to go out on the boat or even in their pool. Being out here on the ocean, tossed around by these enormous waves, must be a special kind of hell for him.

"I don't know. I don't think so." Felix choked out the words. "Are we going to die out here?"

Probably, Marlowe thought, but she didn't want to tell him that and add to his terror. She grabbed his hand and pressed it in hers. "Maybe the Coast Guard will be able to get to us."

"Can we steer the boat back to shore?"

Marlowe shook her head. "No, the engines cut out." She tried to think of what to do through the haze of panic, her head still throbbing. Help. She needed to call for help. And then she remembered. She had a phone.

Marlowe grabbed it out of her wet pocket and tried to turn it on. It didn't light up. The water that had soaked through her clothing must have damaged it. Marlowe threw the phone to one side in frustration.

Think, she told herself. The *Dreamweaver* had a communication system, but she doubted it was working. Marlowe tried to remember Lee's tedious lectures on boating safety. "There's an emergency beacon in the helm. I need to get to it."

Marlowe struggled to stand as the boat continued to pitch wildly from side to side. She staggered toward the cockpit, where Bo had been seated just moments before. The beacon was the size of a remote and was always stored in a small drawer to the right of the steering wheel. Marlowe held on to the wheel, trying to keep herself upright as she grabbed at the drawer. Her fingers found the beacon inside, and she pulled it out, praying that it hadn't also been damaged in the storm.

After she pressed the power button, there was a long terrible moment where she thought that this, their very last chance, was going to fail.

The control panel on the beacon lit up.

Marlowe pulled out the antenna and pressed the button that deployed the signal to alert the Coast Guard that they were in distress, along with the coordinates of where they were located. She felt her legs going beneath her, sliding her onto the ground, but she held the beacon tightly in her hand, praying they would be able to stay onboard long enough for help to reach them.

"We should go down below! We'll be safer down there!" she yelled to Felix, who was still cowering on the deck, his arms wrapped over his head.

Felix shook his head back and forth. "I can't go back down there," he shouted back. "The boat will tip over and sink, and we'll be trapped down there."

If the boat capsizes, we'll be dead wherever we are onboard, Marlowe thought.

"At least come into the cockpit," she called back.

Felix crawled toward her on his elbows, dragging his feet behind, until they were both under the protective shell of the sun cover. He was trembling, and Marlowe wrapped her arms around him. They sat there, huddled together.

Time seemed to stretch on forever, the boat still rising and pitching treacherously on the enormous waves, the seawater drenching them over and over again. Each time the boat tilted to what seemed like an impossible angle, Marlowe thought, *This is it—this is the moment we're going to capsize.* And yet each time, the boat somehow managed to right itself and stay afloat. Marlowe's mouth was parched, and she wondered if she'd ever taste clean, cold spring water again.

She wasn't sure how much time had passed or when she and Felix had last spoken. Their world had been distilled down to the rolling waves, the dark blanket of sky around them, and the roaring of the wind over the water. Marlowe was so weak and exhausted that when she heard the sounds of an engine, she thought her mind was playing tricks on her. She lifted her head and squinted into the night.

That was when she saw a light off in the distance. Was it a light or just more lightning flashing in the sky? Marlowe blinked and wiped at her eyes with the wet cuff of her shirtsleeve.

No, it was a light. The sort of light that shone out from boats navigating at night.

And it seemed to be growing closer.

EPILOGUE

One Year Later

"Thank you for all being here today," Marlowe said, speaking into a small black microphone that sat perched on a Lucite podium. "My parents, Thomas and Katherine Bond, loved art, and they traveled all around the world to collect it. As you'll see when you walk through the Bond Wing here at the Norton Museum, they had eclectic taste. They were just as likely to buy a street scene painted by a local artist as they were to purchase a formal portrait painted by a master. It was their dream to one day donate their collection here to the museum. After they passed away, I decided to make sure that dream was realized. Today, the Bond Wing is open."

The audience, who sat in rows of bamboo chairs facing Marlowe, clapped politely. June—who had come from Vanderbilt for the occasion—let out a loud whoop, and Marlowe beamed at her. Tom, who still lived at home with Marlowe while he worked at a local surf shop, clapped enthusiastically. Felix sat to June's other side, holding her hand in his.

"Our world is often not an easy place to be during these divisive times. But art is the one thing that can bring us together. It inspires and enchants us. It reminds us every day that there is still beauty all around," Marlowe concluded. "Thank you all for being here, and please enjoy the collection. I hope you love it as much as I do."

The audience applauded again and then stood and chatted among themselves as they turned to walk around the airy room to view the paintings on display. Catering staff began to circulate, carrying trays of glasses of wine.

Marlowe smiled and walked over to her children. They were doing far better than she would have hoped after everything they had been through. June had settled into her freshman year away at college, and Marlowe thought she looked healthier, even having gained back a little of the weight she'd lost in high school. June was seeing a counselor on campus, and although Marlowe didn't pry into what they discussed during their sessions, June seemed positive about the experience. Tom was tanned, and his hair was streaked from hours spent in the sun, giving surfing lessons to kids and adults. When he'd told her he didn't want to go to college, at least not right away, she hadn't fought him. She wanted both of their children to find their own way and to spend their lives doing what they loved.

"That was great, Mom." June was wearing a long floral tiered sundress in a vibrant-orange print, and her arm was linked casually through Felix's.

"Are you sure? I was really nervous," Marlowe said. She smoothed down the white linen dress she'd bought for the occasion. "I've never been a fan of public speaking."

"You nailed it, Mrs. Davies." Felix looked dapper in a pink-and-white-checked shirt and blue khaki pants, and he smiled easily at her.

Marlowe had no idea how long she and Felix had sat on the *Dreamweaver* waiting for the Coast Guard to arrive on the night of Hurricane Celeste. The boat had nearly capsized several times as it had been tossed around on the rolling waves. Marlowe and Felix had sat huddled together, unable to speak, both wondering if their lives would end as Bo's had. Two more bodies at the bottom of the sea. It was a miracle they'd survived until the storm quieted down enough for the Coast Guard to rescue them. They hadn't known it at the time, but Elyse

O'Donnell had risked the flooded roads to drive Tom and June to the police station in her Range Rover. By the time Marlowe had activated the emergency beacon, the Coast Guard had already been alerted to the possibility that Bo might try to escape by boat.

A few weeks later, when life had been returning not back to normal exactly but at least to a point where the police had finally taken down the crime scene tape from around the house, Marlowe had hired a private criminal defense attorney to represent Felix on the car-theft charges. She had already let him down once when she hadn't taken Felix's side after Lee had banned him from their home, and she'd wanted to make it up to him. Besides, Felix had saved her life. If he hadn't been there on the boat that night, she had no doubt she would have died. The attorney had managed to get all the charges against Felix dismissed, and he had eventually been awarded a full academic scholarship to the University of Florida. If he hadn't, Marlowe would have been more than happy to pay for his education. He was a lovely young man, Marlowe thought. She didn't know if his relationship with June would endure, with them living so far apart and going to different colleges, but she hoped so. They seemed right together.

"Are they serving food?" Tom asked. He looked slightly uncomfortable in his suit, and he fiddled with his cuffs. Marlowe noticed that he was wearing the watch his grandparents had given him for his sixteenth birthday.

"There are appetizers around here somewhere," Marlowe said. "Are you hungry?"

"Starving," Tom said.

"I could eat," Felix said.

"What a surprise," June said, rolling her eyes comically.

Neither of her children had mentioned Lee's absence from the event. As far as Marlowe knew, Lee was still living in the apartment he'd rented for Isabel while he was out on bond and awaiting his sentencing hearing. He'd already pled guilty to conspiracy charges in exchange for the felony homicide charges being taken off the table. Marlowe wasn't sure if the judge at his sentencing hearing would be as lenient as he'd been with Darcy, as she hadn't played any part in the planning of what happened on the night of the hurricane. She had already begun serving her two-year sentence, which had been a gift considering the charges she could have been convicted on. Marlowe wondered how Lee was coping with the uncertainty of his future and the long prison sentence he was likely facing, but they weren't in contact. The last time she'd seen him was at the courthouse when their divorce had been finalized.

Marlowe hadn't been able to forgive Lee, but she hoped that for her own sake, she would at some point. It was hard not to hate him for his infidelity, for bringing monsters into their home, and most of all for Zack's and Mick's deaths. But the anger felt like poison to her, and she wanted it out of her system. Marlowe had once read a quote on social media—*forgiveness is the gift you give yourself.* She wanted to believe that and hoped she would get there one day.

She wondered how she would feel if Bo had survived the storm. Would her hatred for him have consumed her? There was no way to know. But she was very glad he was dead and she was still alive.

"Where did they hang the Cézanne?" June asked.

"It's there," Marlowe said, nodding toward the far end of the gallery. A group of people were clustered in front of the sketch, blocking it from their view. "You know, I almost didn't include it in the collection."

"Why not?" Tom asked.

"This is going to sound silly, but I was afraid to let go of it. It's always meant so much to me. But then I decided it really needed to be here. The collection wouldn't have been complete without it."

And besides, she thought, as much as she loved the Cézanne, it would always remind her of the night of the hurricane. The night the guests arrived and tipped her world upside down. She didn't need a daily reminder of Bo, and Isabel, and Lee's betrayal hanging in her home.

The four of them walked down to join the crowd admiring the sketch. It hung on its own wall, with a placard mounted next to it describing the work and its artist. It was so simple and yet so exquisite, Marlowe thought. There was a plaque next to the sketch: **DONATED IN LOVING MEMORY OF ELIZABETH "LIZA" DAVIES.**

Marlowe felt tears rising to her eyes, and she quickly wiped them away before Tom or June saw them. She didn't know why she'd never told them about their sister—maybe it had been too painful for her to talk about, or maybe she had wanted to protect them from knowing that you could do your best to be a good person and lead an honorable life, and terrible things would still happen along the way. But everyone found out that lesson eventually. Tom and June had learned it on the night of the hurricane.

"This is all amazing, Mom," June said. "You did a great job."

"Thank you. I just hope it's what my parents pictured when they first came up with the idea."

"I think they'd be really proud of you," Tom said.

Marlowe smiled at her children, feeling the same rush of love she always did when she saw them, especially when they were together like this.

"So what now?" June asked. "Your big project is done. What are you going to do now?"

"I hadn't really thought about it," Marlowe said. She had been so caught up in all the events of the past year she hadn't spent much time thinking about what would come when everything was done.

And it had been a tumultuous year. The crime investigators swarming their house after the hurricane. Attending Zack's funeral and seeing his parents' grief-stricken faces, and then going to Mick's funeral, which had been well attended by men he had served with in the marines. Lee's prosecution. The divorce proceeding, which had been mercifully swift. And, on a happier note, the anticipation of June applying to colleges and receiving her acceptance letters. Tom's excitement when he'd gotten the job at the surf shop. All the work that had gone into making the Bond collection a reality. But now, Marlowe had the rest of her life to consider.

It felt overwhelming. The life ahead of her looked so different than she'd thought it would before the hurricane. It was a bit like when Liza had died and everything had permanently, irrevocably changed. Her life had yet again split into a before and an after.

"I've always wanted to paint," she said.

"You did?" Tom asked. "I never knew that."

Marlowe nodded. "I used to when I was younger. I wanted to study it in college, but I was afraid I wouldn't be good enough. But that's not a good reason not to do something, right? I was thinking about signing up for a class at the community college. See how it goes."

"That's a great idea. I think you should," June said.

Marlowe put an arm around each of her children as they all gazed at the Cézanne. Marlowe knew that it wasn't the last time she'd see the sketch. But it still felt like one more goodbye, after a year of goodbyes.

She wondered what would have happened in an alternate reality, one where Celeste had worn herself out over the Atlantic, her deadly spiraling circle first dissipating and then fading away before the storm could roar up onto shore, raining down destruction. Would she still be married to Lee, ignorant to how deceptive and craven he really was? It was possible. Or maybe he would have left her by now, for Isabel or some other woman, ready to shed his old life and begin a new one. It was impossible to know, but the question had kept Marlowe up and awake on more than one lonely night.

Bo and Lee had led very different lives, but they'd had a similar core. Both men had thought they were entitled to the life they wanted, without ever feeling the need to work to attain it.

Five months after the hurricane, Marlowe had spent an afternoon searching through the old business records of Bond Marine. She wanted to know what had really happened to Bo's and Jason's father. Bo had part of the story right. Peter Connor had been a welder at Bond Marine. Her parents had hired him six weeks after he'd been released on probation from the Glades Correctional Institution, where he'd been serving a sentence for manslaughter. Connor had drowned his wife in the bathtub in front of their two small boys, Bo and Jason.

Marlowe couldn't figure out why Peter Connor hadn't been charged with murder—the preinternet records were spotty, at best—but from what she could piece together, Connor had pled guilty in exchange for being charged with the lesser offense. She would never know if Bo had remembered this part of his past or if he'd been so young that the memory of that time had become blurred with age.

On November 5, 1994, Peter Connor had arrived for his afternoon shift at Bond Marine after his lunch break. He had been visibly intoxicated. His coworkers had attempted to stop him from resuming work, but Connor had become belligerent and pushed past them. He'd picked up his blowtorch and carelessly ignited an oil spill on the factory floor. Before the fire had been put out, one of his coworkers, Roy Dunworth, had been consumed with flames and suffered third-degree burns on 80 percent of his body. Dunworth had died a few months later. Two years after that, Peter Connor had died too.

Marlowe knew her life was a gift. She'd had good, caring parents and a stable, love-filled childhood. Before the night of the hurricane, she'd never had to deal with violence. Maybe if Bo had had a better start to his life, one where he'd been loved and protected, one where his father hadn't held his mother's head under fourteen inches of water until she stopped fighting and her body went still, he'd have become a productive member of society. Or maybe, like Lee—who'd had a perfectly ordinary childhood with perfectly ordinary parents—he'd still have turned into a monster.

She would never know.

"Come on," she now said, patting her children's shoulders and turning away from the exquisite Cézanne sketch. "Let's go find something to eat."

ABOUT THE AUTHOR

Photo © 2017 Robert Holland

Margot Hunt is the *USA Today* bestselling author of *Lovely Girls*, *Best Friends Forever*, *For Better and Worse*, and *The Last Affair*. Her work has been praised by Book of the Month, and her Audible Original *Buried Deep* was a #1 bestseller. You can stay up to date on Hunt's books and upcoming projects on her website: www.margothunt.com.